Revenge in the Cotswolds

D1634409

By Rebecca Tope

THE COTSWOLD MYSTERIES

A Cotswold Killing • A Cotswold Ordeal
Death in the Cotswolds • A Cotswold Mystery
Blood in the Cotswolds • Slaughter in the Cotswolds
Fear in the Cotswolds • A Grave in the Cotswolds
Deception in the Cotswolds • Malice in the Cotswolds
Shadows in the Cotswolds • Trouble in the Cotswolds
Revenge in the Cotswolds • Guilt in the Cotswolds
Peril in the Cotswolds • Crisis in the Cotswolds
◆
A Cotswold Casebook

THE LAKE DISTRICT MYSTERIES

The Windermere Witness • The Ambleside Alibi
The Coniston Case • The Troutbeck Testimony
The Hawkshead Hostage • The Bowness Bequest
The Staveley Suspect • The Grasmere Grudge

THE WEST COUNTRY MYSTERIES

A Dirty Death • Dark Undertakings
Death of a Friend • Grave Concerns
A Death to Record • The Sting of Death
A Market for Murder

Revenge in the Cotswolds

REBECCA TOPE

Allison & Busby Limited
11 Wardour Mews
London W1F 8AN
allisonandbusby.com

First published in Great Britain by Allison & Busby in 2015.
First published in paperback by Allison & Busby in 2016.
This paperback edition published by Allison & Busby in 2019.

Copyright © 2015 by Rᴇʙᴇᴄᴄᴀ Tᴏᴘᴇ

The moral right of the author is hereby asserted in accordance with
the Copyright, Designs and Patents Act 1988.

All characters and events in this publication,
other than those clearly in the public domain,
are fictitious and any resemblance to actual persons,
living or dead, is purely coincidental.

All rights reserved. No part of this publication may be reproduced,
stored in a retrieval system, or transmitted, in any form or by
any means without the prior written permission of the publisher,
nor be otherwise circulated in any form of binding or cover
other than that in which it is published and without a similar
condition being imposed on the subsequent buyer.

A CIP catalogue record for this book is available from
the British Library.

10 9 8 7 6 5 4 3 2 1

ISBN 978-0-7490-2437-6

Typeset in 10.5/15.5 pt Sabon by
Allison & Busby Ltd.

The paper used for this Allison & Busby publication
has been produced from trees that have been legally sourced
from well-managed and credibly certified forests.

Printed and bound by
CPI Group (UK) Ltd, Croydon, CR0 4YY

For Gemma, Luke and Kola

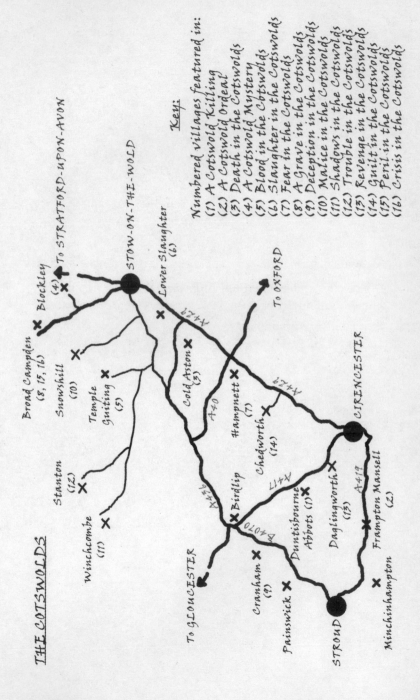

THE COTSWOLDS

TO STRATFORD-UPON-AVON

Blockley
(4)

Broad Campden
(8, 15, 16)

Snowshill
(10)

Temple
Guiting
(5)

Stanton
(12)

Winchcombe
(11)

STOW-ON-THE-WOLD

Lower Slaughter
(6)

A429

Cold Aston
(3)

A40

Hampnett
(7)

A429

Chedworth
(14)

TO OXFORD

Birdlip

A417

Duntisbourne
Abbots (1)

Cranham
(9)

Painswick

Daglingworth
(13)

CIRENCESTER

A419

Frampton Mansell
(2)

TO GLOUCESTER

B4070

STROUD

Minchinhampton

Key:

Numbered villages featured in:

(1) A Cotswold Killing
(2) A Cotswold Ordeal
(3) Death in the Cotswolds
(4) A Cotswold Mystery
(5) Blood in the Cotswolds
(6) Slaughter in the Cotswolds
(7) Fear in the Cotswolds
(8) A Grave in the Cotswolds
(9) Deception in the Cotswolds
(10) Malice in the Cotswolds
(11) Shadows in the Cotswolds
(12) Trouble in the Cotswolds
(13) Revenge in the Cotswolds
(14) Guilt in the Cotswolds
(15) Peril in the Cotswolds
(16) Crisis in the Cotswolds

Author's Note

As with all the titles in this series, the setting is in real villages with real pubs, churches and other public buildings. The individual properties, however, are invented and all the characters are imaginary.

Chapter One

There had been other times, in the past, Thea supposed, when everything had felt out of control, but on nothing like the current scale. Her house, garden and bank account were all defying her feeble efforts to manage them. Her dog was in urgent need of a trim and her car was overdue for its MOT. Even her body was misbehaving, with alarming hormonal surges at unpredictable moments. 'This is what comes of being in love,' she muttered ruefully. It had been a shock to discover that romance could make life so unreasonably complicated. Such a very large element to be factored into everything one did called for considerable adjustment. It hadn't been like that with Carl – probably because she had been twenty when they decided to get married, and at twenty life tends to be fairly straightforward. In one's mid forties, it was a very different matter.

Money had become a serious issue, requiring that she continue with her career as a house-sitter, like it or not, because otherwise she might not be able to dress herself in anything other than jumble sale clothes. Worries over her little house in Witney escalated because there was a clear need to make it pay for itself. Either she must rent it out or sell it, and whichever course she chose, the window frames had to be replaced and the whole building redecorated inside and out.

All of which explained her Saturday morning drive to the little old settlement of Daglingworth in the Cotswolds. For two weeks, she was to take charge of a small house at the lower end of the village, containing one arthritic corgi and a hibernating tortoise while the owners were in Australia attending the wedding of a niece. Her own spaniel was with her, as always, although the homeowners had expressed some concern at this, during Thea's preliminary visit, three weeks previously. 'Gwennie isn't very good with other dogs,' they said.

Gwennie moved slowly, her rheumy eyes unfocussed. Thea did not admit to simmering concerns as to the behaviour of her own pet. Hepzie had been guilty of outrageous unprovoked aggression a few months earlier. There had been no warning and no explanation for it, other than something to do with canine hormones. 'I'll keep a close eye on them,' she promised. 'I bet they'll soon be firm friends.'

The tortoise was asleep in a glass tank in the garage. 'But she'll probably wake up while we're away,' said Mrs Foster. 'If that happens, you'll have to make sure she's all right. If it's sunny, put the hibernation tank outside to get warm. Then if she wakes up, give her a tepid bath, and get the vivarium ready. It's in the spare room.' A quick guided tour and a comprehensive set of instructions followed.

Thea noted it all carefully, with a little glow of excitement at this new experience. The prospect of a reviving reptile was definitely appealing.

There had then been a minor bombshell. 'Oh, and is there any chance you could keep an eye on my sister's house in Bagendon as well?' asked Mrs Foster. 'Just for the first week. She's going to the wedding as well, but coming home the next day. We're staying on for a bit. There aren't any animals, so it would just be a matter of popping over every other day to water the plants and collect the post. It's only a mile from here.'

The wedding must be midweek then, Thea thought, as she tried to keep track of everyone's movements. So, straining for a businesslike response, she agreed, firmly adding that another hundred pounds would be payable for the extra service. Did the sister not have neighbours, she wondered. And was it really only a mile away? She had never had any reason to discover the exact location of Bagendon. If it was as close as that she might walk across country between the two houses, exercising herself and her dog in the process. 'Let me have the address, then,' she concluded. 'And tell me where I can find the key.'

The Fosters handed over the keys to their own house, which they emphasised was the first priority, and explained in exhaustive detail how the Bagendon property could be found, with a hand-drawn map for good measure. 'We'll get Mary to write everything down and leave it here for you when you come,' they promised. 'Along with her front door key.'

For the past year or more, it had become clear to Thea that she had a distinct reputation in the area. She had featured in a number of reports in newspapers, even been glimpsed on the television, as a result of various violent crimes committed in villages where she happened to be. There had been a time when she feared it would put people off employing her, seeing her as some kind of jinx. But instead there appeared to be a notion that she was useful to have around. Nobody admitted to truly believing that any of the crimes happened *because* of Thea Osborne. But when they *did* happen, she waded in and asked questions or made connections that nobody else seemed capable of making. Her role as outsider gave her an objective picture of motives and relationships that others found hard to spot.

So it was that she waited for Mr or Mrs Foster to say something about this. They were a quiet couple, he over sixty and she somewhat under. They were unmistakably excited about their trip – very much further afield than they had ever been before. They had lived in this same house since they married, which in itself endeared them to Thea. They'd never had children, and Gwennie was the last of a dynasty of Pembroke corgis, many of which had their photographs displayed on the walls. They made no mention of work or careers, but they seemed unlikely to be retired.

Nothing was said about Thea's reputation. 'We don't anticipate any problems,' was the nearest they came. 'Please don't contact us, even if something happens to Gwennie. The vet in Cirencester knows her. We've left the number.'

'I ought to have some sort of contact for you,' Thea pointed out. 'Don't you think?'

They gave her the name and phone number of Mrs Foster's Australian sister in Canberra, reluctantly. Mr

Foster gave his wife a look, with eyebrows raised, and said, 'Can't think of anything that couldn't wait, can you?'

His wife shook her head and laughed.

It was agreed that Thea would arrive during the morning of the day of their evening flight, an hour or two after they had departed for the airport.

Which she duly did, wondering at the level of trust implied in this. After all, if something had prevented her from turning up, poor old Gwennie might have died of dehydration before anybody realised. The house faced north-east, set back from a small road that seemed unlikely to boast much traffic. A century ago it must have been the main route into Cirencester, and probably fairly congested as a result, but now the A417 had taken over completely. She drove her car into the garage, which stood separate from the house, and closed the door behind it as instructed. Leaving her spaniel on the doorstep with her bag, she went in cautiously, chirruping to the corgi, which was nowhere to be seen.

The hall was narrow and rather dark, but extended some distance to the kitchen at the back. On each side was a door, leading to the living room and dining room. The sort of house a child would draw, or a medieval merchant of modest means might build for himself. There was nothing especially imaginative or surprising about it, but Thea could readily believe that it had provided comfortable shelter for the centuries of its existence. It was warm and quiet and faintly complacent.

Gwennie finally came out of the kitchen, sniffing the air suspiciously. 'Hello, old girl,' sang Thea. She squatted down to let the dog get her scent and gently stroked the head. The coat was warm and dense, the feet very white and the nose very sharp. 'You're a nice dog, aren't you? We'll be all right, won't we? Nothing to worry about.' The crooning came instinctively, and seemed to have a positive effect. The small stump that was all Gwennie possessed by way of a tail moved slightly.

There were two yellow envelopes on the little shelf holding the telephone in the hall. Before reading their contents, Thea collected her bag and dog and supervised the early stages of what she hoped would be a new canine friendship. Hepzie, when brought in from the front porch, made a casual advance, which was not rebuffed. Gwennie did a lot more sniffing, which the spaniel clearly found irritating, jumping sideways to get away from it. She gave her mistress the sort of liquid gaze of reproach that was a spaniel's chief trademark. 'Be nice,' said Thea. 'She's a poor old lady, and she's got no idea what's happening.'

Hepzie sighed and went to explore the living room.

The Fosters kept a reasonably neat home, which was nonetheless well equipped with comfortable places to sit. Sheepskin rugs, soft cushions, heavy curtains all gave it a cosy feel. Nothing looked particularly new, and there was no attempt at a colour scheme. In the living room the main feature was a large, handsome Victorian clock over the fireplace. It was black and gold, with delicate filigree hands and figures of cherubs perched on top of it. It was certain to strike noisily every hour, if not more.

The dining room had a square table just large enough for four, with a set of chairs sporting needlepoint seats. A battered oak bureau stood in one corner, with a bookcase perched on top of it. Another corner held a sort of chest with a domed, hinged lid, which Thea suspected had been a cabin trunk in its former life. With a quick guilty glance around, as if to ensure the Fosters really had gone, she lifted the lid to see what it contained.

It was full of canvas, hanks of thick wool, books of designs and other paraphernalia fit for a keen needlewoman. So Mrs Foster had done the chair seats. Good for her.

When she opened the envelopes, Thea found exhaustive instructions concerning plants, security lights and burglar alarm – more so for the Bagendon house than the Fosters'. She sighed. Alarms and locks and lights were familiar territory for any house-sitter, but she had been lucky in keeping them to a minimum on most of her assignments. She made a speciality of caring for animals, with the actual property taking secondary significance. So long as it didn't burn down or find itself invaded by drug-crazed vandals, everything was more or less all right. Disasters had regularly occurred, but very seldom as a result of Thea's sloppy security practices.

The imposition of a second responsibility began to seem more of a burden than first assumed, with so many additional details to get right. The trick would be to make a virtue of it in some way. If it really was only a mile away, then the best thing would be to walk over the fields from one village to the other, exploring them both in the process.

It was March, Easter still some weeks away, and the trees reluctant to risk much in the way of new leaves. Buds were swelling, barely perceptibly, and the Cotswold gardens boasted their customary displays of crocus, scilla and iris amongst the infinite shades of daffodil. Traditionally a time of promise, combined with the treachery of late frosts and biting winds, it reflected Thea's mood rather well. It was a year since she had first met Drew Slocombe, three years since she first began her career as a house-sitter, and four years since her husband had died. Anniversaries crowded into this time of year, including her own birthday in February. Hitting forty-five had been blessedly untraumatic, thanks to Drew's attentions, and an unexpected celebration provided by a rare collaboration between her daughter and her brother. She had felt loved. What more could anyone ask?

A year ago, she had been in Broad Campden when Drew Slocombe turned up to bury the owner of the house she was looking after. That one, actually, had not involved any animals at all. She had been struggling with the third anniversary of Carl's sudden death and Drew had been understanding. Now his own wife was dead, too, only eight months ago, and he was still in the early maelstrom of adjustment. 'One of the worst things,' he said, 'is that people think an undertaker should handle loss more easily than everybody else.'

His shortcomings in that respect had been starkly symbolised by his inability to bury Karen in his own burial ground, which they had created together. The plans had been altered at the eleventh hour, to the horror and rage of his small son and larger colleague, Maggs. Only Stephanie, his little girl, had understood and shared his feelings. In fact, it had been Stephanie's distress that cemented the decision, in the face of everyone else's wishes and assumptions.

16

Thea trod very carefully around that topic, which continued to cause difficulties. Now and then she caught a look from Maggs that suggested it might all be her fault. Reflecting briefly on her own character, Thea concluded that people often thought she was at fault in a variety of ways. Accused of being impatient, opinionated and even patronising, she struggled to be a better person and to bring out the best in other people. She had learnt to bite back sharp remarks, at least some of the time. Drew, she hoped, had been a positive influence in that respect.

It was one o'clock, and there was nothing important to be done. Gwennie was glumly curled up in her basket, with her back firmly to Thea and Hepzie. Since her docked tail had briefly wagged on Thea's arrival, she had not been friendly. The decision not to take her on a lengthy walk was easily made.

Unfolding the Ordnance Survey map, she calculated the distance across country to Bagendon to be just over a mile. Comparing it with the sketch map provided by the Fosters, she thought she could work out the location of the sister's house. The way was not entirely straightforward, using a combination of footpaths, country lanes and open fields, but she had every confidence. 'Start as we mean to go on,' she told the spaniel. 'Look at that sunshine.' Hepzie glanced out of the open door without enthusiasm.

Chapter Two

Daglingworth was as pretty as a hundred other little Cotswold settlements. Built around the intersection of two insignificant little roads, it enjoyed a peace and quiet that undoubtedly elevated the property values. The map clearly showed how the modern A417 had replaced older routes to Cirencester, with Daglingworth most likely a point of some importance at some long-gone time. But now the little lanes led nowhere but to other secluded villages or simply formed loops back to the big main road. The starting point of the footpath was somewhere close to the Fosters' house, and she scanned the lane for a sign. Back towards the centre of the village was an elevated path running alongside the road, presumably constructed in order to keep pedestrians and their dogs clear of any traffic. The houses in view were mostly discreet stone cottages, the colours showing their age.

Peering at the map, she concluded that the path she wanted was adjacent to the old school a little way further down to the right. She set off that way, and found she'd guessed correctly. Pausing to inspect the converted school, she drifted back in time to when it would have rung out with childish voices and a summoning bell. Now it seemed to have become a single dwelling, boasting very generous living space. 'All right for some,' she muttered.

A grassy lane presented itself, running in roughly the expected direction, but with no official indication that it was a public path. 'Must be right,' said Thea and let the dog off the lead. Hepzie ran ahead a little way and they proceeded comfortably along, enjoying the sunshine and listening to birdsong. The gradient was just enough to make her aware of her breathing. 'Not as fit as I should be,' she sighed. Perhaps if she did this walk every other day, she would notice an improvement.

The lane itself was interesting, and she wondered whether it had once been a well-used thoroughfare. It was hard underfoot even after a muddy winter, and was just wide enough for tractors and cars to traverse if necessary. It crossed the little road on which she had driven into the village a few hours earlier and headed for Itlay, which turned out to be almost too small a place to justify a name of its own. The view became more open and traffic was audible. The uphill slope had levelled out, much to her relief.

Hepzie seemed safe enough running free, and the absence of an eager dog pulling at her arm made it easier to pursue her own thoughts. Thoughts which tended towards Drew, as if to a magnet. Drew's cool, gentle hands; his attentive grey eyes; his easy charm and boyish humour – five years Thea's junior, he did strike her as inescapably boyish. Falling in love had not embarrassed Drew as much as it had Thea. She had still not disclosed the full extent of her feelings to her daughter, nor to any other relatives. The truth was leaking out, bit by bit, but nothing had actually been said to them. Since the dramatic events around Christmas, less than three months earlier, *love* had been a word she and Drew had used a lot, but only in private between themselves.

The future didn't worry them. 'No need to decide anything irrevocable,' said Drew, if the subject arose. She assumed that they intended to set up home together at some point, whilst knowing it had to be delicately arranged. She was not in any rush to take the role of stepmother to Stephanie and Timmy. Motherhood had never entirely suited her, even with her own child.

Before she knew it, there was a large square tunnel before her, and Hepzie was yapping at something inside it, the sound echoing and reverberating alarmingly. The dog herself was bewildered by the noise she was making and quickly fell silent. The squirrel she had spotted made a rapid escape and Thea joined the spaniel under the westbound carriageway of the A417.

'Come on, silly,' she said, quelling the urge to yodel and enjoy making her own echoes.

A second tunnel was a few yards ahead, and then they emerged onto another lane, with a dramatic and unexpected sight to the right. Through the spindly bare trees, a huge stone quarry fell away below them. Massive chunks of yellow rock were lined up and giant diggers sat waiting to be activated. Such an industrial scene was entirely alien in this soft self-indulgent region – and yet Thea had been aware all along that the lovely stone houses had been built from material dug out of the ground on their very doorstep.

There were quarries galore throughout the Cotswolds. Her map showed them on all sides. And yet this one was simply marked with a few discreet squiggles that only then did she interpret as suggesting stones. She recalled a road sign saying 'Daglingworth Quarry' and concluded that this enormous hole in the ground was the site it referred to.

A minute or two more walking brought her to a specific viewing spot, with a fence and chippings of yellow stone to stand on. She stood and peered over, wondering how many feet above the quarry floor she must be. Too many for comfort, as a nearby sign warned. You certainly wouldn't want to fall that far. She glanced around for Hepzibah, hoping the dog wouldn't find a hole in the fence and go bouncing down the rock face. Her pet was close by and met her eye with a reassuring wag, as if to say, *I wouldn't be such a fool as that.*

They wandered on and exactly as the map predicted, the lane soon emerged onto a proper road, which was apparently part of 'The Welsh Way'. Somewhere there should be a stile into a field on the left, a dotted red line showing a direct path to Bagendon's Upper End. 'Not far now,' said Thea. The quarry was on her right, shielded by trees, and she soon forgot all about it.

A footpath sign confirmed her map-reading skill, albeit standing in the middle of a thicket of brambles that was impassable even in early spring. 'Huh!' Thea complained. 'How do we get through that?'

Hepzie sniffed the ground, and trotted a few yards along the road. She then veered to the left, and jumped onto a pile of stones. Following her, Thea realised that this was the way into the field – not a stile, but a gap in an old wall, which you could simply step through. 'Okay,' she murmured.

A very faint path showed in the grass of the field, which sloped gently down to a strip of woodland. No further signs could be seen, but there was no alternative to entering the wood and finding a way through. Hesitantly, with another close examination of the map, she stepped beneath the leafless trees. Just to her left, two large upright square stones showed where shepherds of a century and more – probably a lot more – ago had built a permanent barrier to exclude or contain their sheep. She wished Drew had been there to see them with her. Such small indications of long-ago human activity always delighted them both.

Hepzie's yapping drew her attention to people sitting amongst the trees on the horizontal trunk of a fallen birch or ash. They were talking intently together, and took almost no notice of Thea and her dog, apart from a visible flicker of irritation. Two young women were perched there, eating bread and swigging from a wine bottle. The conversation was obviously too absorbing to allow anything to interrupt.

'He'll get around to it in his own good time,' said one. To Thea's interested gaze, she appeared to be somewhere in her mid twenties, with hair rolled up and tucked inside a woolly hat. Long flexible limbs, straight back and high ringing voice.

'That's not good enough, though, is it?' replied her companion. 'Nella's going mad, waiting for him to get his act together. And you can't blame her. It's been *ages* now.'

'Less than six months. Loads of couples stay engaged

for years without fixing a wedding date. I don't know why she's in such a rush.'

'She wants a proper old-fashioned wedding, that's why. And it can take a year to arrange it all. She thinks she'll be middle-aged before they get around to it, at this rate.' The second speaker was shorter, plumper and younger than her friend. She had a peaches-and-cream complexion and fair hair.

Thea knew she was expected to simply keep walking past them, but two things stopped her. One was that she genuinely wasn't certain as to where the path had gone. There were narrow ways going off in at least three directions, and she could not see where any of them led. The trees might be bare but they were close together, screening anything further than a few yards away.

The other reason was that she felt it rude of the twosome to ignore her so completely. She wanted them to acknowledge her, to be friendly and interested. So she simply stood there, looking at them, waiting for a pause in which she might ask the way.

The conversation continued in the same vein for another minute or two – the hesitant fiancé, the increasingly frustrated would-be bride, each with a defender. Thea found herself siding with the younger girl who favoured a quick wedding, despite an irritation with the idea that it would take a year in the planning. *Just tell them to get on with it*, she wanted to call out. One lesson she had learnt was that delay was seldom a good idea. You never knew what might happen to snatch away your security and well-being. If the engaged couple really loved each other, they should sweep aside all doubts and grab every available moment together.

And then she quietly tutted at her own maudlin thoughts. After all, she and Drew were at a standstill in their own relationship. Undue haste could be just as bad as a moderate delay. Perhaps there were good reasons for this man to take it slowly.

In the end, Hepzie took the initiative and decided to introduce herself to the two women ahead, and ran between them, with complicated results when she tried to jump up at the longer pair of legs, stretched out from the tree trunk. Always awkwardly balanced, the spaniel twisted and landed back on the leaf-strewn ground with a squeak.

'Good heavens!' snapped the girl. 'What on earth are you trying to do?' She looked directly at Thea for the first time. 'Is this yours?'

Silly question, thought Thea. 'Sorry,' she said. 'This is Hepzie. She thinks it's time she made friends with you.'

The interruption was plainly unwelcome, though more to the older person than her friend. The two seemed to be at least five years apart in age, Thea judged. The younger one was perhaps only about nineteen. She had a pretty mouth and grubby jeans. She laughed and bent down to play with the spaniel's long ears. 'Hello, Hepzie,' she said. 'Pleased to meet you. I'm Tiffany.'

'And I'm Sophie,' said the other one, considerably less enamoured of the dog.

Thea seized the chance for a bit of information exchange. 'I'm Thea Osborne. I'm house-sitting in Daglingworth, and thought we'd go for a good walk. Bagendon's just down there, isn't it?' She pronounced it with a hard g, as seemed the obvious way to say it.

'It's Ba*jen*don, actually. Soft "g". Not that there's much to it,' said Sophie, with a little sigh. 'Where do you live normally?'

Thea repeated the village name to herself, recalling that Mrs Foster had also said it with the 'g' sounding like a 'j'. 'Witney,' she answered. 'But I've done a lot of house-sitting in the Cotswolds. I like to explore these tiny villages – especially the ones nobody's heard of. I was in Hampnett a year or so ago. Nothing could be smaller than that. Except possibly Itlay,' she added, with a backward look towards the place she had recently passed.

'Hmm.' The scrutiny Thea was receiving reinforced her assessment of this Sophie woman as decidedly rude. 'You value the countryside, then, do you?'

'Pardon?'

'You must be aware of the threats to it from all sides. Wind farms, hunting ban, barn conversions, badger culls, fracking, new roads, gated communities . . .' The list seemed set to continue, but Tiffany interrupted.

'Steady on, Soph,' she laughed. 'You're sounding like a crackpot.'

Sophie frowned, but said nothing more. Thea sensed something unexpected and made no move to walk on. 'That's a lot of threats,' she remarked. 'I agree about badger culls and wind farms – but I can't believe they'd put any up around here.'

'Nowhere's sacred. The whole thing has become so totally corrupt, you can't rely on anyone. They say one thing and do another. Broken promises as far as the eye can see. And as fast as you see off one lot of developers, there's two more popping up. All you can do is go to the source.'

'*Sophie*,' begged her young friend.

'How would you ever be able to do that?' Thea was intrigued. 'Even if you change the government, things won't alter very much. Nobody's going to lift the ban on hunting, for a start.' She was struggling to devise a unifying theme to Sophie's list of outrages. 'Besides, since when was hunting so good for the countryside? Don't they break fences and make holes in hedges? All those thundering great horses churning up the fields, as well.' Personally, she had never felt much sympathy for the practice.

'You have to undermine them at the roots.'

'Gosh.' It sounded almost frighteningly serious, the way she said it. 'Nothing short of revolution, eh?'

'Ignore her,' said Tiffany. 'It's nothing like that at all. We just want to look after things like landscape and heritage, don't we? And the badger cull's barbaric, obviously.'

'We?' Thea was quick to ask. 'Just you two, or a whole lot of friends and workmates as well?'

'There's a lot of us,' Tiffany began. 'Students, and loads of others.'

'I'm not a student,' Sophie said, as if the idea were demeaning.

'No, you're not,' her friend agreed peaceably.

Thea's unspoken enquiry as to what she was then went unanswered.

'Come on, Sophie, we need to get a move on,' Tiffany urged. 'Nella's going to be waiting for us.' She and her friend stood up, brushing at their legs, and in unspoken accord, all three trod the obscure footpath in single file. 'It's this way,' said Tiffany superfluously. 'It comes out in a field just over there.'

'The badger cull is appalling,' Thea said. 'You would think they could find a better way. All those experts and scientists ought to come up with something.'

'"Experts and scientists"!' scoffed Sophie. 'Just a lot of self-interested idiots, that's all *they* are.'

If Thea hadn't heard the woman sounding perfectly sensible ten minutes earlier, when discussing their friend Nella, she would have begun to wonder about her sanity. As it was, she was rapidly concluding that Sophie was obsessive and unbalanced, at the very least.

'You need to talk to Nella,' Sophie went on. 'She puts it all a lot better than I can.'

'And Danny, of course,' said Tiffany. 'Between them, they can convert just about anybody.'

'Danny just does what Nella tells him to,' said Sophie with scorn.

'Apart from fixing a date for their wedding,' Tiffany flashed back. 'She's really cross about it, you know. You didn't see her last night.'

Thea was losing interest in the romantic tribulations endured by the oddly named Nella. Her dog was running impatiently ahead, and the western horizon was filling with unwelcome grey clouds. 'How far is it?' she asked. 'That looks a bit ominous over there.'

'We can be at the church in ten minutes if we bustle.' Sophie's long legs began to stride out, regardless of her companions. Thea was regretting the impulse to grab any chance of conversation, reproaching herself for such a bad choice of local informants. Sophie and Tiffany were apparently deeply involved in some sort of protest activity against a bewildering array of issues. Whilst faintly aware of a major feeling of disaffection in Middle England, she had hardly expected to walk into a hotbed of revolution in the rolling wolds of Gloucestershire.

Feeling very much surplus to requirements, she began to allow a space to develop between herself and the others. Fiddling with Hepzie's lead gave her the excuse to hang back. She had a murky sense that she ought not to advertise the fact that she was responsible for Mrs Foster's sister's house, or that it was empty and vulnerable for the coming week. Tiffany glanced back and gave a little wave as Sophie increased her pace. They disappeared through a gap into another field, and Thea imagined she would never see them again.

Upper End turned out to be a loop of quiet road due west of the rest of Bagendon, with the church and a huge manor house on rising ground above it. On a whim, Thea decided to carry on past the house she was supposed to monitor, and walk down to the church for a quick look. For all she knew it would rain for the next ten days and she wouldn't fancy any more walks. According to the map provided by the Fosters, the house in question was to her left and around a curve. She would come back to it and give it a good inspection, before walking back to Daglingworth. The day would be almost done by then.

It took a further five minutes to arrive at Bagendon

Church, past a selection of large houses plainly owned by people of means. A massive barn conversion, and a second defunct village school destined to become a house caught her eye. To her relief the clouds had come no closer. A shiny Freelander was parked outside the church, and Thea could see her new acquaintances standing beside it with a third young woman. She chewed her lip, wondering whether they would object to her following them again. Then she squared her shoulders and marched forward, with Hepzie firmly on the lead. She had every right to go and have a look at the church, after all.

It was very obvious that Tiffany had muttered a quick explanation as to who she was, before she came into earshot. The third woman looked enquiringly at Thea and her dog and said nothing. She was older than the other two, and very thin. Her dark hair was pulled back in a straggly ponytail and her eyes had shadows beneath them. She wore green wellingtons and a blue duffel coat.

'Here you are again,' said Sophie. 'She's a house-sitter,' she told the thin woman. She flipped a hand and added, 'This is Nella.'

Thea had already understood that this was the would-be bride, who did a sideways little nod of acknowledgement, and patted the vehicle behind her.

'Why've you got Danny's motor, anyway?' asked Tiffany.

'He wanted me to take it for its MOT and then meet him here. He's walking back from Woodmancote, apparently. There's a badger sett up there that they missed in the culling. He's trying to camouflage it.' Nella's explanation was certainly comprehensive, Thea thought, imagining the absent Danny as a bearded, sandalled protester with more money than was good for him, if he could afford such a vehicle.

'They'll find them, in the end,' said Sophie bitterly. The slaughter of hundreds of badgers should have been old news by this time, but it had continued to remain in the forefront of people's minds. Thea suspected it was because of a wholesale sense of shame that proved surprisingly difficult to shake off. Inevitable stories of appalling injuries and lingering deaths had circulated widely, as well as rumours of underground workers saving animals as if they'd been wartime resistance personnel. Even at a remove from the centre of the action, Thea had gleaned something of the heightened emotion and dogged determination to obstruct officialdom that rippled through the countryside.

'So – what are we doing?' asked Tiffany. 'I've got an essay to write by Tuesday. I can't be out here all day.'

'We'll wait a bit longer. What did you find for me at Itlay?' Nella's voice was low, and her gaze roamed across the rising ground towards Daglingworth and all the places Thea had traversed during her walk.

All three then glanced at Thea, as if fearing she might be a spy. 'Tell you later,' said Sophie.

'Well, so this is Bagendon,' said Thea heartily. 'I'm going to have a quick look at the church, while I'm here.' She smiled vaguely and went to the small gate into the churchyard.

'Nice meeting you,' said Tiffany. Of the three, this was definitely Thea's favourite. The other two both seemed faintly bonkers.

'Danny's behaving himself, then?' asked Sophie, as Thea tried to operate the unusual latch.

She caught Nella's laugh as she finally got through and up towards the small low-slung church. 'Oh yes. You should have seen him this morning. Really apologetic. He's going to be fine from now on. It was all just a silly mix-up.'

Tiffany's yelp of pleasure echoed in Thea's ears as she entered the porch.

Chapter Three

The church was probably very historic and interesting, for an aficionado. Thea liked wall paintings, gargoyles, and the ungrammatical little leaflets and notices that were sometimes to be found. In this one, she liked the red kneelers, each with a different animal or bird embroidered into the centre. She thought the kneelers were lovely. And then, idly reading the memorial plaques, she found one dedicated to a man called Rev. John Lewis Bythesea and his brother Edmund. She almost crowed with delight, much as Tiffany had just done outside. She wished passionately that Drew were with her to see this incredible name fixed for eternity on a marble slab. The brothers had been born in the 1760s, she calculated. John had previously lived in Wiltshire – which was not at all by the sea. How, *how*, did anybody acquire such a surname? She was transported and fascinated. Here was a glimpse of eighteenth-century rural life in a single surname. Did anybody still carry it, centuries later? Almost certainly not, she assumed. They'd change it to Blythe or Birtlesea or something.

With a final giggle, she went back to retrieve the dog she'd left in the porch and retrace her steps back to Upper End – which was also vaguely eighteenth century, she supposed.

The three women had disappeared, along with the vehicle. The village was deserted, as all Cotswolds villages habitually were. People remained indoors or in their back gardens, if they weren't away in London, where their real daily lives were conducted.

Mrs Foster's sister's house was a large traditional stone building, with the usual tidy garden and well-kept paintwork. It was more recent than the Daglingworth one, but still a good century old, she guessed. She extracted the key and long list of instructions from her backpack and took a deep breath. The door opened smoothly, and she went into a shadowy hallway, feeling unusually apprehensive. After all, she had never met the owner, and had not even been told her name. The arrangement struck her as uncomfortably ad hoc, on reflection. If the woman was only away for a week, couldn't the plants manage on their own? Was there some sinister ulterior motive for bringing her here? Was she being foolishly naïve, or foolishly nervous? The burglar alarm had to be deactivated, and she carefully keyed in the numbers she'd been given, wondering what her chances were of successfully setting it again when she left.

Her worries were allayed as she tiptoed into the living room. Hepzie had been left on the doorstep, her muddy feet rendering her ineligible to walk around a strange person's house. It turned out to have been a wise decision. The sofa and chairs were upholstered in spotless fabric of a creamy colour, surrounded by spindly antique objects all too easily knocked over. A deep window seat was full of exotic indoor plants. Beyond that room lay another, containing a massive oak dining table and a lot more plants. It smelt of polish and frangipani and air freshener; clean, fresh, hygienic smells that betrayed nothing organic or agricultural. Modern oil paintings hung on the walls and a shelf of books bridged an alcove next to a fireplace. Underfoot, there were short-pile rugs in colours that echoed those of the curtains. The walls were neutrally painted in almost-white shades.

Who were these people, Thea wondered. How much time and attention did they devote each day to maintaining this perfection? What else did they do with their lives? Except, there had been no reference to a husband. Just a sister. Had she cleaned up after a divorce, perhaps? A guilty man handing over his house and cash at his injured wife's insistence? There was no trace of children, no family photographs. The niece in Australia presumably stood to gain quite a substantial inheritance from these two country aunts, if there were no others in her generation to share the spoils.

She gave the plants some water, picked up the meagre scattering of letters and flyers from the doormat, and prepared to leave. At the last minute, she realised she needed a pee, and found a downstairs lavatory with immaculate modern accoutrements. So modern, in fact, that when Thea tried to remove the plug from the bathroom basin after washing her hands, she could not see how to do it. There was no chain, no little lever, nothing to grip hold of. There had to be a trick to it, but she could not for the life of her work out what it was.

Why on earth had she pushed the plug down in the first place, she asked herself. The answer was that her hands had been rather grubby from the various things she had touched during the walk, and she had very much liked the smell of the soap provided. So she had made a thorough production, half filling the basin in the process. The only thing she could think of was to bail out as much as possible of the water with a small glass she found in the kitchen, and pour it down the loo. It left a puddle of rather grey water that she could not scoop up. Shrugging helplessly, she left it, promising herself to see to it on the next visit.

When she emerged from the house, having used extreme care in resetting the alarm, she found that rain had set in to an uncomfortable degree. A mile's country walk with a reproachful dog and only a flimsy jacket was not a happy prospect, and she hovered on the front doorstep, unsure what to do. Already the return walk was acquiring a daunting new prospect. The first part would be uphill, the gap into the woods probably difficult to find. She had taken no precautionary notice of landmarks on the way down. The bare trees would drip on her and provide very little shelter from the rain. And her shoes were hardly more resilient than her coat.

She extracted the map from her bag and peered at it. Walking back via roads was hardly any longer, and probably much more sensible. Negotiating the big roundabout where several small roads joined the new A417 would be the biggest hazard. On the map a tangle of green and yellow lines made it look worse than she remembered it from that morning. So long as she had Hepzie firmly on the lead, it should be all right.

She went back down to the church and turned right towards something called Perrotts Brook on the map. Her shoulders were already wet and Hepzie was turning frizzy. Her mood, which had lifted somewhat during the past few hours, dropped back to worry and frustration. She should have prepared better for such weather. She should have got a move on, and simply checked the house and turned back. If she'd done that, she'd have dodged the rain completely.

When a noisy engine came up behind her, she was in a narrow part of the lane, so dragged Hepzie closer and turned to face the vehicle. It was a muddy Land Rover, of an age and condition seldom seen in the affluent Cotswolds. When it stopped beside her, a man in his fifties with greyish-ginger hair and a lean face leant over the passenger seat and pushed the door open. 'Want a lift?' he asked.

A black-and-white sheepdog was in the back, pushing its face eagerly towards her with a wide grin.

'Yes, please,' said Thea without hesitation. 'I'm getting soaked.' She didn't have to apologise for her dog or her wet feet, as she might in a proper car. She lifted Hepzie in ahead of her, and climbed up onto the grubby seat. When she slammed the door behind her, she was aware of a rich smell that could only be labelled as 'farmyard'. It was lovely, and she sighed.

'Where to?' he asked.

'Daglingworth. Lower End, if that's all right. Is it terribly out of your way?'

'Terribly,' he said cheerfully. 'I was going to North Cerney. Totally different direction. You'll owe me.' His accent was that of any educated middle-aged Englishman, with no rolled rs or archaic grammar. 'This is Rags,' he added. 'She's an old girl now.'

Thea reached back and gave the collie her hand to sniff. 'Hello, Rags,' she said.

'Did you break down or something?'

'Oh, no. I decided to walk across the fields. I had no idea it was going to rain. It was fine when I set out.'

'Not local, are you?'

'No. I'm house-sitting for a couple of weeks. I like to explore when I'm on a job. It gets a bit boring otherwise.'

'House-sitting?' He repeated it as if the words and the concept were both entirely new to him. 'Who for?'

'They're called Foster. Do you know them?'

He frowned. 'He's not the auctioneer, is he? The Cheltenham one. Does antiques and stuff.'

'Might be. I don't know what they do, actually. If it is him, there aren't any antiques in the house.'

'Don't worry – I'm not planning to burgle them.'

'Oh no – sorry. I didn't mean that.' She was hot with embarrassment and he laughed. She babbled on. 'They've gone to Australia for a wedding. Makes a change from cruises, at least. They seem to be a real growth industry.'

He snorted. 'Chance'd be a fine thing.'

She managed a faint laugh of her own, thinking this man was just about the last person ever to find himself on a cruise liner. 'Anyway. I'm Thea Osborne. It's very nice of you to give me a ride, I must say.'

'Doesn't happen so much any more. You were brave to take me up on it.'

'Desperate, more like. I was talking to some women an hour ago. I should have asked them to take me back, if I'd known it'd rain.'

'You mean those idiot protesters, I suppose? I saw them in that Freelander, outside the church.' He shook his head. 'You don't want to get mixed up with them. They're all crazy.'

'I did wonder,' said Thea, feeling briefly disloyal. Tiffany, for one, had been perfectly nice and not at all crazy.

'You can't imagine. There's a dozen or more of them, men as well. Never sure who's going to join them next. All they do is find things to complain about. They make a lot of people very angry, I can tell you.'

'Including you?'

'Yes, including me. They've got no idea what it's like trying to run a decent farm with a bloody great debt around your neck and prices going nowhere. Do they think I *want* to sell land? Nobody wants to do that. My dad'll come back and haunt me for it, any time now. But it's a scrappy bit, off in a corner, and *they* asked *me* if I'd part with it. It was never my idea. Some bloke knocks on the door one day and says it's worth a hundred grand as a building plot. Good access, nice outlook – all the boxes ticked. So what am I going to do? That sort of money doesn't come along more than once. It's *one acre*, for God's sake. I've got another hundred and four that's still going to be part of the "natural landscape", as they keep calling it. You know the latest thing – they told the council they'd found a rare orchid growing there, which couldn't hope to survive being moved or built around. All I had to do was put some bullocks in there and that'd be curtains for the orchid. Madness. What else can you call it?'

They had turned right onto a similar lane, and then right again. The road had trees on one side, reminding Thea of many others across the region. She looked out at the wet scene and said nothing. The driver was ranting every bit as excessively as Sophie had done. Had she blundered into a wholesale war, in which nobody could think of anything other than their grievances?

'Sorry,' he said, as her silence finally registered. 'You probably don't have any idea what I'm talking about.'

'I got the gist,' she said.

'It's a nightmare,' he went on. 'Though there's other farmers who get it even worse. The ones who support the badger cull are lucky if they ever get a decent night's sleep. They harass them in the small hours. But the police say nobody's breaking any laws. We just have to stick it out and wait for the gang to move on to some other obsession somewhere else. What do they expect to gain, anyway?' he burst out loudly. 'Do they want to stop all new building altogether?'

Silently, Thea tried to justify the protesters, having always instinctively sided with any efforts to preserve the landscape, and having found most newly built Cotswolds houses to be too big and far too yellow. They were ostentatious demonstrations of wealth, in most cases, she judged. Probably owned by wealthy Russians or Saudis, and no use at all in providing homes for ordinary local families.

They were at the big intersection, with late-afternoon traffic quite heavy along the main road. The Land Rover driver seized a small gap and got hooted at as a result. 'Careful!' squeaked Thea.

'Don't worry. I know what I'm doing.' He sounded offended.

'Sorry. I'm a nervous passenger. Ignore me.'

'Just take my advice and don't get involved with those loonies. They're parasites, you know. They'll drag you in if they think you can be of any use to them, and then just drop you again. They do nothing but harm. Most of them come from the other end of the country – what brings them here, I can't imagine.'

'I'm only here for two weeks,' she said. 'I doubt if they think I'm worth bothering with. They didn't seem very keen to talk to me, anyway, when I met them. They were too busy talking about somebody's boyfriend.'

He gave a huff of impatience, and turned left at the crossroads that was Daglingworth. 'Up here somewhere, are you?' he asked.

'That's right. But you can drop me here, where it's easy to turn. I can walk the last bit.'

'I'm Jack Handy, by the way.' He pulled up at the side of the road. 'Thanks for listening to me. I s'pose I sounded pretty much of a nutcase myself, going on like that.'

'No problem,' she said. 'And thanks for the lift. You're very kind.'

He grinned at that. 'Not many people think so,' he said.

Chapter Four

The nameplate on the Fosters' front wall, announcing 'Galanthus House' was not as welcoming as 'Bide A While' or 'Journey's End' might have been, but she was glad to get back into its sheltering portals. She had forgotten to enquire as to the significance of the name – some sort of plant, she suspected.

It was half past four. Nearly time to feed the dogs and think of something for herself. It would be eight or so before she could phone Drew, as she was itching to do. The intervening hours would pass slowly, as she knew from past experience. Supervising dogs, taking Gwennie outside, unpacking, working out how to operate the various controls for the television – all these diversions and more only took her to six o'clock. Accustomed to similar spells of inactivity in the first days of a house-sit, she pottered in the kitchen, frying herself two eggs and a fishcake, that came from her own grocery supplies. The Fosters had made it clear they expected her to see to her own catering requirements, only using condiments and sauces from their cupboards.

She elected to listen to the radio, rather than sit in front of the TV, with the news full of the usual extreme weather events and alarming economic figures. Nothing she need bother about, she decided.

Her mobile was fully charged and very much more central to her existence than it had been before things had started to happen between her and Drew. She sent him a steady stream of texts and even photos from time to time. But nothing came close to the pleasure she derived from a real conversation and hearing his voice, as far as satisfaction went. And that was a poor second to being in the same room with him, meeting his gaze and touching his skin.

There were other people she could contact, of course – first amongst them being Jessica, her police officer daughter. She had neglected Jess rather seriously in recent months, feeling guilty mainly because she didn't feel guilty about it – which made Drew laugh. The girl was twenty-three, qualified, busy, sociable. She didn't need her mother very much. But other women still hovered over their daughters well past that age, expecting to know every detail of their lives and to have their advice heeded. There was definitely a rule of some sort somewhere that Thea suspected she was breaking. The breaking of rules was part of her nature, it seemed, especially in recent times of surveillance and interference and intolerance of differences. Every time she heard anybody talking about it as an age of individualism, she scoffed. As far as she could see, it was the exact opposite. To run counter to the prevailing tide of opinion was to attract the most extreme opprobrium and even the attention of the police, if they suspected you of hating someone.

When the mobile trilled at her, she leapt to grab it, thinking Drew had found a moment to call her earlier than usual. But it was a different number showing on the screen. 'Hello?' she said.

'Thea. It's Damien. Where are you?'

'Damien? For heaven's sake – what's happened? Is it Mum?'

'No, no. Don't panic. It's nothing like that. Where are you?' he asked again.

'A little place called Daglingworth. You won't have heard of it. Why do you want to know?'

'Just curious. I can never keep track of you these days, with that boyfriend and everything.'

Were older brothers meant to supervise their sisters, then, like a mother with a grown-up daughter, she wondered irritably. Damien had always been someone to avoid as much as possible, with his prissy judgements and tendency to over-control everyone. As older brother to three sisters, he had assumed responsibilities that nobody had ever actually accorded him.

'So . . . ?' she prompted. She didn't like to have the phone tied up for long, when all she wanted was to speak to Drew.

'Listen. I've got some news.' His voice was oddly unsure, even shy – which was highly unusual.

'What?' Already she had guessed that he was going to take holy orders, or sell all his goods and become a hermit. Damien had embraced religion some fifteen years ago and had become difficult to talk to ever since. Occasional attempts to convert one or other of his sisters never came to anything.

'Judy's pregnant.'

'Good God!' Despite repeated requests that everyone in the family refrain from such expletives, the habit was far too deep to change. And perhaps this time, he would deem it appropriate anyway. 'That's amazing.'

'I know. We can hardly believe it. It's due in August, which doesn't seem very far off. We had no idea until last week.'

Thea tried to do the calculations. 'She's four months on, then?'

'Sixteen weeks,' he agreed.

'And she's forty-four – is that right?'

'Not quite, but she will be when it's born. A baby, Thea! At our age!'

'Yes,' she said faintly. 'It's hard to imagine.' And it was. Judy had a PhD in numerology, which had apparently fitted quite readily into Damien's religious faith and practice. She worked as some sort of consultant to a perfectly mainstream financial institution, which supposedly did at least involve an understanding of numbers.

'We never even *dreamt* . . .' He was obviously trying to say something about how the creature had been conceived, but was too embarrassed. 'We thought it was . . . you know, the menopause.'

At least he didn't call it The Change, Thea thought. 'I gather that happens a lot,' she said, wondering with a distinct horror whether it could ever happen to her. 'People seem to cope pretty well. You're both in good health, at least.'

'You are meant to offer congratulations,' he said, sounding stiff and awfully old.

'Take it as read. What does Mum think? Have you told Jocelyn? What about Emily?'

'Mum's delighted. She likes babies. And I'm calling Jocelyn next, after you.' The question about their other sister was ignored.

'You're right about Mum. Well, thanks for telling me. I appreciate it. I'll come and see you sometime. Maybe over Easter. I need to go now – sorry. You'll be fine. Tell Judy from me, she'll be a great mother.'

'Thanks.'

She pressed the red button and sat back on the sofa where she'd gone from the first moments of the call, thinking a long relaxed chat with Drew was about to take place. How in the world had Damien's God made such a drastic mistake as to send them a child? Her brother and his wife were like a couple from the pages of Charles Dickens. She was tall and angular, he short and wide. Neither of them managed the details of daily life especially well. Their house was untidy and disorganised, with books, papers, unopened letters, empty CD cases and assorted accumulations on every surface. Damien earned a modest salary as a counsellor for a church charity, helping people through various crises. Thea had often wondered how good he was at listening or giving advice. Perhaps, she thought optimistically, he was much better with strangers than he was with his family.

At last it was time to call Drew. His children would be in bed and he would be sitting with his feet up, wondering how to pass his lonely evening, just as she was herself. One day, she promised herself, they would spend every remaining evening of their lives together.

He did not answer the phone immediately. When he did, it was breathlessly. 'What's the matter?' she asked him.

'The usual,' he said. 'Body for removal and not enough of us to do it. For some reason, it won't wait till the morning.'

'Can't Maggs and what's-his-name do it?' There was a new assistant, required to be on perpetual standby for just such contingencies. Thea had never met him, but he had sounded reliable.

'Peter. He's called Peter. And he's in A&E according to his wife, because he dropped a sledgehammer on his foot.'

'Den, then.'

'Leave it, love. It's not your problem. I'm getting Hilary from the village to come and babysit. I've got twenty minutes to wait, before she can get here. Let's talk about something else. What's it like in sunny Daglingworth?'

'It was sunny for a bit, and then it rained. Luckily I got a lift from an irascible red-haired farmer.'

'You were out in the rain? Why?'

She gave him a quick account of the day, emphasising the delights of landscape and architecture, and remembering to report the Bythesea name in the church. 'It's a hotbed of revolution, surprisingly. I met three eco-warriors, or something of the sort. They object to practically everything – not least the red-haired farmer's efforts to sell a very small field as a building plot.'

'Don't get involved,' he warned her.

'I wasn't going to.'

'I ought to heed my own advice, I suppose,' he said, with

47

a preoccupied tone. 'I think I might have done something I'll regret.'

'Oh?'

'There's a nursing home not far from here. I've dealt with them since I started, on and off. But a year ago they were bought by a bigger outfit, with new management and a lot of staff changes. Well, in the past four weeks I've done three funerals for them. And yesterday they called with another one.'

'That's good, isn't it? They must like you. Is it them you're going to this evening?'

'No, no. A different one. But when we went one day last week, one of the inmates collared me – I know most of them, anyway. Quite a few have booked places in the field. The thing is, they're all terrified of the new people. And the woman who died before this latest one – she was called Mrs Hepton – she was absolutely skin and bone. They said something about it being due to an infection, which made no sense at all. She must have died of starvation. And she was always quite a large lady. So – I made a call to the police about it.'

'Blimey, Drew!'

'Well, I didn't see I had any choice. I can't let that sort of thing go on and just turn a blind eye, can I? Even Maggs thinks it's sinister, and she's always on at me to leave sleeping dogs alone.'

'Well . . .'

'The thing is, there's always been an understanding that undertakers don't ask awkward questions, particularly where nursing homes are concerned. We need their business,

48

after all. Daphne Plant would throw a fit if any of her team did such a thing.'

'Yes, but you're not Daphne Plant, are you.' It wasn't a question. Thea had heard something of the ambitious female undertaker who had originally introduced Drew to the business. He had left her employ after a year or so, determined to create his own much more ethical concern. On the whole, he had succeeded handsomely.

'No. And those poor old things in the home do need somebody on their side. It's much too easy to make their remaining days a complete misery.'

'And we can't have that, can we?'

'Thanks. I knew you'd understand.' He still sounded worried. 'I'm hoping the police won't reveal the source of their information, but it's bound to get out. Or they'll figure it out for themselves. And if the place is closed down, that's not going to help the inmates, is it?'

'Too late to worry about it now, love. Listen, it must be nearly time for you to go. I'll call you again tomorrow. But first I have two quick questions.'

'Fire away.'

'First – do you know what galanthus is?'

'Um . . . snowdrops, isn't it? I remember when Karen planted them all along our bank, she said that was their proper name.'

'Great. Thanks. It's the name of this house, you see. The other thing is – have you come across a newfangled type of washbasin – you know, in a fancy modern bathroom, where you push the plug in and then can't get it out again?'

'Not that I can recall.'

'Well, there's one in the other house I'm minding. I couldn't for the life of me see how you do it.'

'Try pushing it down further. It might be on some sort of spring.'

'No, no. That can't be it. It's already right down.'

'Just try it, okay. If everything else fails, try the counter-intuitive angle.'

'That would never have occurred to me in a thousand years. I can't wait to go back and see if you're right.'

'I think it's called lateral thinking.'

There followed two minutes of sentimental exchanges along the lines of how greatly they approved of each other. Then Drew said, 'Oh, I think that's Hilary now. I'll have to go.'

'One last thing,' she called, wondering how she could have left it so late. 'My brother Damien's wife is pregnant. She's forty-four.'

'Good for her. So is Maggs. She told me not to tell you, for reasons I don't understand. Speak to you tomorrow, sweetheart. Sleep well.'

And he was gone.

Chapter Five

She woke next morning, still thinking of the two new babies soon to force themselves into the world, neither of them ever even dreamt of in her own personal scheme of things. If Maggs had a baby, that would hugely impact on Drew's business. She wouldn't be able to drop everything and go on removals at all hours of the day and night. Well – perhaps she could do the nights, when her husband Den could mind the child. And perhaps she could take it with her at other times. Drew had looked after Stephanie at the same time as running Peaceful Repose, when Karen returned to teaching. Den, in his late thirties, was still not entirely settled to any proper career. He had gone into the police initially, but deemed himself a failure at it, in some way Thea had never grasped. He seemed like a man born out of his time, a sort of Dixon of Dock Green set down in the wrong era. Even the uniform must have looked all wrong on him, with his extreme height. He and Maggs made a couple even more physically ill-matched than Damien and Judy. At roughly the time Thea met Drew, Den had found a job at Bristol

Airport, as a security officer. As far as she could gather, he was enjoying it enough to generate some hope that he might stick with it for some time to come. The hours were regular, with overtime available, and the pay substantially more than he had earned for ages. He always had a new story to tell about some benighted passenger falling foul of the surveillance system.

It was awful of her, she realised, not to feel thrilled at the imminent new lives. She did try, but all she could think was that her brother's life would be changed forever, and possibly not for the better. As for Maggs and Den, they would no doubt make excellent parents, and produce a lovely dark-eyed child. But the consequences for Drew were unlikely to be beneficial.

Gwennie was slow to rouse, curled in her basket in the kitchen and barely breathing. 'Don't you dare die on me,' Thea told her. 'Have a biscuit and come outside with Hepzie.'

The corgi slowly obeyed and plodded to the end of the garden and back. Hepzie zigzagged over the lawn, sniffing and wagging and generally showing off. The contrast gave Thea grounds to hope there were many years yet to come in which her dog would be fit and active. One of the few aspects of her existence that found favour with Drew's children was her spaniel.

Her first plan for the day was a brief return to Bagendon's Upper End, by car, to check whether Drew's theory about the plug was accurate. She would take Hepzie and Gwennie and give them a gentle stroll around the village at the same time. Then in the afternoon she might go and have a look at

North Cerney, which was another little place she had heard of but never seen before.

At nine-thirty, she bundled the dogs onto the back seat and set off along the route taken by Farmer Handy in his Land Rover, the day before. Bagendon was comprehensively signposted, and she found the small road up to Upper End without difficulty. She even managed to identify the way onto the footpath back to Itlay and Daglingworth – admittedly made easier by the presence of a group of people standing just inside the field. They were staring in the direction of Itlay, where Thea could hear the whirring of a helicopter once she got out of her car.

She recognised Sophie and Tiffany immediately. They were dressed in the same resilient outdoor gear as before, perhaps even more so. Curious as ever, she called to them, 'Hi! What's going on?'

Sophie turned slowly, reluctantly, and simply shook her head. Tiffany was dancing from foot to foot. 'We don't *know*,' she said. 'Steve heard something on the police radio about the quarry. It must be serious for them to call a helicopter out.'

A man in his mid twenties with very large ears and a scrappy beard looked up, evidently having heard his name. He gave Thea a long look, before nodding to her and going back to the phone in his hand.

'He's got an app that means you can eavesdrop on them,' Tiffany explained cheerfully. 'It comes in very useful when we're . . . you know.' Sophie had slapped her arm lightly, effectively stopping her chatter in mid flow.

Thea winced, still floundering in the ethical morass that

every encounter with these protesters produced. She looked around again at the assorted individuals: nobody over thirty-five, most of them wearing sturdy wellingtons and waterproof jackets. Sophie carried an air of authority, with the big-eared Steve staying close to her, like a deputy. 'Well,' Thea muttered. 'Better get on.' It was all too obvious that the whole group wished her well away from them.

She retreated to the house she had inspected the previous day and concentrated – with an effort – on the burglar alarm and the removal of her shoes, which were sure to leave marks on the spotless carpets.

The little pool of water was still in the basin, cold and greasy and embarrassing. With a sceptical frown, she plunged a forefinger in and pressed the chromium plug down as hard as she could. Then she let go and miraculously it popped up. The water ran away, leaving a grey smear on the porcelain. She ran hot water and swept around with her fingers until it was clean again. 'Just fancy that,' she murmured to herself. 'What a barmy arrangement.'

Thank goodness for Drew's good sense, she thought. Casting a final glance around the downstairs rooms to assure herself that all was well, she wondered again what the owner might have in common with her modest sister. Her taste in decor was dramatically different, but then sisters did vary a lot in that respect. Some took it seriously and others really didn't. But this one definitely had an advantage financially, if the size and condition of the house were anything to go by.

What, then, would the woman think, if anything, about the presence of a gang of anarchists – or whatever they were – on her doorstep? Had they crossed her path before? Did she quietly support or noisily oppose them?

She went back the way she had come, to find the little crowd outside had grown in the past ten minutes, and Thea's car had been joined by two others. Intent on her original plan, she got the dogs out and firmly connected them to their leads. Whatever might be happening in the quarry was none of her concern and she told herself to stop being nosy and stick to her job. Gwennie needed exercise and attention. Gwennie was her prime responsibility. But Gwennie herself showed every sign of curiosity at the assembly of interesting people close by. Her pointed nose lifted and she made enthusiastic little squeaks. It would be cruel to deny her the society, Thea decided, allowing herself to be drawn back to the people.

There were three or four newcomers. One was a blonde woman of fifty or so who stood close to Tiffany. Another was Nella, Sophie's friend, who Thea hadn't noticed earlier. One or two young men loitered on the edge of the group, with hands in their pockets and shoulders hunched, as if it were a much colder day. None of them greeted Thea or her dogs, all their attention fixed on Steve and his gadget. 'Fatality,' he announced loudly. 'There must be a body in the quarry. Wow!'

Tiffany squealed and the woman beside her hushed her as if she were a small child. Must be her mother, Thea concluded.

'We should go and see,' said Sophie. 'We're not going to find out anything standing around here, are we?'

'Tiffany's not going anywhere,' said the blonde. 'She's

not meant to be associating with you people, anyway.'

'Mum, for heaven's sake,' pleaded the girl. 'I'm old enough to know what I'm doing. Why are *you* here, anyway?'

'I saw Nella coming this way, and thought she'd lead me to you. I *told* you to stay in this morning. What about that essay?'

'Come on, if you're coming,' repeated Sophie to the group in general. 'We can go through the woods and be there in ten minutes. It might be somebody we know.'

'We won't see anything,' said Nella. 'They won't let us get close enough. Isn't it rather ghoulish, anyway? It's going to be one of the quarry workers, crushed under a digger or a rockfall.'

'On a Sunday?' queried Tiffany's mother.

'They work weekends sometimes, don't they?' Nella sounded vague, almost offhand. 'But suit yourself. I can't see much sense in standing around like this.'

The man with the phone looked up again. 'They're not saying anything new. It's all going according to procedure, I guess. They're never going to put a name out over this frequency.' He shook his head. 'I don't think there's much we can usefully do.'

'Why did you all come out here in the first place?' Thea asked, mainly addressing Sophie, but sweeping the whole group in an invitation to reply.

'Mind your own business,' Nella snapped back. 'Who *are* you, anyway? Why've you brought those dogs? The last thing we need is dogs drawing attention to us.'

'You met me yesterday – don't you remember?' said

Thea coldly. 'And if this is private property, then you're trespassing just as much as I am, wouldn't you say?'

'I know I met you. But I don't get what you think you're doing, barging in like this.'

'I'm not "barging in",' Thea spluttered furiously, all the time thinking that actually, sort of, she was doing exactly that.

'It's something to do with badgers, love,' said Tiffany's mother, who appeared to think she was a fellow intruder. 'They monitor all the local setts this time of year, so they can sabotage the culling when it comes.' She gave her daughter a gentle cuff. 'Getting themselves arrested, if they're not careful.'

'Not if Steve keeps a watch on where they are,' said Sophie, not looking at Thea, but plainly addressing her. There was something rather dreamy about her delivery, as if events were taking place that she had no part in, but nonetheless found fascinating. At the same time, she could not resist asserting their aims, perhaps in the lingering hope that Thea would become a signed-up member, after all. 'The cops, that is,' she elaborated. 'We're always a few steps ahead of them, you see. Although we've had a few narrow escapes lately.' She finally accorded Thea a long scrutiny, albeit with a strange lack of focus. 'You're not working for them, are you?'

'Who?'

'The cops, of course.'

'No.' Thea thought it diplomatic to avoid revealing that her daughter was a cop, as were others among her friends and relations. 'Do I look like I am?'

'They come in all shapes and sizes. Anyway, let's get on with it. Tiffany – are you coming?'

The girl sighed and spoke to her mother. 'Just an hour, Mum, okay? The essay's nearly finished and I've got nothing else to do.'

'How're you getting home?'

'Somebody'll give me a lift.' She looked round. 'Sophie? Nella?'

The others all looked vague. 'I walked,' said Nella.

'I'm going to be out here all day,' said Sophie.

Nobody else appeared to be willing or able to volunteer. 'I can't leave you the car – I need to get back,' said her mother.

Tiffany looked at Thea. 'You're that way, aren't you? Could you take my mum home, do you think? She's in Baunton. That's pretty well on your way. Then I can have the car.'

Thea had no idea where Baunton was, but saw no reason to object. She was even quite gratified to be so readily included, merely by virtue of standing there with the objectionable dogs. She must, after all, inadvertently have ticked a box marked *One of us*, which gave her a small glow. The idea of joining a band of eco-warriors held some appeal, as she mentally ran through the list of hated targets that Sophie had produced the previous day. Wind farms – absolutely. She would quite cheerfully support any efforts to remove every one of them, onshore and off, for reasons that had evolved over recent years almost without her conscious awareness. But she was far less exercised about fracking. From the odd bits she'd gleaned, there seemed very little reason to oppose it. If the land had recovered from coal mining, there could not be much lasting damage from extracting shale gas, as far as she could see. And as for shooting badgers in the thousands, on the basis of some very unfair and one-sided findings, she was wholeheartedly on the side of Sophie and her friends. But even there, she suspected she would never be quite certain enough to qualify as an activist. She had met a few dairy farmers in her time, and knew there was genuine distress every time a cow developed TB.

'Okay,' she said. 'My car's just up there.'

With some final words to her daughter, the woman followed Thea and the dogs to the car. 'My name's Sheila,' she said. 'Sheila Whiteacre. It's the early form of Whittaker,' she added, as if answering an unspoken question.

'Thea Osborne. I'm house-sitting in Daglingworth. I don't know the area terribly well, but I'm good with a map.'

'What're you doing in Bagendon, then?'

'They asked me to water some plants in a house here, as well as minding the other one. Just for a few days. I walked over yesterday and met your daughter. They seem to be up to a lot of exciting stuff.'

The woman made a tutting noise, seeming to want to downgrade the activities of her daughter and her friends. 'Strictly weekends, pet. Most of the time, they're just ordinary citizens. Reminds me of the eighties all the same, when I was their age and we were fanatically CND. Well, Tiff's dad was. Not me so much. It always seemed to be cold and wet when there was a march. I got out of it when I could. I did go to Greenham Common once.'

Thea had the faintest of memories of her father's sister, Auntie Jen, giving an account of a week spent camping outside the American base. It felt romantic and very long ago.

'They all seem to be very committed.'

'I know. I can't really complain, even though I'm scared they'll get into serious trouble one day. It's all on the side of the angels, isn't it? Somebody has to speak out and put the brakes on, or where will it all end?'

'Mm,' said Thea. 'I'm not sure. Was that the whole group? It seems mostly female.'

'Danny wasn't there. Nor Giles. I think he's gone up to Yorkshire for some reason.'

'You know them all by name, then?'

'Mostly. Tiff brings them to the house for meetings. We've got more space than anyone else. I give them coffee and cake.' She laughed. 'And her brother's involved, too, which adds to the pressure to use our facilities.'

'Was he there just now?'

She shook her head. 'He's working this weekend. Does funny shifts, three days on, three days off. I can never keep track of him.'

They were on the same road as the one Thea had travelled in the Land Rover the day before. The A417 was just ahead. 'Where do I go here?' she asked.

'Gosh – sorry. You should have turned left back at the last junction. I wasn't concentrating. Never mind – we can go through Stratton. It's not much further.'

Thea remembered seeing Stratton on her map – looking rather a sizeable place. She didn't think she'd ever been there. 'Okay,' she said. 'But make sure you direct me in good time.'

It was barely five minutes, along a very straight road, then a left turn to Baunton. Thea was glad of the excuse to see a new place, but was not unduly impressed. There were modern houses and a lot of traffic, compared to Daglingworth. But there were some beautiful buildings, one of which turned out to be their destination. 'Gosh!' she gasped.

'I know. It's been in the family for ages. Costs a fortune to maintain, of course. But it is rather special. We try to share our good fortune, and make good use of it. And we did fill it with children. Tiffany's the youngest of five. We're here all the year round, as well. We do our best to justify it.'

'I'm not judging you,' Thea said softly. 'I think it's gorgeous.'

'Yes, well – I'm not going to argue with you.' They sat for a moment in admiration of the property that was solidly Georgian, with perhaps six or eight upstairs rooms and a well-kept garden surrounding it. Ivy adorned the facade. 'Come in, why don't you? We've got a couple of Labradors who'd like a romp with your two. Well – the spaniel anyway.' She looked over her shoulder at the back seat, where Gwennie was slumped as if she'd walked miles in Bagendon instead of a dozen yards or so. Hepzie was panting in anticipation of being released from the car.

'No, no, thanks all the same. I ought to get back. It must be nearly lunchtime. I don't want to get in your way.'

'We don't do Sunday lunches these days. My husband will be making soup or something. You won't be interrupting at

61

all. And anyway – it's only half past eleven. You could have some coffee.'

There was no reason at all to get back and coffee would be very welcome. 'Okay – you've persuaded me,' she capitulated. 'Thanks very much.'

The inside of the house made her think of her sister Jocelyn, who also had five children. Large families meant scuffs and stains and heaps and things kept for sentimental reasons. Even if Sheila's children were all grown up, their presence persisted. The big kitchen was festooned with pictures, dog leads, coffee mugs, and a dusty board covered in notices and lists. 'How many of them still live here?' Thea asked.

'Good question. I'd have to say two and a half. Tiffany and Ricky are here full time. He's my second one, the one I was just telling you about. He works for what was British Waterways, always out and about, getting wet.'

'Was?' Thea had fond memories of British Waterways and canal holidays with Carl and Jessica.

'It's changed to the Canal and River Trust now, God help us. Much less money available. The usual business of making cuts and fudging everything.'

'Nice job, even so. I love canals and locks and all that.' She was tempted to recount the story of her stay in Frampton Mansell, nearly three years ago, which involved a very close encounter with the Cotswold Canal. But she resisted, finding it more interesting to encourage Sheila Whiteacre to keep talking. Which she did.

'Then there's Win. She's a student, so she's only here during the vacations.'

'Win? Short for Winifred?'

'I'm afraid so. We had rather a thing about names – wanted them to stand out from the crowd. Of course, we boobed spectacularly with Tiffany. It's now in the top five or something, on all the urban estates. It's so difficult to be original. I wish I'd thought of Thea. That's a brilliant name.'

'My parents felt rather the same as you. We're got Damien, Emily and Jocelyn as well as me.' Saying her brother's name made her think again of his momentous news. It was sitting somewhere inside her, a blob of information that was rather like the foetus itself. 'Have you got grandchildren?'

'One. Thomas.' She sighed. 'I'm afraid I was a bit rude when they told me what they were calling him. I mean – how very *dull*.'

Thea laughed, and Sheila made two mugs of instant coffee. She went to the door and shouted, 'Coffee's up, if you want it.' Her accent, which had been puzzling Thea, came out as definite South London, when shouting. In response, two big chocolate Labradors came slouching into the room, shoulder to shoulder. 'I said coffee, not supper,' Sheila told them. 'These are Bert and Jackson. They're monsters.'

Two large male dogs did strike Thea as excessive, and she inwardly resolved to leave Hepzie firmly in the car. Romping with these two might well result in some bruises.

Then a man appeared. 'Thea, this is my husband, Art. He's American. This lady is called Thea and she's house-sitting or something.'

So the house had been in *her* family, Thea concluded

doubtfully. The accent and the bright hair and even the name Tiffany (however accidental) felt at odds with the inheritance of a Georgian mansion.

Art had an unruly grey beard and thick-rimmed spectacles. 'Pleased to meet you,' he said, holding out a hand. 'I'm not really American any more. She just says that as a way of apologising for me. I've been here since I was seventeen. This house belonged to my father's brother, who had no kids, so I got landed with it. It's a long story.'

Thea shook his hand and smiled. She liked him instantly. He was everybody's idea of the perfect father and grandfather. Even his clothes looked soft and warm and embraceable.

'There's been some sort of accident at the quarry,' Sheila said. 'Sounded as if somebody might have been killed there.'

Thea had actually forgotten about the helicopter and the police radio messages. Her heart thumped in self-reproach.

'Good God! They don't operate on a Sunday, do they?'

'Not as far as I know. We'll find out soon enough, I imagine.'

'Guess so. Where's Tiff?'

'I left her there, with the car. They're doing some sort of badger headcount. Thea gave me a lift home. She's got two dogs out there.'

'Bring them in,' he invited, spreading his arms. 'We like dogs.'

'I'd better not. One of them's very old and slow. I'm not sure she could cope . . .'

'Oh, these two are real pussycats. They'd never do any harm.'

64

Thea drained her coffee and got up from the kitchen table. 'Better not. I should go, really. I feel as if I'm deserting my post.' She smiled again and wondered whether she would see them again, and possibly meet their son Ricky.

'What does a house-sitter do, anyway?' Art enquired. 'You make it sound as if you stand guard with a rifle on the front doorstep.'

She laughed. 'No, I don't do that. It's the dog, really. I've got to keep her happy.' *And alive*, she thought ruefully.

'Oh, well, if you get the chance, you should do some exploring. Baunton's got a famous picture in the church, you know. St Christopher. It's quite something. And we're overflowing with fascinating characters. It isn't just me and Sheila, you know.'

'I've met some already. A man called Jack Handy, for instance. Do you know him?'

Two pairs of eyes rolled up to the ceiling. 'Everyone knows Farmer Handy,' said Sheila. 'Makes enough trouble for a dozen farmers. If it's not one thing, it's another.'

'He told me about wanting to sell a bit of land for building. I suppose it's got permission, the amount of money he was offered.'

They both stared. 'He told you all that? When?'

'Yesterday. Why?'

'He must have been drunk. He *never* reveals a word about money.'

'He wasn't drunk – just angry. He needed to get it off his chest.'

'Something must have happened, then. That doesn't sound like the man we know at all.' Sheila was frowning in puzzlement. 'Did he have a ratty collie dog with him?'

'Yes. And he was driving a battered old Land Rover.'

Before any more could be said, a phone sitting on a worktop rang loudly. Art picked it up. 'Hi, Tiff . . . what about that essay? What . . . ?' He listened for several seconds. 'Good grief, girl. Just you get back here right away. Don't have anything to do with it. Take a deep breath and head for the car. You can deal with your friends later. I want you *here*, *now*. Understand?'

After another few seconds, he put the phone down. 'The body in the quarry – they've just heard that it's Danny Compton.'

Chapter Six

Thea hovered near the kitchen door, unable to interrupt the tension to say goodbye, and in no rush, anyway, to leave. She might miss something interesting.

'How can they know so quickly?' Sheila asked first. 'They don't give out names for ages.'

'She didn't say. But there doesn't seem to be any doubt about it.'

'Oh, God. Poor Nella! They were getting married. Tiffany was all set to be a bridesmaid.' She spoke partly to herself and partly to Thea. 'What in the world could have happened to him?'

'An accident, I expect,' said Thea. 'I saw the quarry yesterday. It's a long way down. If you slipped off the path and over the edge, you might easily be killed.'

'But Danny isn't the sort of person to slip,' said Sheila. 'He's super-competent at everything he does. Making placards, drawing maps, checking details. He's the opposite of reckless, whatever that is.'

'Cautious,' said Art. 'Thinks three times about everything.'

'You know him well, then?' said Thea sadly. 'What an awful shock this must be for you.'

'More for the girls. They all adored him. I think Sophie always expected she'd bag him, if anyone did. But he just fell for Nella from the start. It was ever so sweet.' Sheila wiped her eyes with her sleeve. 'What a terrible thing to happen,' she sniffed.

'Hey, honey, don't upset yourself.' Art put an arm around his wife's shoulder and rubbed his beard against the top of her head. 'The girls'll rally round, and make sure Nella's okay. You know what a great gang they are. They'll get her through it.'

'Mm,' mumbled Sheila.

'I'll go,' said Thea. 'It's been lovely to meet you both. I expect I'll see you again. Tiffany will be home in a minute. She won't want me in the way.'

They made no attempt to stop her and, as she drove back towards Daglingworth on the straight – and doubtless Roman – road, she met a car driven by Tiffany. She waved, but the girl showed no sign of having seen her. For the first time, Thea wondered why Art had been so concerned to have his daughter home. Why not encourage her to stay and support her friend instead? It was as if he feared for her safety. Or perhaps it was merely that he wanted to console her, having heard acute distress in her voice. In any case, Thea hoped she would see them all again. She had liked the Whiteacres very much indeed.

The Fosters' house was serenely Sunday-morningish when she got back. A bird was singing in a birch tree in the back garden and daffodil heads were starting to change their angle from vertical to horizontal, indicating an imminent opening into trumpets. A man called Danny was dead in a quarry and would never see such delights again. From the very little she knew of him, she assumed he had enjoyed the natural world, since he was working to protect it. Like her own dead Carl, who had been a conservationist before anything else, the fact of an early death was all the more terrible for knowing that this was somebody who would have made excellent use of a long life.

The dogs had been badly cheated, too. There had been nothing by way of a walk. No new smells or interesting encounters. They had been left in the car together – which had done nothing for their relationship. Corgi and spaniel each curled into a corner, as far from one another as possible. Hepzie leapt out as soon as the door opened, but Gwennie had to be helped down, her body unbending and her short legs unequal to the task of jumping anywhere. She made straight for her familiar basket and sat in it, breathing heavily. There was a subtle air of outrage about her.

'Come on, Heps,' said Thea. 'Let's go up to the church or somewhere for a bit. You can probably go loose, if you promise to behave yourself.' This was unfair, she realised, and added, 'You've been a very good dog up to now.' Memories of the extremely bad behaviour in Stanton made her shudder and resolve to keep a closer eye on the two. Leaving them alone in the car had been rather reckless, on reflection.

There were still plenty of walks they could take in the coming days and she was resolute in her intention to explore them. Westwards lay Duntisbourne Leer, with a more southerly diversion into a large woodland. Beyond that lay Sapperton and Daneway, which she had visited nearly three years earlier with her sister Jocelyn, when they were house-sitting together in Frampton Mansell. That seemed a long time ago, with so many adventures in between, but the chat with Sheila Whiteacre had revived the memories and they now raced vividly through her mind.

That area, in the lower left-hand corner of the Cotswolds map, was wooded and secretive, the levels as dramatically uneven as any she'd since encountered. Starkly contrasting with the open sweeps around Snowshill and the rootedness of Winchcombe, she remembered the Frampton Mansell experience as one of sudden shocks and passions, both personal and geographical. The constantly changing landscape, from wide open wolds to hidden glimpses of long-gone industry, by way of country lanes and characterful churches, was unfailingly appealing. Every mile contained a wealth of interest, enough for a day's contemplation and enjoyment. She didn't have to concern herself with a dead man in a quarry. It had nothing whatever to do with her.

But the image that persistently floated before her inner eye was that of the red-haired farmer, Jack Handy. Red-haired and red-faced, as he raged about the protesters. He wouldn't shed any tears over the death of one of the leading members of the group, that was for sure.

The walk up the gentle rise to the church was brief, but pleasantly distracting. Daglingworth had its own quirks, the best of which was a garden at the central road junction, raised considerably above ground level and full of many different herbs. They were at head height, flopping over the wall beside the road. Rosemary, mint, marjoram were easy to identify, but others were either too dormant or too unfamiliar to put names to. It was original and entirely delightful, making Thea smile.

She had left her mobile behind, carrying nothing but the house key in a pocket. Wispy aromas of Sunday roasts and woodsmoke made her dreamy, drifting back in time, conscious that the same smells would have persisted in this place for countless centuries. The enveloping sense of history was one of the main attractions of the Cotswolds. Everywhere you looked there were ancient stones and earthworks that betrayed the millennia of human activity. The herb garden reminded her that this too was a time-honoured practice. Despite the comfortable affluence of the villagers, they still burnt wood and put lavender in their drawers. They surely maintained some sort of feeling for the particular elements of the past that had created this extraordinary region.

At least I'm not spending any money, she thought to herself, as she turned back to Galanthus House. Mooching around the country lanes with the dog was a gratifyingly cheap way to pass the time and, weather permitting, would amply fill the coming days, without any need to engage with activists, dead or alive.

She automatically checked her phone when she got back. It had been a sporadic progression from never even thinking about the thing to a pitiful reliance on it to maintain contact with Drew. Other people used it to call or text her, but not on the same regular basis. It had some abilities that she had come to value, such as access to websites and use as a camera, but she had not yet dived into the world of apps or games. She suspected she was just too old to feel comfortable letting her whole life be controlled by a small electronic gadget. As for Facebook, she still utterly failed to see the slightest appeal to it.

There was a text message.

HI, MA. WHERE ARE YOU? I'VE GOT A DAY OFF THIS WEEK. CAN I VISIT, TUES? JESS. XX

It had happened before, of course. Not just Jessica, but both her sisters and her mother had joined her on various house-sitting commissions, to a mixed reception. The company was welcome, but the complications that came with it much less so. Her relatives tended to show up with the aim of pouring out their latest troubles. They saw her duties regarding the houses as minimal and unimportant. As far as they were concerned, she was having yet another little holiday, all expenses paid, and they may as well share in the bounty.

Without further deliberation, she called her daughter back. 'I'm in the Cotswolds again,' she said, after brief preambles. 'It's all beautifully springlike and peaceful.'

'So can I come?'

'Of course you can. It'll be lovely to see you. We can investigate one of the pubs.'

'No murders, then?' Jessica teased. Murders did happen a lot when Thea was around.

'No. Some chap fell into a quarry, apparently. That's all.'

'Fell? Are you sure he wasn't pushed?'

'I know nothing about it. I've met a few people who knew him, that's all.'

'Right. So Tuesday, then? Tell me where you are. I want to talk to you.'

'You're talking to me now.' It was a shameful evasion, which she knew even as the words left her lips, but she was in no mood to provide counselling for a young policewoman, even if she was her daughter.

'Come on, Ma. Don't be like that.'

'Don't call me Ma,' said Thea automatically. It was a recent development that she very much disliked.

'I've got a dilemma and I want your advice. That's what you're for, remember? Most mothers never stop giving advice. Why do you have to be different?'

Most mothers jogged Thea's memory. 'Did you hear about your Aunt Judy?'

'What? What about her?'

'She's pregnant. You'll have a new cousin.' Every time she thought of it, it seemed more ludicrous.

'Wow! How did that happen?'

'I'm sure they'll be happy to explain it to you, if you ask them. I had to stop him before he talked me through it.'

'He? Uncle Damien told you? When?'

'Yesterday evening. I think he was working through the family. I imagine Jocelyn will say all the right things. She likes babies.'

'Everybody likes babies when they're your own relations. I think it's lovely. Don't be such a curmudgeon about it.'

'I'll try. It's just such a surprise. I can't really imagine it enough to be happy or excited about it.'

'It's good to have plenty of people in that generation. They'll have to keep you in your old age, remember.'

'So they will. I'd better buy it a lot of educational toys and books, then, to make sure it gets a good job.'

'You'll have to pretend to be pleased. They must be terrified. How old are they?'

'He's forty-nine and she's forty-four. Nearly. You must admit that's awfully old to be first-time parents. I was twenty when I had you.'

'And now you're old enough to be a grandmother. Yes, I know. So what?'

'I don't want to be a grandmother. And your gran's got plenty of grandchildren, so she doesn't need another one.'

'Well, I think it's lovely,' insisted Jessica. 'Now tell me where you are, and I'll be there before lunch on Tuesday.'

'Great.'

The idea that her brother and his wife might be frightened had not occurred to her. Damien had never shown fear in his life. He had embraced religion in his early thirties and sustained an unshakeable faith ever since. This had given him a patina of complacency that caused irritation, bewilderment and occasional envy in his sisters. The message he put out was – *I have everything sorted, and if you are so blind and stupid as to reject what I have to offer, then that's your problem.*

'It's not proper religion,' Jocelyn had complained once. 'Really religious people have doubts and dark nights of the soul, and endless moral dilemmas. He doesn't do any of that. He's so bloody *certain* all the time.'

Thea had agreed. So perhaps this baby was God's way of showing her brother that the way was not always smooth, and that he'd had it much too easy up to then.

What would they do if the baby was found to be defective on the scan? She had no idea what Damien thought about abortion, but the assumption had to be that he was against it. Thea herself, with her low levels of maternal passion, would have found it a gruesome decision to have to make. In the end, she thought she'd have ducked it and kept whatever child fate landed her with. While not actively seeking to have a second baby after Jessica, she believed she would have accepted an accidental one with good grace. She wasn't sure people should have quite that much control over something so fundamental – which she supposed was very much out of line with orthodox thinking. Going against nature, as Carl very often remarked, could rebound on you rather painfully at times.

And then a small voice whispered to her – *Just be careful the same thing doesn't happen to you and Drew, then.* That would be a very neat revenge on her, she realised. It would ally her with Damien, and probably separate her from Drew. The idea gave her the shivers. She was only a year older than Judy. It could happen. But of course it wasn't going to, even if – as everybody knew – births and deaths always came in threes.

She made herself a modest and rather late lunch, and began a list of shopping for the following day. Cirencester was close by, and well worth an hour or so pottering up and down the streets. Except she'd be lucky to find anything so mundane as bread and milk in any of the town-centre shops. There would be a Waitrose somewhere – she knew she'd visited it on previous occasions, but had forgotten exactly where it was.

The afternoon loomed ahead of her, as Sunday afternoons so often did. The risk of loneliness and self-pity made her feel cross and determined to ensure they didn't take hold. She wanted Drew. She could see his face before her, feel his warm hugs and hear his hearty laugh. But Sundays were his sacred time with the children, and she seldom found herself included as part of the family. She was *not* part of the family, with Karen dead so short a time. There had been a few wintry walks since Christmas, and a dozen or more evenings together, which extended into the night, but not to the following morning. She had driven all the way back to Witney in the small hours, feeling both lucky and unlucky, blessed by Drew but thwarted by his children, with whom things were still liable to be awkward and difficult. Stephanie had a way of looking at her that made her itch with embarrassment.

So, not for the first time, she found herself with no choice but to speculate on local happenings. The people she'd met were interesting, to say the least. Sheila Whiteacre was a delight, while Sophie and Nella were intriguing. There were loose ends in abundance, now the identity of the dead man was established. Jessica's immediate suggestion that foul play might be involved was an added ingredient to the story, raising a host of possible motives even amongst the handful of people Thea had met so far. There would be others, if she cared to go out and find them: Ricky Whiteacre, for one, and people she still knew nothing about.

The obvious scenario was that Danny had been prominent in a group intent on forcing a number of issues that locals might prefer left just as they were. Most people grumbled gently about change, but adapted to it well enough when it came. A large proportion of the residents of Cotswold villages were rich and powerful enough to organise life as they wanted it to be and ensure that they kept well clear of any nuisance. A wind farm on the top of Cleeve Hill was never going to happen. Fracking was unlikely. The landscape itself was relatively safe from predation, other than the erection of new houses in large numbers. Nobody liked new houses, however loudly the need for them might be asserted. It was always a need more acute somewhere else. All those neglected, weedy sites in the scruffy end of town – towns such as Reading, Croydon, even perhaps Guildford, but definitely not Cirencester or Winchcombe. They weren't towns at all in that sense. They were oases of history, impervious to the vagaries of population and politics.

Danny would inevitably have fallen foul of Farmer Handy and his intention of selling his field for building, along with the rest of the activists. But it was a big stretch from that to suspecting Handy of deliberately killing the man. Why Danny, when there were so many other protesters who would rise up to take his place? Besides, the house would or wouldn't get built, regardless of who died amongst those who opposed it.

Maybe it was the badgers, then. Dairy farmers wanted the animals dead and gone. The government was cautiously on their side, but very conscious of the opposite view. The whole question of what to do with annoying wildlife – foxes, badgers, squirrels, rabbits – never really went away, and was never properly understood by politicians. It wasn't altogether understood by Thea, either. She just knew that it was very far from simple, with whole new layers involved when it came to badgers and foxes.

The speculating occupied about half an hour, as she sat in the living room with both dogs on the sofa beside her. Gwennie leant a tentative snout on her thigh, and sighed. Hepzie rolled her eyes and fidgeted. Outside it was dry and reasonably bright, with almost no passing traffic. Lower End was apparently in the universal shutdown mode that was the norm for the Cotswolds. Whatever activity there might be at the quarry was quite out of sight and earshot. In any case, it would surely all be over by this time.

Restlessly, she extracted herself from the dogs and went to the door into the hallway. It was a more characterful house than the one in Bagendon, but much less so than the one inhabited by the Whiteacres. Mr and Mrs Foster were not obsessively tidy; not ashamed to let the stair carpet get frayed or the occasional spider to set up home over a window. Curious for more information about them, she went into the dining room and in a heap of papers on one corner of the table she found an opened letter from an estate agent, enclosing details of a house in Frome, Somerset, priced at something very much lower than Galanthus House must have been worth. So they were downsizing, or at least moving to a cheaper area – which happened to be not far from Drew and his green cemetery. It was none of her business, not relevant to her commission, but it aroused her interest. Mr Foster must be retiring, she supposed. Perhaps they knew people in Somerset. Perhaps Drew knew somebody they knew.

Poor Gwennie, she thought. Such an old dog would be dreadfully traumatised by a change of environment. She'd never find her way around. Were the Fosters planning to have her put down before they moved? Or was it all just a tentative plan for the future, scheduled for two or three years' hence, and simply getting a feel for prices and facilities in other parts of the country?

And wasn't it a bit peculiar to have the details sent on paper in a letter? Didn't people do it all online these days? She remembered that her dealings with the Fosters had all been by phone from their first approach about house-sitting. A friend of a friend had passed them her name. She had not come across a computer in the house – but then people used iPads and even smaller gadgets to send their emails these days. And they took them along on holiday, leaving nothing in the house. Even so, Thea began to suspect that here was a highly unusual couple, not so very old, who did not engage in any online activity. It made her smile to think such people still existed.

And so the afternoon drifted by, with no sense of urgency or obligation. At five she turned on the TV, and caught some local news, which made much of the discovery of a body in the Daglingworth quarry, but did not name the victim or the manner of his death. A little while later, a national news summary headlined a police raid on a nursing home in Somerset, which was suspected of either neglecting or actively killing a number of inmates. A whistleblower had drawn attention to the fact of a spate of deaths in a short time, with associated elements that might suggest all was not well.

Thea knew instantly that the whistleblower was Drew. He had been taken seriously, to the extent that within hours the police had descended on the establishment. How did you 'raid' a nursing home? Did they batter down the door and dash down corridors shouting 'Police!'? Almost certainly not. There'd be a quiet approach to the matron, or whatever the top person was called, and a request to see every scrap of documentation, with names of doctors and relatives and medications. But the media had got hold of it from the start. Probably listening in to police radio, she thought wryly.

She broke the rule and phoned him.

Drew was still agonising about his reckless reporting of the suspicious nursing home. The police had reacted quickly, and the place was already being investigated. 'If they don't find anything wrong, my career will be over,' he wailed, plainly suffering from panic and regret. 'They'll know it was me – who else could it be? I'll be blacklisted and scorned. I don't know what made me do it.'

'Conscience,' she said.

'I suppose so. It sounds horribly pretentious when you put it like that.'

'Come on. You wouldn't want your poor old mother

starved to death in such a place – or whatever it is they did to them.'

'No,' he said doubtfully. 'But it's not so simple, is it? I mean – a lot of them probably *want* to get it all over with. They might be refusing food. You're not allowed to force feed anybody, after all.'

'That makes it worse,' she said decisively. 'You can't let the idea catch on that these homes are really places to go to be finished off. They're supposed to provide warmth and comfort and distraction and company in your final years. It's supposed to be happy and interesting for the inmates.'

'Right.' He didn't sound convinced.

'Did they have dementia – your customers?'

'Not that I know of. Let me think – one did, maybe. It was a niece who made the funeral arrangements in advance, but the old lady signed the forms herself. Why?'

'I just thought that might make them more annoying for the staff, and more likely to refuse to eat, maybe.'

They talked around the subject for a few more minutes, before Drew asked how things were going in the Cotswolds.

'A man died in a quarry,' she said. 'They found him this morning.' For the first time, the thought hit her that perhaps the body had been there when she'd walked past the previous day. He might have been just below her feet, perhaps not quite dead. She had actually looked down and thought it a dangerous spot. Had he been inaudibly crying for help? Had she mysteriously heard him telepathically? Until that moment, she had felt entirely removed from the death, only interested in an intellectual, theoretical fashion.

'I passed that way on my walk yesterday,' she added, slightly breathlessly.

'An accident, then?' said Drew, sounding as if he needed that to be the case.

'Probably. He had a fiancée. I met her briefly, and her friends. He was one of the people protesting about local environmental threats. Specifically, a proposal to build a big new house somewhere near here.'

'I see,' he said absently.

'You should go. Where are the kids?'

'Upstairs. I'm meant to be doing supper.'

'I'll phone again tomorrow. Eight o'clock.'

'It'll put the whole place out of business,' he burst out. 'The home, I mean. What have I done? Why the hell did I do it? I must have been mad.'

'It'll turn out right, you'll see. Stop stressing about it. What does Maggs say?'

'Nothing. She's too busy being sick.'

Only then did Thea remember that particular added layer of complication in Drew's life. And if it was in his life, then it was in hers as well.

'I'll ring again tomorrow,' she repeated and left him to his family.

She fed the dogs and took them round the garden. Then she settled with the bland Sunday offerings provided by the television and did her best not to think very much. She wanted life to remain quiet and uneventful while she was in Daglingworth. It didn't seem a lot to ask. But then, she had wanted it many times before and been denied her wish.

82

Trouble followed her on so many of her house-sitting jobs. Trouble and malice and deception and fear had all dogged her footsteps from one village to another. People behaved badly much of the time. And Thea, with her sharp nose for connections and dissembling, was very often the linchpin in teasing out the truth of what had happened.

Not this time, she resolved. If indeed it was a *this time*. If it did turn out that somebody had deliberately hurled the protester into the quarry, she wanted nothing to do with it. She had no reason at all to concern herself with it. She was still mentally insisting on this sort of approach when a police detective came to the door.

Chapter Seven

It was Jeremy Higgins, a familiar face from only a few months before, as well as occasions prior to that. He smiled ruefully and said, 'Me again, I'm afraid.'

'What sort of time is this to pay me a visit?' Her attempt at a lightly flirtatious tone was not a great success. Already she was asking herself how in the world he knew where to find her. And the effort required meant that this must be something serious; something professional to do with a crime. 'Come in, anyway.'

Hepzie seemed to remember him – but then she did the same scrabbling at legs and frantic wagging with every man she met. She was a man's spaniel at heart. Thea wondered whether she still missed Carl, who had known and loved her for the first few years of her life.

Higgins wasted no time. He stood in the hallway and said, 'You met a man called Jack Handy yesterday. Is that right?'

She nodded, waiting with increasing foreboding.

'What time would that have been?'

'Afternoon. He gave me a lift because it was raining. We got back here around half past four.'

'Did you ask him in?'

'No, I did not.'

'Did he talk to you?'

'Yes, a bit.' She was beginning to feel defensive of the farmer, for no good reason other than he had been cheery with her, and went out of his way to drive her home. If Higgins was thinking of him as a murderer, she wanted to show him the error of his thoughts as soon as she could, even if she'd entertained the same possibility herself not long before.

'What about?'

'Something to do with a field he's trying to sell and how people are making objections. Listen, Jeremy – he was a perfectly nice and polite man. What's all this about?'

'You know I can't tell you. Even if you and I do have a history, you still have to answer like an ordinary witness. Okay?'

'A history? Is that what you'd call it?' She and Higgins had never entertained a moment of mutual romance, as far as she was aware. She had been the lover of his superior, Phil Hollis. She had cried on him a time or two. He had rescued her from awkward situations. History was a fair word for all that, she supposed.

'He says he was with you for half an hour or more, from four to half past.'

'He's right. You have to tell me why it matters.'

'We're trying to establish people's movements between two and five yesterday.'

'Because somebody died then? The man in the quarry? Who else can it be? I was there beside the quarry at about half past three. I didn't see anything unusual.'

'Which side of it?'

'Um, the west, I suppose. The little lane joining Itlay to the road the map calls Welsh Way. There's a viewing place. I stood there and looked down.'

'He wasn't far from there.' The detective inspector rubbed his cheek and stared into the middle distance for a moment. 'Along the northern side, actually.'

Thea tried to visualise it. 'Off the Welsh Way, you mean?'

He nodded. 'There are trees alongside it, and a steep drop.'

'And you don't think he just fell, of his own accord?' There was an inevitability to his answer that she found depressing. She realised how much she had wanted this death to be a simple accident.

'There's plain evidence that he didn't.'

'But if you didn't find him until today, how can you be sure of the time of death?'

'We can't. But there are indications . . .' He stopped. 'I'm telling you far too much.'

'Okay. Sorry. But it sounds as if I was around at the crucial time. So were lots of people. The protesters, for a start.'

'Which protesters?'

'A couple of young women. And then another one – the dead man's fiancée, actually.'

He closed his eyes and rubbed the flesh under his chin. It was developing into quite a dewlap, she noted. 'How can you possibly know that? How long have you been here?'

'A day and a bit. I just happened across them and heard them talking. I saw a few more of them today. People tell me things,' she finished simply. 'It's not my fault.'

'Nobody ever thinks it's your fault,' he said tiredly. 'You're like Typhoid Mary. It wasn't her fault, either.'

Her heart lurched. 'Don't say that! That's a terrible thing to say. It *never* has anything to do with me – *as* me. You know what I mean. Besides, you can't generalise. They've all been so different. Until now I thought this one was an accident, anyway.'

He shook his head. 'So did we, for about twenty minutes. But then we had a closer look at his injuries and . . . well, let's just say the quarry was nothing more than a place of disposal.'

Thea frowned. 'He was dead before he got into it?'

'Looks that way. Signs of a scuffle, as well. Blood splashes. Nothing very subtle about it.'

She sighed. 'I suppose I'm not really surprised. Strong young men don't just fall into quarries on a calm Saturday afternoon, do they?'

'Why do you call him strong? Did you meet him as well?'

She put her hands up. 'No, no. But he sounds very capable and outdoorsy. Doing something with badgers. He can't have been anything else but strong.'

'He weighed ten and a half stone, and was five feet nine. Well nourished, apparently. Not exactly a bodybuilder, but capable of putting up a fight, I'd say.'

'How did you establish the time of death?' She was

pressing him, hoping he hadn't noticed that he was revealing a lot more information than he was supposed to.

'He was in the Bathurst Arms in North Cerney until two o'clock. So it must have been after that. And he didn't show up for a date with his girlfriend at five, so we assume he was incapacitated by then, if not dead. She was expecting him and he never showed at the time agreed.'

'You've spoken to her?'

'She spoke to us. Making a fuss, demanding to see the body. The name got out much too soon.' He rubbed his neck again.

'They listen in to police radio. They've got an app.'

'Names aren't sent over insecure radio frequencies, for that very reason. I think they must have been watching through binoculars from the other side of the quarry. The victim was wearing a distinctive cagoule type thing. I imagine they recognised it and ran with it. They operate like MI5, you know. There's a whole big network of them – more so since the badger thing. You can't hope to keep track of them. It's terrorism,' he finished darkly. 'They run rings round us.'

'And they're all quite respectable citizens most of the time. With jobs and houses and cars and money. Tricky for you.' Looking at him, Thea wasn't at all sure where her sympathies lay. The police were handicapped by so many rules and regulations, so vulnerable to accusations of bias and heavy-handedness. No wonder they spent so much time staring at computer screens, trying to catch villains that way. It was far less likely to lead to trouble.

'Yeah. Anyway, there's a problem with this chap's

identity. Or there would have been, if the girlfriend hadn't barged in and told us who he was. Nothing on him to give a clue as to who he might be.'

'Fiancée. She's his fiancée,' Thea corrected. 'Nella something.'

'*Fe*nella, actually. Fenella Davidson, she's called. And he's Daniel Compton. She says his parents are working in Dubai. Still married, apparently, with a younger brother who's at school there. Haven't traced them so far.'

As if poked in the back, Jeremy suddenly stiffened, lifting his chin. 'Hey! I'm not meant to be telling you all this, damn it. You didn't hear it from me, right? All I want from you is confirmation that you can account for Mr Handy's movements, for at least part of the afternoon.'

'Because somebody told you he was the most likely person to bash Danny over the head and chuck him into the quarry? All I can say is, he didn't look like someone who'd just done a murder. He was angry, in a general sort of way, but also rather nice.' She thought about the man, and what she had just said. 'Although he *was* very cheerful at first. As if something pleasing had just happened. Maybe it was relief to be rid of a pest.' She laughed. 'Ignore that. It's not evidence, is it?'

'It's helpful. Anything that adds detail to the picture comes in useful. Well, that's it for now. How long are you here?'

'Two weeks. How *did* you find me, by the way?'

He gave her a patient look. 'Jack Handy told us, of course. We questioned him two hours ago.'

'That was quick.' She narrowed her eyes at him. 'I suppose you've been interviewing people all afternoon.' There was something unsavoury about the whole idea of a hasty police investigation with the intrusive questions and horrible suspicions.

'Sooner the better,' he nodded. 'I expect I'll be seeing you again.'

And he left. She hadn't even asked him to sit down, she realised. They'd been standing in the hallway for fifteen minutes and Higgins hadn't made a single note of what she'd told him.

The regular encounters she'd had with the police over the past three years still left her hazy as to the details of how they went about a murder investigation. The body would not have been properly examined by a pathologist yet – that much she was sure of. So they had no conclusive evidence as to cause of death . . . except it did sound as if the fatal injury was of such a nature as could not possibly have been inflicted by a fall down a steep slope lined with trees, to land on sharp-cornered rocks at the bottom. She tried to imagine the various likely scenarios – the most credible that there was a large hole in his head, caused by his killer, who hoped it would look like damage from the fall. Or perhaps he had been stabbed or shot, with the killer making no attempt to conceal how the deed was done. So, as Higgins had already indicated, the quarry was more or less incidental. Somewhere to hide the body, or a final vicious shove for good measure, sending him over the edge.

She recalled DI Higgins promising that he would see her again soon. With a sigh, she braced herself for further involvement in the violence and mayhem that never failed to accompany a murder.

Chapter Eight

Monday dawned fresh and breezy. Thea enjoyed two minutes of slow awakening before the trouble started. Downstairs, Gwennie began to bark. Not the one-note yap which said *I'm awake, so you should be too* but an urgent string of throaty sounds that suggested there was actually something to be worried about.

Thea got up and went to the bedroom door. 'What's the matter?' she called down the stairs, hoping to quell the animal simply by letting her hear a voice. Instead she heard an odd sizzling sound, which was quickly followed by a bang and the smell of smoke.

'Hey, Hepzie, come with me. Something's burning.'

The spaniel eyed her from the foot of the bed and remained where she was. 'Come here,' grated Thea, grabbing her by the collar. 'Do as you're told, will you?'

Gwennie was still barking, and there were crackling sounds at the bottom of the stairs. Still half asleep, Thea dragged her dog down the stairs after her, to discover a pool of flame in the narrow hallway. A coat hanging near the door seemed to be on fire, but otherwise it was not spreading. Muttering half-remembered instructions about keeping oxygen levels low and getting everybody outside, Thea dragged Hepzie past the all-too-close flames and smoke, and into the kitchen, where Gwennie was standing with her muzzle in the air, barking and sniffing and making small agitated leaps. 'Come on, both of you. Out into the garden,' Thea ordered. She bundled them outside, and went back to the hall. Probably she could smother the flames quite easily with a thick blanket, without the hassle of calling the fire brigade, who would cause much more damage with their overenthusiastic water hoses.

For a moment she stood staring at the fire, which was emitting some nasty black smoke, before remembering a red canister on the wall beside the cooker. Returning to the kitchen, she found a fire blanket, with a metal loop ready to be pulled. When she did so, a rectangle of white material emerged, and she took it back to the fire. It wasn't big enough, but when she threw it over the centre of the flames, it gave her a sense of control, at least. She had bought herself a bit of time and reduced the smokiness. Reaching carefully over the smouldering coat, she unhooked another garment and threw that over the surviving flames beyond the edge of the blanket. 'Hasn't done the carpet any good,' she muttered, standing a yard or so away from the conflagration. It was all now subsiding, the smoke swallowed up by the coverings. She'd have liked to stamp out the small tentative flames she could still see, but her feet were bare. After a minute or two, in which she assured herself that it wouldn't spread any further, she ran upstairs and threw on some clothes and shoes.

Downstairs again, she congratulated herself on her efforts. The fact that the Fosters' hallway was empty of furniture, and the carpet probably flame-retardant, helped considerably. But if she hadn't been there, the fire might easily have crept towards the stairs, by way of the coats and the open door into the living room, and perhaps along skirting boards and banisters, until the whole house was engulfed.

She stamped every last flicker into submission and went to find a brush, with the vague idea of restoring some sort of normality to the scene. But then she stopped. This was not an accidental blaze. It was nowhere near a power point or an electrical gadget. It was quite obviously a deliberate act of arson. Something had been pushed through the letter box, containing petrol or similar, and Gwennie had heard it all. If Thea had run through to the front bedroom and looked out of the window, she would very likely have seen the culprit.

'A Molotov cocktail,' she said to herself, unsure of exactly what such a thing was, nor whether it would fit through a letter box. Didn't it involve a bottle, for a start? She gingerly lifted up the coat and fire blanket, and stared at the awful black mark on the pale-grey hall carpet. In the middle was a misshapen lump of melted plastic, impossible to miss. And she could smell petrol faintly.

Reluctantly, regretfully, she dialled the number for the Gloucestershire police, that was already in her mobile, and asked to speak to Detective Inspector Higgins.

Higgins wasn't there, and the person who took the call was cautious about putting her in touch with him. She wanted to know name, purpose and level of urgency. Thea paused. She didn't need Higgins in person, did she? Any police officer would do. She was required to report the fire if only to gain the due paperwork for the Fosters to make an insurance claim. 'Somebody tried to set the house on fire,' she said coolly. 'I've put it out, but it was undoubtedly a crime, which I am now reporting. It's Galanthus House in Daglingworth. Jeremy – sorry, DI Higgins – was here last night, so he was the first person to spring to mind. But it needn't be him, of course.'

'That's all right, madam,' said the girl inanely. 'I've taken down those details, and somebody will be with you this morning.'

'Thank you.' So she would have to stay in, waiting for the visitation which could be hours away. Inevitably there would be a shortage of available officers, given the fact of a murder investigation. She couldn't even clean up any more of the hallway, because that would be interfering with evidence. She had probably already done too much.

She let the dogs back in, but confined them to the kitchen. 'All clear,' she told them. 'More or less. Well done, Gwennie – you did exactly the right thing.' The corgi wagged its few millimetres of tail, which made Thea feel sad. Docking tails was something she deplored profoundly. She gave them some biscuits and a drink, and tried to eat some toast herself. To her surprise, she couldn't swallow it. Her body was operating on a stubbornly independent track, insisting that the past half hour had been a serious trauma that she would be foolish to deny. Taking more notice than before, she found her heart was beating heavily and quickly, her hands were shaking and tears were gathering behind her nose. The more she noticed, the worse it got. Hepzie came to her side and pressed her soft head against Thea's leg, which worsened things by another notch. A sudden storm of uncontrollable sobs shook her, and she put her head down on her arms and gave way to it.

Then somebody was knocking on the door. Blearily, she went to open it, finding a man in a fireman's suit standing there. He introduced himself with great formality as Fire Officer George Kemp. 'There's been a fire here?' he asked, already looking past her at the mess on the hall carpet. She stood back and pointed. 'Blimey!' he said, which she thought considerably more human and pleasingly unprofessional. All defences falling away, she leant towards him, blindly hoping for a hug. 'Are you all right?' He peered down at her face and tutted gently. 'Looks a bit like a shock reaction to me.'

'You just missed being cried on,' she choked. 'I'm all right really.'

'Sweet tea,' he prescribed. 'I can make it for you, if you like.'

'Go on, then. Mind the dogs.'

He stepped around the blackened patch and let himself into the kitchen, chirping at the dogs. Thea drifted after him, feeling useless. Everything had gone weak – legs, voice, mind. She dropped into a chair. 'It wasn't very bad, really. I don't know why I'm in such a state.'

'It's the might-have-beens,' he explained. 'That's what hits you.'

Deftly, he produced a mug of tea, finding things in the strange kitchen like magic. Then he went back into the hall and started a close examination of the after-effects of the fire. 'Not a very subtle attack. I gather the cops are on their way. They'll want to give it a really thorough look. Could go down as attempted murder, if they knew you were in the house. Is it just you here?' He eyed the coats hanging by the door, as if working out the family structure from them.

'It's not my house. I'm just the sitter. I'm looking after the dog – as well as the house. They're not going to give me a very high score, are they?'

'They can hardly blame you.' He licked his teeth ruminatively. 'And the chances are, surely, that it wasn't you, but the usual people who were being targeted. Looks as if they've upset someone, and this is their idea of revenge.'

'That's horrible.'

'They could have thought the people were away and the house was empty. Where's your car?'

'In the garage. They wouldn't have seen it.'

He made a little shrug and smiled. 'I'll leave the questions to the police. You don't want to have to say it all twice. Congratulations, by the way, on handling it all so capably. Fire blanket and coat – exactly what we'd have recommended. If it's any consolation, I don't think you were in much danger. There isn't a lot to encourage a good blaze just here. Can't have been too much smoke, either. The walls aren't black.'

They were, however, smudged with grey blotches in places. 'The carpet will have to be replaced, though. And one of the coats hanging up was burning when I came down.'

He looked at the coats. 'Lucky that didn't spread, then.'

'It's not a very *Cotswoldy* thing to do, is it?' she burst out. 'I mean – you associate it more with inner cities and family feuds. And gangs. Or insurance scams.' She remembered a dreadful story of a man who set fire to a house and killed a large number of his own children. 'And it's pretty stupid, as well,' she added with feeling. The sweet tea was evidently working, as she stood in the kitchen doorway filling up with anger.

'That's better,' approved Fireman George Kemp. 'Look, I'll stay till the crime chaps show up, if you like. I can sit in there and write my report.'

'You don't have to. I'll be all right. It's lucky I managed to get myself dressed before you got here. I came down in bare feet, when I realised what was happening. As it is, these are yesterday's things. I need to go and change.'

He smiled distantly. 'I've known people die because they stopped to get dressed. Amazing, when you think about it.'

'The power of cultural taboos,' she agreed. 'I can see that a lot of people would rather die than stand in the street stark naked.'

'We give them blankets. One of the first things we do. I'll just hang on for a bit, while you sort yourself out,' he finished kindly.

She went upstairs and pulled on the warmest clothes she'd brought with her, hoping to stop the shivering that still beset her. Hepzie went with her, leaving Gwennie to guard the fireman. Gwennie seemed to be rather enjoying the whole business. Thea's thoughts remained scrambled, fixated on the mentality of a person who could deliberately fill a bottle with petrol and push it into a house, quite unable to predict the exact consequences. Not least, she realised, a very long prison sentence if they were caught. Throughout history, the setting of fire to things had been considered a heinous crime. Children with arsonistic tendencies must always be firmly quelled – she remembered her own brother, in a rare moment of disobedience, getting into extreme trouble at school for throwing a lighted match into a roller towel in the boys' lavatories, and causing a minor conflagration. She had been impressed and rather amused at his mortification. But the abiding lesson was that fire had a mind of its own, and quickly got out of control. You treated it with respect and kept matches in a safe place.

Downstairs, she encouraged George Kemp to get back to his duties and leave her to gather herself together. 'I'm perfectly all right now,' she said.

'If I were you, I'd bale out, and let the house fend for itself. You've earned your fee already, and you're going to be shaky for a day or two yet.'

'I can't do that,' she said, automatically. 'They won't do it again, will they?'

'I don't suppose they will,' he agreed. 'But the cops'll tell you the same thing.'

'I can manage them, don't worry.'

Two unfamiliar police officers arrived at eleven-fifteen, and elicited the whole story from her. Their eyes widened with admiration at her capable behaviour, but they said little. They gathered fibres and carefully bagged the melted plastic bottle. The fire officer had left them an official report, which they read attentively. They measured and re-enacted, one of them going outside and operating the letter-box flap. 'Pretty amateurish,' one of them muttered. 'Lucky – or *un*lucky, I should say – the thing caught light at all. It's not as easy as people think to burn a house down.'

'Was it petrol, then?' Thea asked. She had hovered and watched them, despite being well aware that they would rather she didn't.

'Probably,' said one. 'Put it in a bottle and fit a bung of cotton wool or something. Set light to it and throw. It generally explodes and spreads the flammable fluid over a wide area. Plastic doesn't work as well as glass.'

Rather belatedly, she thought, they asked for contact details for Mr and Mrs Foster. 'Do you have to tell them? It'll spoil their holiday,' she pleaded.

The men gave her a look, almost identical on the two faces. 'This is a serious crime, madam. We have no choice in the matter. We need to know whether they have any ideas as to who did this.'

Thea gave them the Australian phone number the Fosters had given her and left the rest to them. 'They've gone to a wedding,' she said. 'It's in the middle of this week. I think tomorrow, actually. You won't want them to come home early, will you? All that way!'

They were interrupted by a woman approaching from the road. The white coveralls worn by the officers were as big a giveaway as there could ever be, Thea realised. 'What in the world happened?' asked Sheila Whiteacre, her blonde head jutting forward in her eagerness for information.

'Just a little—' Thea began, before one of the men laid a hand on her arm.

'Can't tell you just yet, madam,' he said. 'Nothing to be concerned about. Might you be a neighbour?'

'Not really. Baunton.'

'Right. But you know Mrs Osborne, do you?'

'We met yesterday.' Wide-eyed, she gazed through the open door at the blackened hall carpet. 'Was there a *fire*?'

Thea nodded briefly, feeling like a traitor.

Sheila evidently had little fear of contravening police orders. 'Somebody tried to burn this house down? With you in it? Good God, that's appalling!'

Thea nodded again.

'They must have assumed it was empty, surely? They'd never have done it if they thought you'd be trapped. And the *dogs*.'

'Gwennie raised the alarm. She was a hero.'

'Your people must have done something to annoy somebody, then. Something rather awful, I'd guess.'

'*Madam*,' thundered the policeman. 'Speculation at this stage is very unhelpful. If you have any information that you think would help, please come to the police station and make a statement.'

'No, I haven't. I don't know the people who live here. But I think I might be allowed to express some normal human sympathy.' She addressed Thea again. 'You know you're always welcome to come to us. If you lose your nerve, I mean. I'm sure *I* would.'

'Thanks,' said Thea. 'That's very kind of you.' She resisted a strong urge to just pack up and accept the offer.

'My daughter's coming tomorrow. I'll see what she thinks. But I'm not scared to stay here. I don't think the fire-raiser knew I was here. And I'm quite sure he won't be coming back. Nobody would be that stupid.'

'True.' Sheila nodded decisively. 'Well – the offer remains.'

'Thanks,' said Thea again.

It was one o'clock when she finally had the house to herself again. She was hungry, thirsty and unsettled. There was a real risk that the Fosters would feel so agitated and bewildered that they'd decide to fly home after the wedding and abort her fortnight in Daglingworth. But hadn't they made it clear that nothing whatever would be allowed to do that? Wasn't it more likely that they would content themselves with police assurances that nothing further could be done, and their house-sitter was willing to carry out the original commission?

She found herself hoping they wouldn't be in any rush to come back. Why did she hope that, she wondered? What possible reason did she have to want to stay in a place where people were committing vicious acts of violence? She concluded it was more that she did *not* want to go home to Witney. Doing that would make it impossible to avoid a host of implications, financial, romantic and professional. Everything hinged on everything else, the consequences of one decision spreading across all areas of her life. And she felt unequal to deciding anything without a contribution from Drew.

It was much easier to concentrate on events in the Cotswolds that centred on other people's lives. Even thinking about Damien and his baby, or Maggs and hers, was preferable to estimating how much money her house might be worth and which items of furniture she ought to dispose of. It made her feel like a retired person downsizing, instead of a woman in her prime, with many decades ahead of her.

The dogs ought to be given some attention, she decided. Gwennie was still glowing from her small act of accidental heroism, turning her cloudy eyes up to Thea's face every few minutes in a show of affection. Hepzie was plainly bored and unimpressed, making a big show of her feelings by jumping on and off the sofa and sighing.

'Come on, then,' said Thea. 'We'll go and look at the church again.'

It was a short, easy walk, either by road or footpath, already proving perfect for Gwennie's limited capacity. It was possible to turn it into a circular stroll, which would take well under half an hour to complete. As always, there were public paths in all directions, and for a moment she was tempted to lengthen the walk southwards, where the map showed a dotted line running directly into the famous Cirencester Park. 'We'll do that another day,' she decided. At the back of her mind was the idea that she ought to stay close to Galanthus House for the rest of the day, either as guard, or simply to be available in the event of further police visits.

There were no people about. Nobody jumped out at her to ask why a fireman and two policemen had called at the house early on a Monday. The few scattered neighbours who might have noticed something had probably been off down the motorway to work, or glued to their computers in a back room. The sudden appearance of Sheila Whiteacre began to seem rather odd, the more she thought about it. Had she perhaps been planning to call in for a chat and been deterred by the police officers? Did she have news about the dead Danny, or even questions for Thea about her encounters on Saturday?

Which set Thea thinking all over again about the body in the quarry.

Chapter Nine

To distract herself from futile speculation she went into the church, which she came to from the east along a track which suddenly opened out into a wide area with car park and large houses. She tied the dogs to the porch gate, and pushed open the big wooden door which she faintly recalled as being five hundred years old or thereabouts. Inside there were three Saxon stone carvings which she knew were renowned for their powerful simplicity. She gazed at them for a while, thinking how impossible it was to recapture the passions and motives of the people who made them, a thousand years before. The figures were out of proportion, as if drawn by a child, and it was hard to imagine that they had inspired reverence at any stage of their existence. The main source of awe, she found, was that they had survived for so long. Similar amazing survivals had been preserved in numerous small Cotswold churches, their origins essentially mysterious. The scenes depicted were amusing, more than anything else, in this sophisticated age. Spiritual inspiration or encouragement was very far removed after so long.

Outside again, she felt a sudden chill from an easterly breeze and thought how typically March it was. It would be nice to light a log fire and spend a cosy evening with a book and warm dogs. Although any thought of setting a fire going gave her pause. *Don't be silly*, she scolded herself. It would be very inconvenient to go through the rest of her life afraid to strike a match.

She caught herself counting the hours before she could phone Drew again. Despite breaking the rule the previous evening, she knew she mustn't do it again. Nobody could blame Stephanie and Timmy for objecting to their father spending an hour on the phone instead of reading them their bedtime stories or supervising their bath time.

She took the dogs down the little road to the junction where the appealing herb garden beckoned. No traffic passed, and she let the dog leads droop loosely from her hand. But she was careful not to let them go altogether. A painful lesson had been learnt in Lower Slaughter about the hazards of escaping dogs. Gwennie might well have hidden energies, capable of making a dash for it if the whim seized her. Old dogs could take you by surprise, as she knew from experience.

As Galanthus House came into view, she felt a strong disinclination to go back into it. 'Where *do* I want to be then?' she muttered to herself. The answer was so obvious that she smiled. Drew's little house, with its burial ground full of saplings and bulbs and pieces of stone and wood, was her favourite place in the world now. Time spent away from it was simply a waste, a sort of treading water that left her feeling detached and unemotional. The shock of the fire was an exception; the discovery of a dead man in a quarry was not. She found herself really not caring very much about Nella and Sophie and their fellow protesters. They didn't seem particularly pleasant people, anyway. Only Tiffany and her parents had got through to her, charming as they had been. As for Jack Handy, she rather wished she had not accepted his offer of a lift and thereby got herself peripherally involved in the whole business. Whatever possessed the dratted man to give her as some kind of alibi, when it was obviously not enough to clear him of suspicion?

Jeremy Higgins probably hadn't even heard about the fire at Galanthus House. He would be spending every minute on interviewing witnesses, reading background information on the victim, and searching for evidence to incriminate a murderer. Thea had been close to many such investigations over the past three years, but still had a shaky grasp of precisely how the police arrived at their final conclusions. So often it turned out that somebody unexpected gave the game away, or the truth emerged sideways, associated with something else entirely. This line of thought took her to a very unappetising idea: what if the fire she had been faced with that morning was connected to the death of Danny Compton two days before? However hard she tried, she could not see how this might be, unless some idiot thought she had killed him and was wreaking revenge. That was laughably unlikely. Danny had definitely been murdered – as Higgins had confirmed – and probably it was because of his activities as a protester. He had driven somebody beyond the point of reason. It ought not, she thought, be too difficult to pin down the individual concerned.

She found herself looking forward intensely to seeing Jessica again and running everything past her. There were so many questions hanging in the air and the wait for answers was paralysing. What would the Fosters do about the fire? Were the police going to question her again? How much should she tell Drew about it? However hard she looked, she could find no certainty in any direction.

She made herself a mug of tea and a small stack of cheese sandwiches when she got back indoors, thinking that her eating habits were becoming rather odd. There was a randomness to the timing that some people might think eccentric. The prospect of a substantial pub lunch the next day with Jessica began to gain appeal and she consulted her map to find a likely venue. The Bathurst Arms in North Cerney looked the most accessible. They might even walk to it if the day was fair.

And then DI Higgins himself was at the door again, with a female person slightly behind him. Thea assumed it was a new young detective she had not yet met. 'This is DC Gordon,' he introduced. 'She's only just started in CID, so she's observing, that's all.' He looked as if the presence of the observer was something of a trial to him.

'Come in, then,' Thea invited. 'You'll have come about the fire, I suppose.'

'Not really. That's all in hand, as far as I know. It's more of a long shot about the victim in the quarry.'

'Danny Compton,' she agreed. 'What about him?'

108

'Just wondering whether you've heard any more about his background. Seeing the way you get people to talk, I thought you might know more than we do about it.'

'Not a murmur,' she admitted, with a pang of regret. 'Sorry.'

'Doesn't matter. We've got all we need from the girlfriend, when it comes to it. There's not really a problem – just that it seems a bit odd the way the parents don't seem too bothered about him.'

'Don't they?'

He rubbed his brow. 'Actually, I'm not sure they've been told the full facts. There's been some trouble getting to see them face-to-face. We get the feeling there's some sort of rift.'

'Awkward,' Thea sympathised. 'I suppose lots of people don't speak to their parents.'

Higgins nodded and chewed his lip. 'Right,' he said reluctantly. 'But when there's a murder, we need to find out as much as we can about the victim. Friends, relatives, employers. All the obvious stuff. Miss Davidson told us almost every detail of the past year of his life, took us to his flat, and explained all about his freelance job. Not entirely useful.'

'What was the job?'

Higgins grinned. 'He's a locksmith, specialising in cars. Makes new keys when people lose theirs. Goes all over the country, apparently. Not been doing it long. Set up for himself, with all the gear.'

'So what's the issue? Assuming there is one, or why would you be here?'

'Just a feeling there's something missing. Something we're not being told about him.'

'He's a protester, remember. It comes with the territory, keeping a low profile.' She found the whole idea of avoiding leaving much of a trail rather exciting, already impatient to tell it all to Drew. 'What else would you expect to find?'

Higgins looked uncomfortable. 'Phone, car – for a start. The car's registered in the girlfriend's name. She said it was an insurance thing, because he already had the van full of locksmithing stuff. And the phone's a pay-as-you-go thing. Anonymous.'

Thea shrugged. 'Doesn't sound very unusual to me, especially the phone. I've seen the way they use them – they'd be daft to advertise where they were, and who was using them. They do break the law, I imagine, quite a lot of the time. They *harass* people in the night.'

'So I understand. Not that any of them would say anything about that.'

'Loyal,' murmured Thea. 'So what do you want from me?'

He went back to his original point. 'Just checking that you didn't catch anything that might help from the girls you met on Saturday. We know you, Mrs Osborne, and your skills at getting people to chat. Did they talk about this bloke at all?'

She cast her mind back. 'They were discussing him when I first came across them, as it happens. How he was dragging his feet about fixing a wedding date. He and Nella got engaged recently, but that's as far as he'd go, apparently. It didn't sound especially unusual to me, but Nella was impatient to get planning the whole thing.'

'That's all?'

'Something about badger setts in Itlay. He was meant to be checking them, or counting them.' She paused to think. 'Actually, they said he was camouflaging them somehow to stop the culling people from finding them.'

'Not my problem,' said Higgins. The trainee detective, sitting at a remove from them, made a little sound of disapproval, which he ignored. 'That's it, then, is it?'

'More or less. Nella said she'd been taking the car for its MOT, and was supposed to meet Danny at the church in Bagendon. I guess he never showed up.' She shuddered at the closeness of death, on an afternoon that had felt perfectly normal.

'MOT? On a Saturday afternoon? Where?'

'No idea. Doesn't it show up on your searches?' For some reason, Thea looked to the new detective for an answer. Perhaps she automatically assumed that it would be a junior like her who made that sort of computer check. DC Gordon was late twenties, dark-haired and solid. She did not smile and only fleetingly met Thea's eye. She appeared anxious and tense.

Her mentor rubbed his throat in the familiar way and sighed. 'I'll get somebody to have a look when I get back. Don't suppose it matters.'

'I don't think I've helped,' Thea said. 'The fiancée must be distraught, poor thing.'

'Right. Angry as well, actually. Saying all kinds of things about locals – farmers, to be precise. Blames them for all the ills in the world, not to mention murdering her beloved.'

'That Sophie is a ranter as well. There's a lot of it about.'

'Sophie Wells,' he nodded. 'She wasn't much help, as far as I can see. It wasn't me who interviewed her.'

'Is Farmer Handy off the hook?'

He gave her a warning look, and said nothing. Belatedly, Thea understood that the junior tagging along with him could possibly be seen as a spy, reporting any deviations from procedure that he might commit, wittingly or otherwise.

'Well . . .' She was at a loss. 'Would you like some tea?' she finished feebly, assuming they'd be much too busy to accept.

'A quick one might be nice,' he nodded. 'You can tell us about the fire.' He'd already spent half a minute staring at the blackened hall carpet and the smudges on the wall. 'Must have been scary.'

'I was shaking. The fireman made me drink sweet tea. It really does work.'

'Never fails,' he smiled. 'There's a team working on it, obviously. Funny you've got your name connected with two different investigations. Must be a record.'

'Don't say that,' she pleaded. 'You don't think they could be linked, then?'

'Can't imagine how. Even if both crimes are due to some kind of grudge – which they do seem to be – we can't find a connection.'

'Except me,' groaned Thea. 'Which is quite a nasty feeling.'

'Don't think of it like that. You're not involved in the quarry thing. Not really.'

'Nice of you to say so.' They laughed gently together,

excluding the solemn-faced Detective Constable. Higgins was a straightforward man, thorough, well intentioned. Sandy-haired and undeniably overweight, he would work methodically through a case, seldom losing his calm demeanour. Thea had not known him to show any great brilliance or insight, and he harboured much the same unthinking prejudices as most police officers, but she liked him. There was hardly anything not to like.

They all drank the tea quickly, with DC Gordon making some careful notes on a reporter's pad. Higgins rolled his eyes at Thea, but made encouraging remarks to the young woman. Then they were gone, and it was four o'clock and the day's end almost within reach.

She phoned Drew at eight, and he was a long time answering. 'Sorry,' he panted. 'Stephanie's got a sore knee and she's been milking it shamelessly ever since she got home. And now the evenings are lighter, she's not so keen to go to bed at the usual time. Says all her friends stay up until nine. I always thought they should go at the same time as their age.'

'Um . . . ?' Thea was slow to understand.

'You know – seven o'clock for seven-year-olds and so on. Of course it soon stops working.'

'She's eight, isn't she?'

'And three quarters, nearly,' he said glumly. 'Practically grown up.'

If only she was, thought Thea. *Everything would be a lot simpler.* 'So what's happened about that nursing home, if anything?' she asked him.

'Nothing yet. Give them a chance! It won't be one single act of vengeance. It'll just be a slow reduction in business, when the word gets round that it was me who blew the whistle. Every nursing home in Somerset is going to be wary of me and think I'll report the slightest little thing.'

'But the choice of undertaker isn't always down to them, is it?'

'It is, mostly, unless the deceased has already signed up with a particular one.'

'Talking of vengeance, it looks as if my employers have upset somebody themselves.' And she told him, lightly and quickly, about the fire.

He was not deceived. 'Lord, Thea. You might have died. Was it very smoky? Did you see a doctor?'

'It was a very small patch of burning carpet. A very amateur arsonist must have done it. But it's a rotten thing to do, even so. The police are trying to contact the Fosters, and I suppose they might come home early.'

'What about the other house? In the other village?'

'What about it?' She hadn't given it a single thought all day.

'Well – if it belongs to the same family, might that not be vulnerable to something similar as well?'

The suggestion made her feel weak and out of control. She couldn't be in two places at once. 'I would have heard if that had happened,' she said optimistically.

'Would you? How?'

'Higgins would have said something.'

'Okay.' He sounded doubtful, and she was already well on the path of imagining a variety of ways that a house could be damaged, other than by pouring petrol through the letter box.

'And listen – you were right about the plug in the washbasin. What a bonkers arrangement!'

He laughed. 'Glad I could be of some use. So what else did you do today?'

She described the church and its Saxon carvings, and then ran out of things to say.

'No progress on the murder enquiry, then?'

'The chap must have been a very dedicated campaigner. They can't seem to find out much about him.'

'DNA? Teeth? Fingerprints?'

'He didn't say.' She paused. 'They wouldn't bother with all that, surely? Not when his fiancée's identified him. It's only that they can't get much background. Since it seems almost certain that somebody from around here killed him, it probably doesn't matter very much, anyway. They've found his parents, apparently, even though they're not bothered enough to drop everything and fly here from Dubai.'

'I guess they think it's a bit late. Not much they can do, apart from arranging the funeral.'

'And Nella can do that, I imagine.' Then she remembered to tell him about Jessica's visit the following day. 'We can go and investigate the local pub. Except it's not very local, really. Must be a couple of miles' walk away.'

Drew tutted. He did not regard walking for its own sake as a very appealing activity. 'Take the car, then,' he said. 'You're less likely to get into trouble that way.'

'Not so,' she reminded him. 'Car trouble was fairly extreme in Stanton, if you remember.'

'You won't do that again. Anyway, it'll be good to see Jess. Say hello from me.'

'I will. She's sure to ask after you. My family are beginning to realise there's something going on between us. You'll have to meet Jocelyn and Damien at some point.'

'Even Emily, *eventually*,' he said softly.

Thea's older sister was at a remove from the family circle, at least for a time. Her name was mentioned as seldom as possible. 'Even Emily,' Thea agreed.

The conversation rambled on for another half hour, with repetitions and jokes and a few endearments. *We're like a pair of teenagers*, thought Thea, when they'd finished. It was talking for the sake of talking, maintaining the contact, strengthening the bond. It made her feel warm and secure and excited and optimistic. Only when it came to a solitary bedtime, with the problems and worries that beset them once again looming large, did she find herself facing a reality that gave scant grounds for optimism.

Chapter Ten

Jessica had to drive from Manchester, which would take her into late morning. The day was dry but cloudy, perfectly suited to a brisk March walk. Thea formed a plan, whereby they left a car at North Cerney, for the return trip after a lunch at the pub. She was so full of it that she gave the girl little time for preliminaries before spelling out the logistics of what she proposed. They hadn't even made it into the house.

'Hey, Mum, slow down!' Jessica protested. 'I've hardly said hello yet. Let me look at you, at least.'

It was the sort of thing a mother generally said. Thea laughed and stood still for the inspection. At the same time, she gave her daughter a similar long look. Jessica was definitely grown up now. Taller than her mother, fairer and less obviously attractive, she had a confidence that was new. Her choice of a profession with the police had come as a surprise, with both parents quietly unnerved by it at first. There had been rocky times, which included an unfortunate choice of boyfriend, but on the whole the profession seemed to suit her quite well. The uniform gave her a presence she had not possessed before, and the authority that any police officer finds herself invested with sat comfortably on her. Jessica had always been a well-balanced person, not inclined to extremes. She liked people, but as an only child, could get along without them when necessary. Thea gave her a little pat of approval. 'You'll do,' she said.

'You look okay, a bit tired,' Jessica judged. 'How's it going with Drew?'

'Same as ever. Jogging along. I'm not really tired – not in general, I mean. I didn't sleep very well last night, that's all.'

The girl became alert. 'Why? What's happened?'

'Come and see.' She led the way indoors and pointed at the singed carpet. 'A sort of petrol bomb, apparently. It didn't work very well.'

'Well enough.' Jessica had gone pale.

'I didn't want you to know about it, really. Maybe I should have found a rug to throw over the place. You'd never have noticed.'

More details were demanded and provided, with Jessica visibly biting back a lot of concern. 'What about the people? Aren't they coming back?'

'I don't know yet. I don't think they should. It's happened now. What good can they do?'

'They can give names of people with a grudge against them, for a start.'

'They can do that by phone, can't they?'

'Maybe. Okay, then. Who's this poor old doggie?' The corgi was at her feet, trying to catch her attention. Jessica bent to stroke her. 'Nice coat,' she said.

118

'She's called Gwennie, and she's a sweet old thing. No trouble. She sleeps most of the time.'

'Old dogs break your heart, don't they? When you think back to them as puppies, with all that energy and trust, to see them deaf and blind and witless is so awful.'

'Yeah.' Thea recalled a witless dog she'd minded in Hampnett, and the sadness that he carried with him, and sniffed.

'Sorry. Hepzie's got ages before she reaches that stage.'

'I wasn't thinking about her, actually.' She gave herself a shake. 'There's a tortoise as well, out in the garage. If the weather's nice, it's liable to wake up from its hibernation.'

'I'll have a look at it after lunch. Now come on, then. I'll be hungry soon. Are we really walking two miles?'

'We really are. First we have to drive both cars to the pub. Then we come back here in one of them, and do the walk. We should get there by one, if we bustle. We'll take Hepzie with us. I think the pub allows dogs, but she can stay in the car if not.'

It was duly accomplished, but it was half past one before they got their lunch. Thea walked her daughter past the quarry, which still had lingering signs of a police operation in the form of a notice on the small road to the north of it, asking for any witnesses to an incident the previous Saturday. 'What's this?' Jessica asked. Then she remembered. 'Oh – you said something on the phone. A man fell in, is that right?'

'They think he was murdered, actually.' Thea had been very ambivalent about letting Jessica know the details of the latest drama. 'I haven't been especially involved in it. It was a young man called Danny, and it happened on Saturday afternoon. He was in a protest group, campaigning against new houses and all sorts of other things. I met some of his friends when I first got here. It's my old friend Higgins in charge. I'm not involved at all,' she insisted.

'Really? That doesn't sound like you.'

'They're thinking it might have been a local farmer that did it. He's been targeted by the protesters. I honestly don't know much of the detail.'

Jessica was trying to get a look down into the quarry through the bare trees. 'Looks like quite a drop. He went in from here somewhere, did he?'

'Further on, as far as I know. Now come on. We have to climb over a wall and cross a field next.'

'This is a very small road. What if a big lorry came past and hit him, knocking him over the fence and into the quarry? That would look like murder, wouldn't it?'

'Jess, for heaven's sake, leave it. It's all in capable hands. They'll know by now exactly how he died. The post-mortem must have been yesterday.'

'Neat way to do it, though,' Jessica persisted. 'Maybe the farmer sent him over, with a Land Rover or tractor or something.'

'Look – we have to get over this wall and through those woods. We're not even halfway yet. I ought to have a quick look at the other house, while I'm here. Ten minutes max, okay?'

'Other house?'

'Didn't I say? Mrs Foster's sister has gone away as well. She's got a very smart place just down there. You can hold the dog while I water the plants again.' She didn't say anything about the nagging worry she'd fought against in the night, that the Bagendon house might have been attacked in some way by the same arsonist who'd been at large the previous day.

'I hope they're paying you double, then.'

Thea laughed ruefully. 'Not quite,' she said.

The house appeared undamaged at first glance. Apprehensively, Thea unlocked the front door and deactivated the alarm. She sniffed and detected no signs of smoke. A rapid circuit of the ground floor showed all windows intact and nothing in the least disturbed. Breathing more freely, she reproached herself – and Drew – for ever thinking there was the slightest reason for concern. Whatever the motive for the fire, it made little sense to think a second house might fall victim to the same thing, even if owned by a relative. Where would that end, taken to its logical conclusion? The plants were still in damp soil, but she dampened them again, thinking they would last until Friday quite easily. After that, the owners would be back, and she could forget the place completely.

'Looks all right,' she reported to Jessica. 'Thank goodness.'

'What's a house like this worth?' the girl wondered aloud. 'Must be half an acre of garden. And look at that view.' She pointed to the gently sloping fields behind the house, with trees along the upper ridge. Everything was still and timeless. The first greening of spring was visible in patches, and a flock of sheep dotted one field with picturesque patterning.

'Easily half a million,' said Thea, with only a slight twinge of resentment.

'Crazy.'

'Makes them all paranoid about anything that might come along to lower the value. That's basically what the protesting is about, I assume. Although . . .' she frowned. 'It's all back to front, isn't it? The activists or whatever they are should be on the side of the common people, not the local plutocrats – and that's who they're representing, when it comes down to it, opposing new houses.'

'Yes, but they're opposing it because it'll be big and expensive, and no use at all in relieving the housing shortage,' Jessica explained. 'Surely that's obvious?'

'You're right. Except that a whole other lot of locals would go berserk if a new estate of cheap houses was proposed instead.'

'You're sure it is housing that they're campaigning about, then?'

'Not really. It's badgers as well. And fracking. And wind farms. And quite a few other things. A girl called Sophie gave me a list. It's just that Jack Handy's sold some land for a big new house around here somewhere, and the police think that's the most likely reason for this chap being killed. As far as I can tell,' she finished with some uncertainty.

'Not much danger of wind farms in the Cotswolds,' said Jessica. 'Aren't they moving them offshore now?'

'I don't know. I just keep thinking of what your father would say about them, now we know the damage they do to birds. He'd have been horribly torn about it.'

'I think he'd take the side of the birds. What's the point

of building things meant to help the planet if they kill the creatures we're trying to be protect?'

'Right,' said Thea with relief. The whole question of wind farms made her tight with complicated feelings, that were all the more uncomfortable for being a turnaround from six or seven years previously. At that time, there had never been any question about the virtue of the modestly sized turbines. Since they had grown to insane proportions, most of her original assumptions had been overturned.

Everything to do with environment and climate seemed to have at least two excellent and contradictory arguments to be made, and everyone held impassioned positions one way or the other. In the past few months, it had all begun to seem like too much hard work, and she was inclined to let other people work it all out, regardless of what she thought herself. She had a growing feeling that the planet was not in the slightest danger anyway. Some of its inhabitants might be, but that didn't appear to be any different from the reality of the past umpteen billion years in any case.

'Keep walking,' Thea ordered. 'We don't have to go down past the church, like I did before. The road to North Cerney goes off before we get that far.' With a firm eye on the map, she marched them around the loop that was Upper End, and sure enough a small road was signed to the next village. It was an awkward walk with the dog, though, due to the lack of a footpath, and they kept to single file for much of the way.

North Cerney turned out to have a powerful appeal in another individualistic twist on the theme of endless variety that the region boasted. 'We don't have to look at the church, do we?' asked Jessica, as they passed it.

'Maybe on the way back,' Thea threatened. 'I expect it's wonderful. Most of them are. But I don't know any stories about this one.'

'They'll have stopped serving lunch if we don't get on.'

The Bathurst Arms was a substantial building, offering accommodation, a garden and a perfectly adequate menu. As a bonus, there was no objection to dogs in the bar. On a March Tuesday, there were only two other patrons, neither of whom Thea recognised.

They ordered a large meal and spoke little as they waited for it. 'That was quite a walk,' Jessica observed after a few minutes. 'I bet it was more than two miles.'

'I don't think so. Have you got a deadline for getting home?' Already the inevitable bleakness of being left alone again was threatening to undermine the moment.

'Not really.'

'Are you working tomorrow?'

It was as if the girl had been waiting for this precise question. 'I am, yes. We've got something on, so there's not much free time just now. I'm only off today because there are rules about maximum hours.'

'Something on?'

'I can't talk about it. It's an operation, with a big "O". Exciting.'

'You don't look very excited.'

'I can't *talk* about it, Mum. I'm just a small cog in a big machine. I don't even know exactly what the aim of it is. But it's important. Some of us are doing stuff we've never done before. It's a challenge.'

Thea frowned. 'I'm not at all sure I like the sound of it. Ought I to be worrying about you?'

'No more than I should worry about *you*. I don't think anybody's going to burn me in my bed, for a start.' There was a little crease of unease between her eyes, which Thea hadn't seen before.

'Are they making you do more than you feel competent to tackle? I mean – sorry, Jess – I *don't* mean I think you're not up to the job. But you're still quite new to it all. And it's not always the most ethical line of work, is it?'

'What makes you say that?'

'I don't know. You just looked sort of . . . guilty, for a minute. Queasy.'

'Stop it – okay? I really am forbidden to talk about it. They'd shoot me if they thought I was giving anything away.'

'I do hope not,' said Thea lightly. 'I think that's the army – and even there I have a feeling they abandoned firing squads a while ago now.'

Jessica gave a tight smile and took a swig of beer.

Thea watched her, rerunning the conversation in her head. 'You brought it up, so you must have wanted me to know at least a little bit. Something's bothering you, by the look of it. We could try a hypothetical approach. Something abstract.'

Her daughter thought for a minute. 'You mean, I tell you about a friend of mine who's got herself into an awkward spot, and has been asking for advice?'

'That sort of thing, yes.'

'O-o-kay. Well, what would you say if a person told you she'd been given something to do by her superiors that she's not sure is fair?'

'Fair?'

Jessica nodded.

'Fair to who?'

'People. Suspects.'

'You mean dishonest, don't you? What's the word – entrapment? Are you . . . sorry, is this person being asked to pretend or tell lies in order to catch a criminal?'

'Too much detail, Ma. Can we keep it general?'

Thea's heart was thundering with a sudden rage against the superiors who were corrupting her innocent girl, forcing her into some shady scam that would deceive suspected delinquents into incriminating themselves. It was shabby at best. But she knew, albeit dimly, that this kind of thing went on all the time. It was indeed unfair, playing dirty, and ultimately self-defeating. If the enforcers of the law couldn't keep themselves clean, then what hope was there for society at large?

'It's disgusting,' she snapped. 'They should be ashamed.'

'It's the system. It's the way things work. They say it justifies itself ten times over. Nobody gets hurt, really. I'm a means to an end.'

'So you'll do it?'

'I don't really have a choice. You're supposed to understand that. And it is a big operation. If it pays off, a lot of bad people will be off the streets.' She looked more sure of herself as she spoke.

'I can see that,' said Thea, aware that she ought to back off, but still wondering why the subject had been raised in the beginning. 'It doesn't sound as if there is much of an alternative, then. Let's hope it all works out as planned.'

'I keep hearing Daddy's voice in my ear, going on about the right thing, and integrity and all that sort of stuff. I've even been dreaming about him.'

'Oh dear.' Carl's unwavering morality had been a key element in his make-up. It had made life easy for his wife and daughter, always knowing how he would react and what line he would take in virtually any situation. 'I think he knew this sort of thing would arise, from the first moment you said you were going into the police.'

'Uncle James had a chat with me, two or three years ago now, warning me about the grey areas. I don't have much cause to complain, now it's happening. I expect it gets easier.'

'Your father never really had to make any nasty choices,' Thea realised. 'He chose a line of work where it was all perfectly plain.'

'It's not like that now, though, is it? The whole Green business has got pretty murky in some departments. Like we were just saying about wind farms.'

'Yeah.' Thea thought of Drew Slocombe and how similar he was to Carl in many ways. It was both unsettling and reassuring to see the pattern that was forming. 'It goes with growing up, I guess. Sooner or later you have to get your moral hands dirty, if that makes sense.'

'That seems to be the general idea.' Jessica smiled. 'That helps, actually. People on the moral high ground can be rather awful. Not Daddy, but a lot of them. Complacent. Superior. The rest of us just have to do the best we can. Right?'

'Right.'

The food had arrived in the middle of their exchange and they were eating absently, all their attention on each other and their thoughts. 'Not bad,' judged Jessica, holding up a forkful of lasagne. 'I was starving.'

'More beer?'

'Why not? I'm not driving again for hours yet. Is Hepzie all right down there?'

The spaniel was flopped bonelessly on the floor under their table, worn out from the walk. 'She's fine,' said Thea. 'She likes a good walk.' It was sufficiently inane to mark a break in their conversation. 'Did I tell you about Maggs?'

'Who? Oh – the girl undertaker. I must meet her sometime, she sounds unusual. What about her?'

'She's pregnant. I always thought she'd abjured children for ever, but it seems not.'

'Is she married?'

'Oh yes. Her husband was in the police. Den, he's called. Very tall, with a Devon accent. He must be ten years older than her, at least. He used to help collect bodies in an emergency, but now he works at Bristol Airport and isn't very available.'

'Why did he leave the police?'

'I never really found out. There was a murder, and Drew's wife got shot, and somehow Den lost his vocation. That's all I know. He drifted around for years before getting this job. They've got hardly any money, same as Drew.' Down below the surface, she had a sudden notion that Den was one of those to whom the moral high ground was the only place to be. Like Drew. And Carl. And possibly not Jessica. She sighed.

'Complicated,' said Jessica, without any discernible interest. 'At least Uncle Damien's not skint.'

'Not exactly flush, either. I don't know anybody who has enough cash, these days. You can't make proper plans without money,' she complained. 'You just have to take life a week at a time.'

'Like most of the human race,' Jessica observed dryly.

'I'm not happy to think poor Maggs has to live like someone in the Third World. At least they're all in the same boat in Africa and places.'

'They don't call it the Third World any more, Ma. And there are quite a few rich people in Africa these days. China's throwing money at them in Zambia and Botswana, for a start.'

'Really? I'm very out of touch, then. I had no idea.'

Jessica waved this aside and finished off her meal before speaking again. 'You and Drew – what's the plan?' she asked.

'Plan? Some hope! Everything's on hold until the kids are older. We carry on as we are for the foreseeable future.'

Jessica shook her head. 'Can't see that happening. Treading water for years – what sort of a life is that? How often do you expect to see him, on that basis? What a waste!'

At your age, Thea heard the unspoken words. She sighed. 'Nothing like often enough. But neither of us can see any option. The children are still so young, and shell-shocked by losing their mother. He can't do anything that unsettles them even more. He has to put them first, obviously. He *wants* to.'

'Maggs has unsettled him, by the sound of it, getting herself pregnant. What'll his kids think about her having a baby of her own? Presumably she's a sort of mother substitute for them at the moment. That'll change, won't it?'

'I don't know.' Thea felt like wailing at all the complications and frustrations in her life. She and Drew were so *right* together. Jessica's generous and open reaction to the relationship had been wonderful – almost *too* wonderful, given that it was such an interrupted and sporadic affair.

'Kids don't mind change as much as people think, you know. They kick up a lot of fuss at first, but then they get on with it, no harm done. And at least there are two of them. They still have each other, whatever happens.'

'I don't think that's true. They *look* all right, maybe. But I think it does a lot of damage, deep down.'

Jessica shrugged. 'It's the same point, isn't it – the theme for today. Something about the discrepancy between the ideal and the reality. That's what we're really talking about.'

Thea was impressed. 'That's very clever,' she said.

'I've been thinking about it quite a lot lately. Could be it's a vital part of growing up – letting the ideals fade a bit.'

'Which these eco-warrior people haven't done. Does that mean they're immature?' She thought about it. 'They'd be furious at the idea.'

'They're nowhere near as admirable as they think they are, that's for sure. I don't claim to know how their minds work. It's something the police find rather frustrating, actually.'

Thea laughed. 'I can imagine.'

They sat for another half an hour, after which Hepzie revived and grew restless. 'Better go,' said Jessica. 'Are there any local attractions you want to show me?'

Thea's mind went blank. 'Cirencester's rather nice. Lots of ancient Roman associations. A museum I've never been to. Wool. A big park . . .'

'And a church. Don't tell me.' Jessica rolled her eyes. 'No thanks. Why is it always the church that people focus on?'

'I never mentioned the church. I agree with you, more or less, that they're irrelevant in a lot of ways. But they're also very beautiful, and they do show something of how people lived a thousand years ago, if you know how to find it.' She felt a fraud, after her lack of response to the two churches she had visited that week. 'Or how they thought, anyway,' she amended.

'Let's just go back to Daglingworth and have some tea. I haven't talked to that corgi properly yet.'

'And the tortoise. Did I tell you there's a hibernating tortoise?'

'Yes, you did. Sounds fascinating.'

'I haven't even looked at it myself yet. I think it needs my help before it can start coming back to life. Something weird about giving it a bath. I've got everything written down.'

'There's a first time for everything,' said Jessica, her attention fading yet again.

Thea's car had been elected as the one to take them back, mainly because the fact of a muddy dog was less of a problem for her. The back seat had a sturdy cover designed to withstand whatever Hepzie might deposit on it. After years of ineffective nagging, Thea had eventually succeeded in persuading the animal to stay on it when wet or dirty. Which in fact she was not on this occasion, luckily for the floor of the Bathurst Arms.

For variety they followed a different route, alongside the River Churn, before turning right. 'This is where Sheila Whiteacre brought me,' Thea remembered. 'Did I tell you about her?'

'One of the protesters?' Jessica guessed.

'Mother of one of them. No – two, actually. There's a boy as well, who I haven't seen. They live in Baunton. Fabulous house. Really nice people.'

'All the houses are fabulous,' sighed the girl. 'Didn't we already decide that?'

'Oh, goodness. Look!' Thea interrupted. She slowed the car, and craned her neck to look through a field gate on their left. 'That must be Mr Handy's Land Rover. I recognise the dog.'

The vehicle was parked crookedly just inside the open gate, and the collie was standing behind it. There was no sign of the farmer.

'So what?' said Jessica.

'So nothing, really. I just . . .' She realised she felt slightly guilty towards the man who had kindly given her a lift in the rain. She had thought bad things of him, thanks to DI Higgins and his questions. 'I rather liked him,' she muttered.

'So?' said Jessica again. 'Are you going to stop and talk to him or what?'

'No. I'd better not. I wouldn't know what to say.'

Another car was coming up behind them, hooting for

them to get out of the way. 'Ma – you'll have to move. You're blocking the road.'

'No need to hoot. Can't he wait a minute?' She looked into the rear-view mirror and caught a glimpse of a man's face, bracketed by large ears. 'That's one of the protesters,' she said. 'Steve. Nobody could miss those ears. He must get caught on CCTV all the time.'

Jessica laughed. 'Just move,' she insisted. 'Unless you want to stop and talk to them.'

Still Thea was caught in a sort of paralysis. She *did* have things to say to Jack Handy, if only she could articulate them. She had questions for him as to where he stood with the police, and what, if anything, her testimony had done to help. The impatient Steve was a complication that rendered her stubborn. She pulled the car as far into the verge as she could, and turned off the engine.

'Ma!' Jessica protested, sounding far more alarmed than necessary.

'Don't worry. I won't be a minute.' She looked over her shoulder, wondering why Steve didn't squeeze past her in the mud-splashed white car he was driving. He was sitting there, staring through the gateway at the Land Rover, with horror on his face.

Chapter Eleven

'Something's wrong,' Thea said. 'He's seen something.' She got out of the car and went to the gateway. Instantly, she saw what Steve had seen and gave a cry.

Jessica followed her, seeming to take far too long to open her door and leave the car. Together they stood for ten seconds, making sense of the scene a few yards away.

A man was sitting on the ground, with his hand to his head. Blood was pouring through his fingers and he was moaning. His dog stood close, but not close enough to touch. The man's other arm was extended as if to ward the animal off.

'What happened to him?' asked another voice behind Thea. 'I saw his feet and legs, through the hedge.' It was the big-eared, scrappy-bearded protester. 'Uncle Jack? It's me, Steve. What happened?'

Uncle Jack, Thea repeated to herself, noting a slight similarity between the two that would never have struck her without help. The question being asked did seem to be the only rational one and she waited for an answer before moving.

Jessica, however, showed no such hesitation. She knelt beside the farmer, and pulled his hand away. 'Can you see?' she asked him. 'Can you tell me your name?'

He mumbled something, and she nodded. 'All right. I'm calling an ambulance for you. You don't have to talk, but try not to go to sleep, okay? Stay upright if you can.' She extracted a phone from her pocket and was soon giving an account of the situation to an emergency person. 'Where are we?' she asked Steve. 'Exactly.'

'It's the A435,' he told her. 'Just north of the A417. They'll find it.'

Jessica shook her head briefly and relayed the information, repeating it twice. Finishing the call, she turned back to the injured man. 'They shouldn't be very long. One of us can go back to the junction and wait for them. They might not see us otherwise.'

'I'll go,' said Thea, but Steve was quicker. He got into his car and reversed the short way back to where they had turned off the larger road. Shrugging, she looked at Jack Handy. 'Did somebody hit you?' she asked.

He gave no reply and Jessica threw her a sharp look. But Thea was already deep in thought, the murder of another man very prominent in her mind. If Handy had been attacked in a similar way – perhaps even intended for a tumble into the same quarry, which was barely a quarter of a mile away – then didn't that prove that he had not killed the first victim? Didn't that suggest that the original assumptions as to motives were awry?

The man was terribly pale, his skin almost grey under the streaks of blood. The shoulders of his jacket were splashed with red, and his fingers looked as if they'd been stuck together by the congealing gore from his head wound. He was taking deep noisy breaths, which appeared to be calming him, but he swayed more and more until he flopped onto his back. But he was still able to lift his head at Thea's question and his eyes met hers.

'There was a gang of them,' he said clearly. Then, 'Ouch!'

Jessica was gently inspecting the wound, which was to one side of his crown. Most of his hair was matted and dark on that side, and the girl had pulled some of it slightly. 'The bleeding's nearly stopped,' she reported. 'Did you black out?'

He frowned. 'Might have done. They'd all disappeared when I opened my eyes. That bloody dog was no use,' he added thickly. 'Just danced around them barking. Got hold of one lad's ankle for a minute, that's all. He soon kicked her off.'

'It's a collie,' Thea defended instinctively. 'What did you expect? And besides, she's old. They might have hit her as well if she'd got too close.'

'Could be,' he admitted. 'Anyhow, looks as if I'll live.'

'Your skull might be cracked. There could be a swelling of the brain. You'll have to be watched,' Jessica said briskly. 'But the signs are fairly encouraging,' she added. Thea suspected it was more for the sake of providing reassurance than an accurate observation. After all, he was obviously no longer able to sit upright.

'A *gang*?' Thea repeated. 'Did you know them?'

'Those protesters,' he panted. 'Girls, mostly. A couple of blokes. Shouting about their mate Danny and how it must've been me who chucked him in the quarry. Warning me I'd not get away with it. I told them to bugger off, and then one chap hit me with my own stick. Not just the once, either. The girls pushed me at him and he laid into me.' He put a hand to his cheek. 'Hurts here,' he said. 'And I've lost a tooth.'

Mother and daughter peered closer through the obscuring blood, and found swellings in several places on his face. 'Nasty,' said Jessica. 'You're going to have to press charges against them. I assume you know who they are?'

'Are you police?' he asked thickly. His eyelids were fluttering and his mouth hung open after he'd spoken.

'He's losing consciousness,' said Jessica urgently. 'Where's that ambulance?'

'I can hear something,' said Thea. 'No siren, though.'

'No need out here. It's only intended to get traffic out of the way.'

Less than half a minute later, an ambulance came down the road, only just getting past Thea's car and into the gateway. Two bulky paramedics jumped into action, asking staccato questions and festooning the patient with devices presumably designed to record his vital signs.

'Where's Steve?' asked Thea. 'Chap in a dirty white car.'

Nobody replied and she forgot him in the excitement. The ambulance people seemed worried, and one of them went to speak on the radio in the vehicle.

'Where will you take him?' Jessica asked the other one.

'And what about his dog?' wondered Thea. The shaggy animal was pacing restlessly, making little growls and whines. There was mud up its legs and around its neck.

The ambulance man ignored the question that was beyond his remit and answered the other. 'John Radcliffe, most likely. Don't like his readings, to be honest with you. Don't you know him?'

'Not really,' said Thea. 'I've met him once, that's all. He was talking to us two minutes ago, perfectly lucidly.'

'That's good,' said the man unconvincingly. 'The police are aware there's an incident. They ought to show up any time. We'll make sure they know it's a case of foul play.'

'There must be people around who'll take the dog, if they have to,' said Jessica. 'Hasn't he got any family?'

Thea blinked. 'I really don't know,' she said, racking her brains for any mention of a wife or child during their brief ride four days ago. 'I don't even know where he lives.'

'Won't be too difficult to find out,' said Jessica stoutly. 'We know his name, don't we?'

'Jack Handy,' nodded Thea.

'I wasn't sure I'd heard him right, but I thought he said "Dandy",' smiled the girl. 'Lucky you know better.'

The sheepdog came slowly up to them and nudged Thea's arm with her nose. 'Poor Rags,' Thea murmured. 'We'll see you're all right, okay?' She stroked the black-and-white head, and then ran her hand down one side. 'You're very matted, aren't you?' she muttered. 'I bet you live in an outside shed or something. Might not even be house-trained.'

'You know its name?' Jessica was surprised.

'We were introduced. I remembered because it's a male name for a female dog. And I've got a thing about dogs, in case you haven't noticed.'

The ambulance was preparing to leave. 'Not coming?' they asked, not expecting a positive reply.

'Where did Steve go?' Thea wondered afresh. 'Did he meet you at the junction, to show you where to come?'

The paramedics shook their heads. 'We saw your car down here,' they said, 'and assumed that was where we were needed.' Then they drove off, leaving Thea to try to calculate how far away Oxford must be. It had to be thirty miles at least.

'Doesn't that seem suspicious?' she asked, thinking about the Steve person.

Jessica confirmed this with a frown. 'Weird,' she said.

'We can vouch for him,' Thea said slowly. 'I mean – that he wasn't one of the attackers. He drove up behind us. But he might have known it was happening. They were his friends. Although, he called him *uncle*. He might have been deliberately left out, because of that.'

Jessica was standing with her arms wrapped around herself, leaning against Thea's car. 'I hope he comes round and tells the local chaps the whole story,' she said. 'I don't want to get drawn into it.'

'Do we have to wait here? Why are they taking so long?'

'They've got my number, so they'll find us, in any case. Or I can call again, and tell them where we are. Give them another couple of minutes and then we can go.'

'We'll have to take Rags. And what about the Land Rover? We *can't* go, Jess.'

'Right. Sorry. I ought to have thought.'

They hung about for five more minutes, trying to reassure the worried sheepdog, until a police car finally materialised.

Two uniformed officers got out and asked a lot of very basic and not very relevant questions. 'I'm with the Manchester force,' Jessica told them, after a while. 'I know how this goes. Can we find out Mr Handy's address and take his dog home? We'll do it, if you tell us where to go.'

The men blinked at the deviation from protocol. They were slightly older than Jessica, their uniforms neat and clean, their faces bland. They said 'madam' a lot, to both Thea and her daughter. They showed very little sign of grasping the significant features of the incident, and kept staring at the Land Rover as if expecting its owner to be somewhere inside it.

'You can find his address through the vehicle registration,' Jessica said helpfully.

'Have you got ID?' one of them asked her. 'Anyone could say they were a police officer.' He scratched his cheek. 'Around here, it wouldn't come as a surprise, either. You could be one of these eco-idiots, for all we know.'

'We're not,' said Thea crossly. 'And we're getting cold and a bit impatient, quite honestly. Neither of us lives around here. We've just got involved by accident. The man was attacked. He knows at least some of the people who did it. We can help you to get it straight, if you just listen for a minute.'

'All right, madam,' said the man ponderously. The ghost of a mountain of paperwork hovered before all their eyes. 'Might this be connected to the death of the man in the quarry at the weekend, do you think?'

'Almost certainly,' said Thea. 'The same people are involved. Mr Handy was – last I heard – one of the prime suspects for having killed him. I think you probably need to speak to Detective Inspector Higgins, and get yourselves up to speed on it all. This is wasting everybody's time.'

The effort to remain polite was plainly considerable. 'Mother!' Jessica gasped. 'Behave yourself.'

'Well, they're impossible. We've stayed here waiting for them in the cold; we've offered to take the dog home, when that's obviously their job; we're trying to explain what's happened and all they can do is ask for identification and what our mother's maiden names might be.'

'DI Higgins?' said the second man, who was smaller and quieter, but no quicker on the uptake than his partner.

'Yes. He knows me. I've seen him very recently. Haven't you got access to the case file about all this? Didn't anybody even make the connection when Jack Handy's name came up?'

'It didn't come up, Ma,' said Jessica. 'I didn't give a name when I called the nines. They have no way of knowing.'

'Well, now they do. Just get his address, and we can go. Jeremy knows where I am if he wants me.'

The use of the DI's first name was a calculated gamble. She hoped it would intimidate these constables into a better quality of attention. It could easily have gone the wrong way, but it seemed to have worked.

'That's your car?' queried the talkative one.

'Yes. And the spaniel inside it is mine as well. This dog here, named Rags, belongs to Mr Handy. We're hoping he has a wife or other relative at home who can take custody of it.' A thought struck her. 'A person who presumably by now is aware of his injuries and might be on her – or his – way to

Oxford, or wherever they've taken him.' The ramifications began to overwhelm her. 'Oh, God,' she groaned. 'This is too much. How do we know what to do, if you can't even get the simplest details sorted?'

The officers decided to give up. 'We have your contact details. We can call you when we know more about Mr . . .' he glanced at his notes 'Handy's situation. If you could kindly take charge of his dog in the meantime, that would be appreciated. We need to secure this crime scene and wait for back-up.'

'We can go?' Thea could hardly believe it.

'They don't need us, Ma,' said Jessica tightly. 'Let's get back to the house. The corgi will be feeling neglected.'

'God, yes. So she will, poor thing. And stop calling me Ma,' she added. It was bad enough in a text – out loud in front of policemen, it was outrageous.

Rags climbed onto the back seat beside Hepzie with a look that said *I will do as you say, but I'm not at all sure it's wise*. Thea sighed. Intelligent dogs always bothered her, the way they could see through human failings, and yet still maintained their loyalty. This one was muddy and scruffy, as well.

'That was a completely ludicrous business,' she snapped, as they drove away. 'Why were they so *stupid*?'

'They weren't really. They had to get things in the right order. It was us as much as them. We were wrong to assume they knew who the man was. That was fairly stupid, actually. They'll get it all straight in no time and let us know what to do with the dog.'

'Oh, Lord,' Thea's sense of losing control gained

ground as she imagined the next few hours. 'I can't just introduce a strange dog into the Fosters' house. It might kill Gwennie. It might pee on their carpet.' Looking at the road layout ahead, an association struck her. 'I know! I can go to Baunton and see if the Whiteacres can help. They'll know where Jack Handy lives, for a start, and whether he's got a wife. I might even leave Rags with them.' The dog was licking urgently at a front paw on the back seat. When Thea glanced back, she whined, and rubbed at her nose with the licked foot. 'I hope they didn't hurt her,' she worried. A sudden choking-cum-coughing sound only increased her anxiety. 'What's wrong with you?' she asked. The dog wagged a slow tail, and coughed again.

'It's nearly half past three,' Jessica said in alarm, ignoring any concerns about the dog. 'It'll be midnight before I get home at this rate.'

'More like about seven,' said Thea. 'Does it matter?'

'I need a good night's sleep. I *told* you. There's a lot going on. We're all meant to be on top form.'

'Better than that dozy pair we just met, then.'

'Stop it. Who are these White-what's-it people, anyway?'

'A very nice family who I met on Sunday. I told you about them, remember? They've got five children and two dogs. They seem to know all the local characters, and Sheila turned up just after the fire yesterday. She'll be wanting to know how I'm getting on. I think I can find the house again. It's Baunton. That's left here, on the main road, look.'

'I can't get the geography straight,' Jessica admitted. 'I don't know how anybody managed before there were satnavs.'

'Maps,' said Thea shortly, thinking that Carl would have

been horrified at his daughter's remark. He had taught her how to work a map when she was about six.

'Right. Hey, you two – settle down.' Both dogs in the back were standing up and jumping about, in a dance that was not entirely friendly. They gave Jessica mutinous looks. 'Behave yourselves,' she ordered.

'What are they doing?' Thea asked, trying to see them in the mirror. 'If they start fighting, I'll probably crash the car.'

'They're not happy. Why do your adventures always involve troublesome dogs?'

'They don't. Sometimes I don't have any dogs at all to worry about. Except Hepzie, of course, and she's no trouble when she's on her own.'

'That Steve person,' Jessica said slowly. 'Have I got this right – he's one of the eco-warriors or whatever they are? And Mr Handy said they were the ones who attacked him? So Steve must have known them. That must be why he made himself scarce instead of waiting for the ambulance. But he knew we'd seen him.'

'Right.' Thea was still worrying about the dogs.

'It was a crime scene, in that field. They'll have to go over it – and the Land Rover. And if he stays unconscious, we're the only ones who've got any idea what happened to him. That's awkward,' she concluded. '*Very* awkward, if he doesn't wake up soon and tell the story for himself.'

'He won't *die*, will he?' The idea had not occurred to her up to then.

'Probably not. The John Radcliffe's pretty good, isn't it?'

'Famously so. But it'll take them half an hour at least to get there. He might die on the way.'

'They have a whole mass of machines and stuff in the ambulance. He'll be okay.'

'It must have been a sort of vigilante thing. Taking revenge, because they don't think the police will ever charge him for killing Danny,' Thea mused. 'But it's odd that it's a weekday. They've all got proper jobs, according to Sheila. They only do the protesting and campaigning at weekends.'

'Lunch hour,' Jessica suggested. '*Stop it*, you dogs.'

The sudden shouted order had some effect and things quietened down on the back seat. 'Nearly there,' said Thea. 'It's one of those, if I remember rightly.'

Two large houses stood on opposite sides of the road, and Thea pulled up outside the one on their left. 'Isn't it gorgeous!'

'Looks as if they're in.' Three cars were parked in the generous driveway, forcing Thea to stay out in the road. 'You go, and I'll stay here to keep order,' Jessica suggested.

'Okay.' Feeling overloaded and mildly resentful, Thea walked up to the house. She rang the doorbell and waited.

After a lengthy silence, the door opened and Tiffany was there, looking pale and puzzled. 'What do *you* want?' she asked.

It was difficult to tell the story succinctly, standing on a doorstep, but she thought she did it rather well. 'Jack Handy has been attacked and he's been taken to hospital. I've got his dog. I need to take it home, but I don't know where he lives.'

'Mum!' shouted the girl, into the hallway behind her. 'Can you come here?' She turned back to Thea. 'I don't get why you're involved in it. Why can't you just mind your own business?' She spoke softly, with a furious cat-like hiss. Her eyes widened and her lower jaw jutted. 'You have no idea what you're doing, have you?'

Thea had been spoken to in similar ways many times. It always struck her as very unfair. She *would* mind her own business, if people gave her the chance. Speechlessly, she reran the events of the afternoon, in an effort to justify herself. Surely nobody would simply have driven past that gateway without looking to see if there was a problem? Any normal person would have stopped as she had. Except, she admitted to herself, they probably wouldn't and hadn't. Most people assumed that it was not their concern, that whatever was happening could happen without them. 'It was your friend Steve,' she blurted. 'He saw something, and I thought we should have a look as well.'

Then Sheila Whiteacre was standing beside her daughter, both of them significantly taller than Thea anyway, and even more so from the extra height of the doorstep. 'Where does Jack Handy live?' she asked wearily. 'That's all I want to know.'

Sheila smiled uncertainly. 'Why?'

'She's got his dog,' said Tiffany.

'All right. I'll see to it now. You get back to your homework,' Sheila ordered her daughter, giving her a solicitous stroke on her shoulder. She smiled again at Thea. 'She's didn't go to school today. She's too upset about Danny.'

'The dog,' Thea prompted, after a small nod of sympathy. 'Will there be anybody there? I mean – he's been taken to hospital. Has he got a wife or somebody? I can't really take it to the Fosters', you see.'

'Sorry – I don't see at all. What happened to him? Why have *you* got anything to do with it?'

Don't you start, Thea wanted to say. 'It's a long story. I really wish I hadn't been there, just at the wrong moment. I can leave the dog here, if you'd rather.' This last came with a spurt of exasperation at all the questions.

'He lives in North Cerney. I thought you knew that. It's a farm a little way along the road to Woodmancote. Three or four miles from here, that's all.' Sheila spoke in a calm, deliberate tone, spiced with reproach. She made Thea feel foolish and oddly tainted, as if she had brought something unwelcome onto the doormat.

'Thank you,' she said and turned to leave.

'Wait a minute – you won't find it without more help than that. It's got a cattle grid across the entrance, and you can just see the house at the end of the track, with a big barn and masses of sheep everywhere. He lives with an older woman – I think she's his stepmother. She doesn't go out much. Hospital, did you say?' The belated reaction was almost comical. 'What happened to him?'

'Ask Tiffany,' said Thea abruptly. 'I'll have to go. It'll be getting dark before long, and then I'll never find his damned farm.'

'You've got at least two hours of daylight. Come and see me tomorrow, when you've calmed down, and tell me the whole story.'

'Sorry.' Thea almost wept. 'It's been a difficult week so far – and it's only Tuesday. I've got my daughter in the car. Thanks for the help.'

She slumped back into the driving seat and heaved a

great sigh. 'Back the way we came,' she announced. 'All the way to North Cerney and beyond.'

'For heaven's sake!' Jessica protested. 'That's ridiculous. What if there's nobody in when we get there?'

'What else can we do?'

They were saved further argument by Jessica's phone. She answered it eagerly, and there ensued a conversation that Thea quickly understood was with a police person. The important details of their adventure were conveyed, and then Thea's own name was mentioned. 'She's at a property called Galanthus House in Daglingworth,' said Jessica. 'Oh – right. Of course. There was a fire, yes . . . I suppose so. I really need to get back to Manchester . . . and there's a dog. No, no, I understand. We'll be there in five minutes. Okay, then.'

She pressed the red button and looked at Thea. 'They're coming to interview us. The dog will have to wait.'

'When? Now?'

'More or less. Oh, and I meant to tell you – while I was sitting here, two men came out of the shed, just there.' She pointed to a good-sized building beside the driveway with a door standing open. Inside, a lawnmower, stack of firewood and jumble of tools were all visible. 'I had the window open, because of all the dog breath, so I could hear what they said. They were arguing. I think they were father and son.'

'Did one have a beard?'

'They both did, actually.'

'Probably Ricky and Mr Whiteacre,' Thea guessed. 'So what about them?'

'The older one said "For God's sake, don't let Tiffany know about this. If you and her so-called friends want to go beating up local farmers, that's bad enough, but I'm not having her involved." That was more or less exactly what he said.'

'Did they know you'd heard them?'

Jessica grimaced. 'Probably,' she said.

Chapter Twelve

It should have taken barely two minutes to drive the straight road from Baunton to Daglingworth – a speck of time which saw Thea's mind so thronged with implications and worries that she was confused to find herself back at the complicated junction with the A417. 'Where do I go now?' she faltered. 'This isn't right.' She recalled a left turn at the church which she ought to have taken. It led directly to Galanthus House. Instead, she would have to do a near-circle to reach it.

'Over there, and then left,' ordered Jessica. 'What's the matter with you?'

'About a thousand things,' she snapped back. 'I missed the turn. I've already almost been burnt to death. Now the Whiteacres know that I know that their Ricky attacked Jack Handy. They'll come in the night and shoot me.'

'No, they won't, because they'll know we'll have told the police. They'll deny the conversation ever took place. They'll have worked out an alibi for Ricky. And if Mr Handy wakes up and names him, then that will be that, and you won't be relevant at all. Calm down, for heaven's sake.'

'How can I?' Her mind continued to race over everything she'd learnt. 'I really *liked* the Whiteacres,' she wailed. 'I thought they'd be people I could go to if anything else happened.'

'You can go to the police. Or pack up and go home. Maybe the owners will come back in a day or two, anyway. They won't be able to relax once they know somebody tried to burn their house down.'

'And these *dogs*,' Thea went on. 'I can't just abandon poor Gwennie, can I?'

'You can hand Rags over to the police when they come. It's their job, anyway.'

'Stop saying *anyway*, as if that makes it all less important. The Fosters won't come back, for a start. I'll have to stay here for another ten days.'

'Can't Drew come at the weekend and do it with you?'

'Him and two children, you mean? I hardly think so.' Her voice caught on a choke of frustration. 'What did I do to get myself into all this?'

'I don't know. But I expect it was something.'

They were at the Fosters' house, where Jessica's car sat waiting in the driveway. Thea drove past it and into the garage, without thinking.

'You're assuming you won't have to go out again, then?' said Jessica.

'Hoping,' Thea corrected. 'Rags can stay in the car for the time being. If she's staying overnight, I can shut her in the garage with an old blanket for a bed.'

'Probably her idea of four-star luxury.'

They took Hepzie into the house, and went to find Gwennie. The corgi was on the sofa, fast asleep. For a terrible second, Thea thought she was dead, seeing no sign of breathing, but the panic soon died as she approached and laid a hand on the thick golden coat. The colour was officially known as 'red', she believed – which was miles away from the reality. Gwennie raised her nose slightly and sniffed at the sudden hand. 'She's fine,' said Thea. 'What a good dog.'

Jessica came into the room and looked at the scene. 'She's got a nice coat,' she said. 'Must keep her lovely and warm.'

Thea fingered the dense hair of the white ruff at the back of the dog's neck. 'She's very sweet-natured. Makes you think her owners must be kind and patient with her. She's a sort of canine barometer of the kind of people they are.' Then she thought of the big placid Labradors at the Whiteacres' and wondered if the theory was already collapsing.

'Yeah,' said Jessica dubiously. 'Oh – here they are, look.' From the front window they saw a car draw up and a man get out. 'Is that your DI chap?'

'Higgins,' Thea confirmed. 'Looks as if he's on his own.'

It was obvious that Jessica thought she should do all the talking. She stepped briskly to the door and had it open before Higgins could ring. She almost pulled him inside, introducing herself and waving him into the living room. Thea remembered the way she'd kept him standing in the hallway the day before, and blushed gently as she realised he remembered it just as vividly.

'How is he?' she asked. 'Has he come round yet?'

'Hold on,' he said. 'One thing at a time.'

'Yes, but that's the most important thing, isn't it? You don't need me and Jess if he's telling you the whole story for himself.'

Higgins sat back in a soft armchair and exhaled. 'No, he hasn't. He's in a deep coma. They're operating on him any time now. So all we know of what happened will have to come from you.'

'And Steve,' said Thea, without thinking. 'Steve saw him as well.'

'He didn't hear what he said, though,' Jessica pointed out. 'That was mostly me.'

'I heard it all as well,' Thea objected. 'I was right there.'

'Ladies!'

The effect was impressive. Mother and daughter fell silent and waited for him to take charge.

Higgins extracted a notebook from his pocket and opened it. 'Can we please go back to the very beginning? If just one of you could speak at a time, that would be helpful. Any disagreements or corrections will obviously be listened to, but it would be very much easier to get the main facts from just one of you.' He looked at Jessica as he spoke, and Thea tried not to feel resentful.

The young police constable squared her shoulders and gave an admirable account of the events of the afternoon, none of which gave Thea any reason to argue or correct. What had seemed like a painful muddle was now laid out clearly. It only took a few sentences to explain the essential facts. 'He actually told you who attacked him?' Higgins queried. 'Did he give names? What were his actual words?'

'No names. He said it was a gang of protesters, made up of at least one man and a number of girls. He said a man hit him with his own stick and the girls pushed him around.'

'Some stick,' muttered the detective inspector. 'Did he have any idea why they did it?'

'Revenge for what happened to the chap in the quarry – what's his name?' Jessica looked to her mother.

'Danny,' said Thea.

'They were shouting accusations at him as they attacked him,' said Jessica. 'He definitely said that. And since then I've heard a conversation that suggests an identity for the attacker.'

'And don't forget about Steve,' Thea insisted.

Both the others gave her a look of irritation. 'What about him?' snapped Jessica. 'I've already said it was thanks to him we stopped in the first place.'

'He called the farmer "Uncle Jack", remember. And they look rather alike.'

'All right, but let me get to the part about Ricky Whiteacre.'

Higgins held up a finger. 'Hang on a minute. Let's make sure we've covered everything at the scene first.' He checked the details through again and then invited them to cautiously speculate on what seemed to have happened.

Jessica gave Thea a little wave of invitation. 'Go on – you've met most of these people,' she said.

'I can't add anything useful. The campaigners must be assuming Jack Handy killed their friend Danny Compton, and they were punishing him for it. Maybe they think the police are letting him get away with it. But it does seem rather idiotic of them, doesn't it? Letting him see them, and attacking him in broad daylight. Unless they meant to kill him,' she finished uneasily. 'That's terrible, if so. Those girls – Sophie and Nella and Tiffany – they're all perfectly ordinary respectable people. And Ricky,' she added. 'Although I've never met him.'

'Ricky?' Higgins looked at his notes. 'Now, tell me about him.'

'He's the son of Sheila Whiteacre. Tiffany's brother. Jessica heard him talking about it with his dad, just now. We went there to ask for Mr Handy's address, so we could take his dog home.'

'Dog . . . yes, there's a note about the dog. Where is it now?' He looked around as if expecting to see it.

Thea wrestled with a renewed surge of impatience. 'In my car, in the garage. She can't stay there for long. Apparently there is somebody at the farm to look after her.' She sighed tiredly. 'I suppose I can take her – except it'll be dark soon, and—'

'There is a female relative, but she's gone to be by his bedside in Oxford,' said Higgins. 'She doesn't drive far after dark if she can avoid it, so we sent a car for her.'

'How kind.' The sarcasm was muted, but still unmissable. 'So what am I meant to do with Rags?'

'Normally we'd find a place for it in a rescue or kennels somewhere. I'm sure she'd be happier staying here with you, though. She can go home tomorrow, in any case.'

'Are you sure? What if this stepmother or whatever she is decides to stay by the bedside for *days*? People do,' she finished gloomily.

'She'll be fine for a night in the garage,' Jessica interrupted impatiently. 'That's just a detail.' Even she seemed to be eager to get to the important part.

'Pity she didn't bite any of the attackers,' said Higgins. 'They'd probably have to go to hospital and we'd get a report.'

Jessica had mentioned Mr Handy's disdainful remarks about his dog, in her account of the incident. 'She might have torn a garment,' she surmised. She had also confirmed that there had been no estimate of the number of protesters involved. 'Four or five, at least, the way he was talking,' she concluded. 'Now, can I tell you about what I overheard? It's extremely important.'

'Go on, then.'

It was accomplished in seconds. Higgins made a note. 'Hearsay,' he pointed out. 'Not very useful as evidence.'

'Maybe not, but it gives you a strong lead, doesn't it?' Thea was all too familiar with the slippery business of hearsay evidence. In reality, it seemed to her that the great majority of murder investigations relied on it very heavily indeed.

'Funny they were all around on a weekday,' mused the detective.

'That's what I thought,' said Thea. 'Plus there's Steve and Tiffany. Her mother said she was at home all day.'

'I've been thinking about that Steve,' Jessica offered. 'We wondered whether he'd been meant to take part in the attack, and deliberately hung back because it was his uncle. Or maybe he was told to stay clear for that reason. But he might have known it was going to happen, and gone along to check that Mr Handy wasn't too badly hurt.'

'He looked absolutely horrified,' Thea remembered. 'I saw his face in the mirror.'

'I think he knew where to look. We'd never have realised there was anybody lying in the field, without him behaving as he did.'

'I imagine they had some sort of group message sent round, arranging it amongst themselves,' said Thea, feeling clever. 'So they all gathered in the lunch hour and savaged the poor man en masse.'

'Please!' Higgins called, holding up both hands liked a determined traffic cop. 'You both know better than this. All I want is a dispassionate description of what happened. No wild speculation or accusation. Just facts and sensible hypotheses.'

'You started it,' said Thea. 'Wondering how come it happened on a weekday. Implying they're just weekend campaigners, with proper jobs the rest of the time.'

'It's all very *vague*, though, isn't it?' said Jessica. 'Do you actually know the names and details of everyone in this group, whatever it is? Have they been breaking any laws?'

Higgins merely shook his head and closed his notebook. He closed his eyes too for a moment, and then said, 'Mr and Mrs Foster. We contacted them about the fire. They were very alarmed and upset and wanted our assurances that you were all right.'

'That's nice,' said Thea. 'Weren't they worried about Gwennie as well?'

'Who?'

'The dog. The reason I'm here in the first place.'

'Oh – I think they were, a bit.'

'Did you speak to them personally?'

'No, actually. But it was all written down. They really don't want to come home early, especially as they'd have to pay some enormous amount for emergency seats on a flight. We told them there wasn't that degree of urgency, if they could just try and think why it might have happened.'

'And did they?'

'As a matter of fact, they were very helpful.'

Thea waited impatiently. 'And?' she prompted.

'We're following it up. I can't say more than that.'

'Am I in any further danger? At least tell me that much.'

He smiled. 'I would say the only danger you might get into would be as a result of any further reckless involvement in local crimes. Just stay out of the way and you'll be fine. Leave that garage open, or park in the driveway, so everybody knows you're here – although I imagine they've worked it out by this time. The story of the fire will be public knowledge by now, and when we've completed our interviews, there could well be an arrest, which will probably make the local TV reports.'

'Wow!' breathed Thea admiringly. 'You haven't wasted much time, have you?'

'Murder, arson and GBH since Saturday, all within a mile of this house. We've had to cancel all leave and shout for reinforcements from Gloucester.' He laughed. 'Never a dull moment when Mrs Thea Osborne shows up.'

'Stop it,' she said. 'I'm the victim here, remember.'

'I know you are,' he agreed, suddenly serious. 'Some of us think you're very brave to keep on with this house-sitting malarky at all. There always seems to be some unforeseen hazard.'

'Stop it,' she said again, feeling uncomfortably weak and vulnerable. 'Just catch these baddies, okay? Are the Fosters going to call me?'

'Probably. We did downplay the damage somewhat, though, and told them you were completely unharmed.'

'Thanks,' she muttered. 'I think.'

'Ma – I've really got to go,' Jessica interrupted. 'It's well after five. I hate to leave you with all this chaos, but I suppose you can cope. It won't be the first time, after all.'

I don't want to cope! Thea silently screamed. *I want a nice easy life where nothing like this ever happens.* 'I expect I will,' she said.

She made tea for her daughter, and added sandwiches made from cheese and pickle, insisting she needed something before the long drive. Slowly the events of the day fell into a more manageable pattern, leaving her with nothing demanding her attention except for Rags. Even that responsibility felt lighter, once she'd let the dog out of her car and taken her for a quick walk outside, firmly attached to a lead. She then fed her with some of Hepzie's biscuits. It was a mild evening, so she constructed a nest in a corner of the garage, made of the old blanket and piece of carpet she kept in her car boot. 'You'll be all right here,' she said firmly. 'But you'll have to stay tied up.' The lead was short, so she replaced it with a length of thin rope she found on a shelf in the garage. It was long enough to allow the dog to go to the front of the building for a pee if necessary. It was a bare concrete floor that would easily survive such usage. At least the animal wore a collar, which made things easier.

The fact of a muddy sheepdog tethered in the Fosters' tidy garage was incongruous. If it barked all night, there would be complaints.

Jessica finally left just after six, looking rather more frazzled than Thea was feeling. 'What a day!' she kept saying. 'I expected a nice peaceful walk in the country, and instead I landed up as witness to an assault. I need to give all my attention to my own work, from here on. Compared to that, all this Cotswold stuff is peanuts.'

'Big peanuts,' said Thea mildly. 'You'll have me imagining conspiracies to murder Prince Charles at this rate. Or blowing up Manchester Cathedral. I'm starting to think I definitely should be worrying about you.'

Jessica glanced upwards, in muted exasperation. 'Don't start that now. I've got to go. I'll try to text or something in a day or two. Keep me posted, right? And give my love to Drew.'

'I will.' The evening phone call to Drew was very much at the forefront of her mind, as she waved her daughter off. There was, after all, a great deal to tell him.

Chapter Thirteen

But the phone call to Drew was delayed by visitors. At seven o'clock, the dog outside set up a warning bark that was enthusiastically taken up by Hepzie. Even Gwennie joined in, with a bewildered wolf-like howl. 'Quiet!' Thea ordered, with little effect.

Three people stood crowded together outside the front door. 'Hi again,' said the shortest, youngest one. 'I hope you don't mind, but we'd like to talk to you.'

It was a deputation at best. The mere fact of the number was intimidating; all the more so when the events of the afternoon were taken into account. 'What for?' she asked warily.

'Don't worry. We won't hurt you,' said the tallest, thinnest one. 'We thought we should try to explain a few things, that's all.'

'You really don't need—' Thea began, but Sophie cut her off.

'Please,' she said. 'You must have got a terrible idea about us, with everything that's been happening. This was

Tiff's idea. She said her mum was a bit short with you, when you were there today. They all feel bad about that, you see.'

'All?' Thea shook her head in puzzlement. 'Who do you mean? Sheila was fine. She doesn't have to worry. She told me what I wanted to know.'

'All my *family*,' Tiffany explained. 'Look – we understand how it must seem to you. And when we heard about the fire as well, we thought you were probably feeling a bit vulnerable, here on your own. I mean – Daglingworth is probably the quietest safest place in the world, but even so . . .'

'Two men have been attacked, in the past two days,' Thea finished the thought.

'Three days, actually,' said Nella, who looked gaunt and ill. Her voice was low and croaky, as if she had a sore throat.

'Can we come in, then?' Sophie persisted. 'Just for a few minutes?'

'I suppose so.' Thea was reluctantly curious as to what they might wish to say to her. Were they going to confess to assaulting Jack Handy? Were they going to make another attempt at recruiting her to their campaign, whatever it might be?

She led them into the living room and invited them to sit down, but made no offer of drinks. In other people's houses, the usual laws of hospitality were in abeyance, she had long ago decided.

'We really do want to explain things to you,' Tiffany repeated. 'Ricky wanted to come as well, but we said that would be too much.'

'Your brother,' Thea nodded. She sat forward on the chair and examined each face with care. Tiffany seemed very young; consumed by a need for a good outcome. She had been the one, Thea recalled, who sympathised with Nella's desire for a quick wedding to the murdered Danny. Sophie looked strained and fearful. Of the three, she appeared to have the clearest grasp that things had become alarmingly serious. Sophie did not strike Thea as a very trusting person. That long list of reasons to protest and campaign came back to her. Sophie apparently disliked almost everything about the world as it stood, and saw it as her role to put as much as possible straight.

Her short flat hair suggested regular wearing of a balaclava; her straight back and direct look made it easy to imagine her striding the countryside with a stick or a whistle – all the paraphernalia of harassment and disruption. There was something implacable about Sophie.

And Nella was simply ravaged. Her jaw was working, as if swallowing back tears or screams. She would not meet Thea's eyes, but stared at a point on the carpet and kept her arms wrapped tightly around herself.

'Okay, then. What did you want to explain?' Thea encouraged.

'You found Jack and called the ambulance and police,' said Sophie. 'That was . . . unlucky.'

'Who for? Me or you?'

'Everybody. Steve's told us all about it. You got in the way, you see. He was supposed to do it all, not you. He's related to him,' Sophie added.

'Yes, so I gathered. He's Jack's nephew.'

'Not exactly, but close enough, I suppose. That doesn't matter, anyhow.'

Thea was doing her best to follow the implications, her head starting to throb gently with the effort to understand. 'But what do you mean – he was supposed to do it? Do what?'

'He knew there were plans to show Handy a lesson, warn him off. But Steve couldn't be part of it, could he? Because Handy knows him and there'd be obvious difficulties with the family connections. So we told him to go to that field and watch, without being seen. We thought that made sense. Handy wasn't supposed to be *killed* or anything.'

'Although he almost was. He might die yet. His skull was broken. Who hit him, anyway?' She looked straight at Tiffany. 'Your brother, was it? It all points to him, doesn't it?'

But the girl did not react, and when nobody replied, Thea ploughed on. 'But he *knows* all of you. What made you think he wouldn't tell the police who attacked him?'

Nella spoke up. 'He wouldn't dare. Not after what he did to Danny.' She reached out a hand, which was grabbed by Tiffany and rubbed warmly.

'So you beat him as punishment for killing your fiancé?' Thea summarised brutally. She had dwindling patience for this trio of self-righteous women. 'Is that it?'

'You don't understand,' said Sophie. 'You think any of *us* was there? That's quite wrong. Tiff was at home. I was at work. And Nella . . .' She looked worriedly at her friend.

'I was in Cirencester,' said Nella shortly.

Thea felt herself floundering. 'But you persuaded others

from your group to act for you – is that it? People Jack doesn't know. Except, surely he knows Ricky?'

'Stop talking about Ricky,' ordered Sophie. 'You've got no idea what actually happened. Jack Handy got what he deserved. The police questioned him and let him go. Apparently there's not enough evidence that he killed Danny. That made a lot of people very angry.'

'So you're vigilantes,' Thea accused. 'Taking the law into your own hands.' She sighed. Hadn't the whole group of them been doing just that already, disrupting badger culls, bullying landowners? 'As usual,' she finished.

Sophie took a deep breath and held it for several seconds while she sat rigidly upright. Her jawline was sharp, and the look in her eyes held nothing soft or yielding. 'We do what we have to,' she said, eventually. 'Once you really look into things, and see the depths of corruption and greed, you have no choice. Everything becomes simple and obvious.'

Thea felt limp in the face of such stark fanaticism. 'But Jack Handy isn't corrupt, surely? All he did was to sell a small plot of land. There will be any number of regulations to make sure the house that's built there will be perfectly in keeping with the area. How can it be worth all this trouble?'

'It's not,' said Sophie. 'We weren't too bothered about that. One or two of the group raised token objections, on the grounds that it's yet another example of fat cats getting the cream, with nothing of the slightest use to people who really need a home. But it's not *housing* we care most about.'

'What then?' Something had slipped out of any remotely logical track. 'Why do you think Jack killed Danny, in that case?' She was hanging on desperately to the theory at the core of the whole business.

'He's the obvious one,' said Nella, still husky. 'And not just because of his building plot.'

'It's wildlife that matters most,' said Tiffany loudly. 'That's our main concern. Sharing the planet. Leaving them some space and letting them live their natural lives. The cull is barbaric. Anyone involved in it deserves all they get.'

'And that includes Jack Handy?'

Tiffany groaned. 'You still don't understand. It's not just one thing. Handy hasn't kept the marksmen off his land, but he's fairly neutral about the cull, because he isn't in dairying. We didn't do the night calls with him.'

'Night calls?'

'We phone them every hour or two, through the night,' said Sophie. 'Legal and effective. Makes them think twice.'

'Don't they just unplug their phones?'

'Only for a while. Most people are afraid to miss important calls. We used their mobiles mainly, anyway, and nobody turns them off for long, do they?'

'Harassment like that *must* be against the law,' Thea objected.

Sophie shrugged. 'Not unless it becomes threatening. Even then, it's not high priority. The police have better things to do than keep tracing phone calls and trying to make a case.'

'Better things like catching a murderer,' said Thea. 'I'm surprised you seem to have forgotten that your own friend – your own *fiancé*,' she addressed Nella directly, 'was killed. Maybe you've all got alibis for the attack on Mr Handy, but you were there in spirit. You know people who were there, and what they did to him. You know quite well who it was that used the man's own stick against him.'

'It doesn't matter. We work together. The act of any individual isn't important.' It was Sophie again, sounding as if she were quoting from some Little Green Book.

Tiffany lifted her chin and spoke bravely. 'I know you think it was my brother. I can face the truth. Besides, he says he didn't hit him at all hard,' she added childishly.

'It's never a good idea to hit a person on the head,' said Thea. 'A lot of skulls have thin spots that break easily. He might die, you know. And then what will you do? How will you feel about being involved with a violent killing? Your brother will go to prison. The police don't share your ideas about collective responsibility.'

'I wasn't involved!' Tiffany cried. 'I wasn't even there.'

'But your friends were. He said there were several girls, pushing him.'

Nella jerked forward, her eyes bulging. '"He said"? Who? When?'

Thea regretted her careless words. 'He was conscious when we found him. He told us what had happened.'

'Did he give names?'

'I don't think I should tell you that.' Suddenly she felt frightened. These three could easily hurt her if they wanted to. The veneer of middle-England, middle-class respectability had already been shredded during their first encounter.

Sophie, at least, was not a civilised person. She could not be trusted to follow any of the normal rules. Nella was hardly any better. Only Tiffany seemed to retain some fragments of sympathy for the casualties of their actions. And even that was probably wishful thinking, Thea supposed. 'It's all in the hands of the police now,' she concluded, hoping to surround herself with an aura of official protection. 'And you would be wise to expect some serious trouble. Even if you're right – and I doubt very much that you are – in thinking Jack killed Danny Compton, it was undeniably criminal to assault him. Whose idea was it anyway?'

Nobody answered that, but the threesome exchanged meaningful looks which made Thea feel even more alarmed. She remembered the rude awakening she had had a day and a half earlier. 'Did you try and burn this house down, as well?' she blurted, knowing the accusation was foolish, but hoping to divert their attention.

It worked. 'What?' said Sophie. 'Of course we didn't. What do you mean?'

'I'm sure you've heard by now that somebody pushed a petrol bomb through the letter box, early yesterday. Tiffany's mother showed up when the police were here.'

'We saw the scorched carpet,' said Nella, non-committally. 'And it smells of fire out there. I had no idea it was done deliberately.'

Sophie shook her head slightly and reached out to touch Nella's arm. 'Tiffany and I knew about it. You've been too distracted . . . you know what I mean.'

'Yeah,' muttered Nella, with a sniff. 'Right.'

'Well, anyway – we thought it must have been those Tanner

people,' said Sophie confidently. 'Taking their revenge.'

'Of course!' endorsed Tiffany, almost gleefully. 'It's the sort of thing they'd do.'

'Who?' demanded Thea. 'Who are they?'

'Oh, it's an old story, really,' Tiffany explained. 'Mrs Foster reported them for deceiving the benefits people. The husband has been claiming disability benefit for years, when there's nothing wrong with him. He was prosecuted a week or two ago and given a prison sentence. It was a *huge* amount of money he swindled out of the government. Of course, it's ruined all their lives. He's got three children and a useless wife. They'll have to move away, to a cheaper area. There are two boys, mid teens. Most likely they did the fire.'

Sophie made a soft tutting sound. 'You've exaggerated the whole story,' she told Tiffany. 'They'll get over it soon enough.'

Thea was justifiably curious. 'How did they know it was Mrs Foster who shopped him?'

Sophie took over from her friend. 'The stupid woman told people she was going to do it. Everybody knew. She was terribly righteous about it. And of course it was a totally dishonest thing for him to be doing. Most local people didn't know what to think about it. They don't believe Mr Tanner was being deliberately criminal – he just sort of got into the habit. He probably did have backache at some point. And they do make it terribly easy, don't they? The social services, I mean. Or they did, before it got tightened up a bit.'

The ethical morass became painfully apparent to Thea and she thought again of her conversation with Drew, who had done something similar. It took courage, obviously, to report a neighbour to the authorities for such a transgression. It was also perhaps suggestive of arrogance and other not-so-nice aspects of character. It didn't altogether chime with what she had seen of Mrs Foster. 'Where do they live?' she asked. 'The Tanner family?'

'Stratton,' said Tiffany. 'Not far from us.'

'How did the Fosters know them, then?'

'Everybody knows them. And she's just retired from being a social worker. She was in child protection, I think. She couldn't do anything while she was working, but now she's free to say what she likes.'

'Most people join a bridge club and have long lunches with their mates,' said Thea. 'She must have really let this family get under her skin.'

'I think the real problem was that they were so *blatant* about it. It was a sort of challenge.'

'So now, surely, everybody will know it was them who tried to burn this house down.'

'Sort of,' Tiffany agreed. She frowned. 'Stupid, when you think about it.'

'Very much so. Just as bashing Jack Handy was stupid, because it's obvious that your people must have done it.'

'We only wanted to make him admit to killing Danny,' said Sophie. She reached out again to take the hand of Nella, who sat next to her on the sofa. 'We all felt we owed Nella that much.'

'But you didn't have the courage to be there yourselves,' Thea pointed out angrily. 'And do you feel any better now, knowing he's fighting for his life in hospital?'

'I'm not going to answer that,' said Sophie. 'I told you – we never meant him any serious harm.'

'You're implicated, anyway, even if you weren't there yourselves. You'll all be prosecuted.'

'Bullshit!' Nella's eyes were sparkling. 'That's the strength of a group. Safety in numbers.'

'Right,' confirmed Sophie. 'Everyone loved Danny the same as Nella did.' Her face darkened.

Tiffany chipped in. 'We all feel the loss of Danny, and we all want to make sure his killer is punished.' She did indeed appear to be in the grip of genuine shock and grief as she spoke. All three were pale and looked exhausted.

'You'd be much better off helping the police, then.' Thea sounded pompous to her own ears, but the sentiment was sincere.

'Which brings us to our reason for coming,' Sophie said, with a self-mocking smile at the realisation that this had taken so long. 'Tiffany's mum reckons you're quite in with the cops – which we never clocked when we saw you on Saturday. The way they dropped everything to come here when the fire happened shows they think you're someone special. And now you've got yourself in position as a witness to what happened to the Handy bloke, whether on purpose or by accident. We're not sure how you're doing it, but it looks to us as if you've been sent deliberately to watch us.'

It was like a slap on the face. 'No! Of course that's not true,' Thea shouted. 'The idea's utterly ludicrous. I'm a house-sitter, for God's sake. That's *all* I am.'

'Oh, yeah,' sneered Sophie. 'So prove it. Stay away from us from now on. Just mind your own business and leave us alone. It was bad about the fire – I'll give you that. It's not connected to our group in any way, though. And by now the Tanner boys will have been caught. Even if there's no evidence it was them, they'll be scared off doing anything else. You're perfectly safe, just so long as you let things alone.'

Thea was still shaking with frustration and rage at the suggestion that she was a spy. 'You've confused me with Mrs Foster,' she accused. 'She might have sneaked, but that's not the kind of thing I'd do. It's underhand. It's . . .' She remembered, all over again, that her own beloved Drew had done something very similar himself. He had reported a nursing home for suspicious behaviour. And Drew was the most upstanding, moral, ethical man imaginable. 'It's just not the way I do things,' she tailed off awkwardly.

'Bullshit!' said Nella again. The word seemed strangely foreign in her plummy English mouth, as well as very forceful. It conveyed a lot of meaning in two small Anglo-Saxon syllables. Funny, Thea reflected foolishly, the way it had been taken over by Americans.

'It's a surveillance society,' said Sophie, with a didactic glitter in her eye. 'We live like people in the Soviet Union used to, watching everything we say, never trusting anybody. Surveillance on every corner, telephones bugged, computers monitored. Everywhere you look, it's corrupt and dishonest. There's no goodness left.'

It was a tragic way to view the world and Thea felt a stab of pity for this young woman, who managed to sound like a Soviet citizen herself much of the time. She also felt angry at the way Tiffany Whiteacre was being drawn into the same outlook at far too early an age. No doubt there were many others lured by the adventure and sense of setting things to rights. Sophie, Thea thought again, was a dangerous individual.

'Of course there is,' she argued hotly. 'There are a million examples of goodness and beauty in every little village in the world. People being kind and generous, working together, laughing, loving . . .'

'"What a wonderful wo-o-orld",' sang Sophie satirically. 'Listen to yourself. It's sickening.'

'You're the one who's sick,' said Thea, feeling a physical nausea rising in her throat. 'Besides, you don't really believe it yourself. Why would you be spending all your time fighting and arguing like this if you didn't think there were things worth saving?'

Sophie scowled and shook her head. 'That's enough. We're going now. Just remember what we said. Stay out of our business. We don't want to see you again.'

'The feeling's mutual,' Thea spat childishly.

She slammed the door behind them, and kicked an angry foot across the burnt patch in the hall, wondering what she ought to do next, if anything. Nothing was clear any more. A man had died and another was unconscious in hospital, somehow as a result of a twisted morality that until that week she might well have endorsed. The character of Danny Compton remained mysterious, but she remained fairly sure there was nothing wicked in Jack Handy's make-up. Sheila Whiteacre and her husband had seemed thoroughly pleasant people and yet their son was apparently capable of hitting a man's head with a large stick. Their daughter had recovered sufficiently from the trauma of a violent death to defend her brother's actions. Who *were* these people, then?

The need to find at least a partial answer to this question would very probably ensure that she defied their order to mind her own business.

Chapter Fourteen

Somewhere in the kitchen her phone was warbling, and she couldn't find it. Her bag and coat had been carelessly slung over the back of a chair, and forgotten. The sound was faint and muffled, and she only heard it because she'd gone to boil the kettle and was trying to remember whether she'd given Gwennie her early evening walk. 'Go out anyway for a bit,' she suggested, and opened the back door.

The phone wasn't in her bag, and by the time she located it in her coat pocket, the ringing had stopped. But the clever phone informed her that Drew had been the caller, and suggested she ring him back. Which she did.

'Sorry!' she said, the moment he answered. 'I couldn't find the phone.'

'No problem. How are you?'

'Fine,' she said automatically, before correcting herself. 'No, that's not true at all. I'm angry, exhausted, confused and slightly scared. How are you?'

'Surprised, concerned, excited and frustrated,' he listed thoughtfully. 'Sounds as if I've had a better day than you.'

'Could hardly be worse, actually. So tell me the good things that have been so surprising and exciting.'

'No, no. You go first.'

'Honestly, I don't think I can bear to go through it all again. I am all right, really. Just a lot to think about. You can cheer me up.'

'Okay,' he said reluctantly. 'It feels a bit selfish, though.'

'Drew! Get on with it.'

He laughed. 'Well, you remember the business with the nursing home?'

'Vividly.'

'It's turning into something amazing. I've had about ten phone calls from a whole lot of people congratulating me for being so brave and honest. Some of them say they'll definitely use my services when the time comes. One has an ancient mother expected to die any day now. Everybody insists they're *grateful* to me for sounding the alarm.'

'Blowing the whistle,' said Thea.

'Actually, I don't like that image. It makes me sound like a traffic cop or a football referee.'

'Better than a sneak or a spy.'

'What?'

'There's been something similar happening here, with much less positive results.' She explained about Mrs Foster and the felonious Mr Tanner. 'They're sure that's the explanation for the fire yesterday. His sons were taking revenge.'

'Nasty,' he said slowly. 'I was expecting something of the sort myself, only yesterday. Now I seem to be a hero.' He sounded puzzled. 'Hard to account for the difference.

Doesn't anybody *admire* Mrs Foster for what she did?'

'I don't know. There appears to be sympathy for the Tanner family, in some quarters at least.'

'It's weird,' he said. 'I feel totally helpless. None of it is within my own control, and yet it was me who made it all happen in the beginning.'

'And I didn't do *anything*,' she whined. 'I might have burnt to death and been an absolutely innocent victim.'

'Horrible.' He sounded thoroughly rattled. 'And you've implied that more nasty things have happened since then.'

'Yes, they have. And now the whole community seems to be angry with me.' She gave a very brief summary of Jack Handy's assault and the visitation from the three protesters. 'And I've got his poor dog tied up in the garage. The old woman at the farm must be wondering what's happened to her.'

'Her herself or her the dog?'

'The dog. Rags. She's very good, but obviously bewildered.'

'Couldn't you have taken her home?'

'I could, yes. But it was dark and I'd had enough for one day. Sheila said I might have trouble finding the farm. It isn't really my job, anyway.'

'You made it your job when you put the animal in your car.'

'Did I?' She gave this some thought. 'Is that where I go wrong, then? Doing that kind of thing?'

'Some people might think so. I just regard it as a very admirable wish to help.'

She laughed. 'Thanks. But you're right about it all

getting out of control. I can't see any way to help now. I feel strongly tempted to just drive home – or down to you – and let them go to hell in their own sweet ways.'

'You'd be welcome,' he said with a gentle purr.

'The kids might not agree.'

'The kids adore you,' he protested. 'How could you think otherwise?'

'They don't, Drew. That's a huge overstatement. They mistrust me, and quite right too. I have outrageous designs on their father.'

He chuckled, then turned serious again. 'No sex talk on the phone, please. I've warned you about that before. It does nobody any good.'

'Quite right,' she said primly. 'But it's nice to hear your voice, all the same. It makes an enormous difference.'

'Likewise. But you're wrong about the children, you know. Mistrust is quite the wrong word. They're just unsure about what happens next.'

Thea's heart thudded. 'Nobody can predict the future,' she said quickly. 'It's bad enough trying to keep up with what's going on in the present.'

'Okay,' he said, before falling silent for a moment. Then he came back more strongly, 'So, listen. I realise you haven't told me everything, and I am definitely concerned about you, but I guess you can take care of yourself. You've got that big strong police detective watching your back. He's much more use than I would ever be, even if I was by your side. Lock the doors and pull the duvet over your head. They say it'll be warm and sunny tomorrow. Take the dogs somewhere peaceful and enjoy it.'

'I never told you about Jessica,' she realised. 'But that can wait. I'll be fine – you're absolutely right. And it's great that you've been hailed as a hero. Richly deserved.'

'Not really. You know – I was expecting something awful to happen in retribution for my treachery. I was all for moving to Broad Campden and giving up this place altogether.'

'If you did that you'd get retribution from Maggs. You can't escape.' She spoke lightly, but the idea of Drew living in the Cotswolds, far from his old life in Somerset, was one she often entertained as a highly appealing answer to their difficulties.

'One day,' he said quietly. 'One day, we'll have everything just as we want it.'

'There you go again,' she said lightly. 'Although you can't let that poor house sit there empty for much longer.'

'I know,' said Drew.

She finished the call and dropped the phone into her bag as if it weighed twenty kilos. Her body felt heavy too. Weariness flooded through her, as if the mere act of remaining alive were a hugely burdensome effort. 'It's all too much,' she muttered, not entirely sure what she meant.

She had been sitting at the kitchen table, the dogs sharing Gwennie's bed, keeping her company. Outside, Rags was silent and Thea hoped she was asleep. Whatever had possessed her to take on the responsibility for yet another dog? What sort of rescue fantasy had she been following this time? Was that what Drew had been hinting at, she wondered. Did she regard herself as some kind of female Sir Galahad, righting wrongs and solving murder investigations? It was perfectly evident that other people behaved in different ways, blithely ignoring suffering and injustice and appalling crimes, so long as it did not directly concern them. They knew, better than Thea did, that there were repercussions and consequences to small acts that went against the general grain.

She recalled an incident, years ago, in a hardware shop. A man wearing a baggy mackintosh had calmly gathered a selection of three or four tools and clasped them to his chest, underneath the coat, obviously intent on stealing them. Thea had seen him clearly. She had met his eyes, so he knew that she knew what he was doing. He did not wink, or grimace, or make any sort of silent plea. He simply let her see him, and make her own decision. Jessica, aged about ten, had been with her, but had been looking in another direction, missing the whole thing. Thea had done nothing. She had ordered her brain and conscience to stay in abeyance, thinking nothing, blanking her own knowledge. It worked long enough for her to move to the other side of the shop with her daughter, giving the man his chance.

Gradually she had filled with anger – against the man and herself in equal measure. How did he dare? And why had she let him? Something had paralysed her, and it was months or even years before she grasped something of what it had been. It came back to her whenever there was a news item about public collusion in crime, or the opposite. Every time an individual stepped forward and tried to do the right thing, it seemed they got hurt in some way. Chasing after a thief, reporting a wrongdoer, standing up when everyone else remained seated – it put you in danger. Except for golden boy Drew Slocombe, of course. He was the exception. He excepted himself, singled himself out for judgement and vengeance, and found himself covered in glory as a result.

'Well, good for him,' she murmured, meaning it both literally and cynically. Then she heard the collie outside yap and remembered that she too had done a good thing that day.

She went through the house, room by room, straightening ornaments, fingering plants, wiping a smudge off a window with her sleeve. She was keeping it all safe as instructed, earning her pay. Everything was clean and orderly, waiting for the return of its people. Apart from the hall carpet, of course, and even that had been saved from much worse damage thanks to Thea's quick response. She had nothing to reproach herself for.

She rewarded herself with a film showing on Channel Four, both dogs on the sofa beside her and a large mug of coffee placed securely on a small table. The film involved a surprise pregnancy, which inevitably sent her thoughts back to Damien and Maggs and the vast change there would be to the futures of both couples. Assumptions crumbled to ash, new plans were forced upon more people than the two couples at the centre. As aunt, Thea herself would be drawn into the destiny of her brother's new child. Another person to buy for at Christmas; another source of news and opinion from her mother. Another little hostage to fortune, too. The child might have problems, mental or physical. The family might be required to rally round to an uncomfortable degree. If nothing else, the poor little thing should have some respite from its father's obsessive addiction to religion. Aunt Thea might supply that, she supposed – although Auntie Jocelyn was likely to be a much better bet, with her own disorganised litter of cousins who would show the newcomer as much of real life as it could bear, given that Damien allowed it anywhere near them.

And Maggs – the arrival of a baby in that household would, she hoped, carry even more direct implications for herself and Drew. She hoped she would still be important to him by the time the baby was born. She hoped she might be allowed some direct involvement with the work, learning the arcane rituals surrounding even the simplest of funerals. She could replace Maggs, in the early part of the baby's life. It would be sweet to do so, a new direction she would be delighted to embrace.

In the film, everything worked out for the best, the final shots of optimism and conciliation a Hollywood necessity. Perhaps there was hope in real life too, thought Thea with a sigh.

She went to bed early, deliberately not thinking about Rags or her injured owner. Nor did she obsess about protest groups, quarries or arsonists. For the time being, she assured herself that everything was quiet. Malefactors would be going to bed, too, hoping the nagging images and anxieties created in their own hearts by their actions might be blanked out by sleep. It was an aspect of crime that Thea sometimes dwelt on – the effect of an extreme act of violence on its perpetrator. She never got very far with her deliberations, unable to place herself in the skin of these people. But one day, she promised, she would gain some useful understanding of it. Until then, even the thought processes of a shoplifter remained obscure to her.

But when she did fall asleep, her own dreams were filled with worrying scenes of fire and failure. She was entrusted with a baby, only to leave it on the very edge of a sheer cliff where it would certainly roll to its death unless rescued. A dog somehow materialised, covered in a foul brown slime, adding to her responsibilities. Her feet refused to move, mired in something heavy and clinging.

She fought back to wakefulness, like someone coming out of deep water for air. Her dog was warm on her feet and everything was silent and still. A clock with green digital figures told her it was barely past midnight. The desperation from the dream mutated into resentment. Why was her mind full of such undeserved anxiety and trauma? She had done nothing wrong. What was she doing taking on other people's guilt and inadequacy? She, Thea Osborne, was innocent. She was tempted to shout it out loud, but Hepzie might take it badly. Punching her pillow angrily, she did her best to slip back into a more restorative slumber.

Chapter Fifteen

The dream she remembered on waking had centred around Danny Compton, lying dead, broken and faceless in a stony indentation at the foot of a high cliff. It was as if her unconscious was reminding her that that individual's death was very much the central issue, amongst everything that had happened. The police would be focusing more on that than anything else. She forced her mind back to Sunday, when Higgins had turned up to ask about Jack Handy. He had told her then that Danny's parents lived in Dubai, and that he had carried no identification with him. Normal practice, she supposed, for habitual troublemakers roaming the countryside disrupting official activities. The fact that they had succeeded quite well in saving the lives of a lot of badgers had doubtless pushed them into new areas of protest. Thea herself was aware of a recent study showing how destructive noise was to the well-being of wildlife. Major roads and railways created large-scale changes to the normal behaviour of creatures great and small. Drainage, verge-cutting, tree-felling – even things that were intended to help sustain the environment – all reduced the numbers and health of animals and birds living in field and woodland. Daglingworth Quarry, she suddenly realised, must obviously be a huge example of disruption and damage, in existence for years and guilty of extreme noise and devastation. Could it be, then, that Danny's death was a quarry-related message of some sort? Had the protest group challenged the quarrying and thereby infuriated its owners?

She presumed that by this time, Danny's parents had been located and the dreadful news conveyed. She wondered if Nella had spoken to them about the funeral. If so, surely there would be a degree of open communication between the absent parents and the bereaved fiancée. Nella would probably make the arrangements once the body was released, and the bereaved couple would fly back in time for the actual funeral.

But she would have liked to know more, for reasons she was reluctant to investigate. Was the nagging curiosity mainly born of the aggressive instruction from the three young women to keep away, causing a perverse wish to do the very opposite? There did not appear to be any other explanation that she could find. It was a deep urge, going right back to early childhood, in which she hated to feel ignorant. She would grow furious at her sisters if she suspected they were keeping anything from her. Anybody whispering in her presence would suffer a torrent of insistent questions as to what they had said. And more than that, she had never liked to be told what to do.

Carl had found ways to soften her obstinacy, patiently explaining that people needed their privacy, that their secrets had nothing to do with her, and that there were more positive ways of channelling her curiosity. He encouraged historical research projects, often conducted purely for their own sake, following a topic as far into the past as she could, by means of the Internet and visits to museums and archives. For much of her thirties, she had made this a passionate hobby, intending to turn it into paid employment. But there never seemed to be a relevant job available, and gradually her interest waned. By the time Carl died, she had more or less abandoned it completely and hardly missed it. Only when the new career as a widowed house-sitter took over her life did she find that the basic nosiness that was her character had not gone away. She had not been able to resist burrowing into people's lives and discovering how they connected and what they had done before she met them.

So here she was again. She was inescapably intrigued. There was enough personal emotion involved for it to matter directly to her. Jack Handy had been friendly. Sophie had been horrible. Sheila Whiteacre was fascinating. How anybody could possibly expect her to simply sit quietly for several days and ignore them all was a mystery.

'Right, then,' she announced to the dogs. 'We'd better see how poor Rags is doing.' It was a rhetorical 'we', because she had no intention of letting all the animals mingle. The spaniel and the corgi were given a few minutes in the back garden, and then shut in the kitchen before Thea went out to the garage carrying a small bag of dry dog food and cautiously pulled the door open a little way.

'Rags?' she called. 'Are you okay?'

The building had originally been a large shed or small barn, separate from the house. The double doors had to be opened manually, with none of the usual Cotswold mechanisms that were operated from inside a car. There was no window, but it did have a light, which Thea switched on. Peering around, she could see no sign of her lodger. 'Rags!' she said again. 'Where are you?'

From the shadows beneath her car, a long nose protruded, followed by a shaggy body crouched close to the ground. The dog whined and remained half concealed. 'Come on, pet. I'll take you home in a little while. You look as if you've had a miserable night.'

Rags glanced towards the door which Thea had closed securely behind herself. 'You want to go out? Good girl. Here, wait a minute.' She produced a lead from her pocket, and fumblingly attached it to the collar that the dog was providentially wearing, in place of the long piece of thin rope she had used as a tether during the night. Then she pushed the door open and led Rags out to the front drive, which was bordered with grass on either side.

Fifteen minutes later, with the collie looking more cheerful, willingly sharing the back seat of the car with Hepzie, they set out for North Cerney. It was nine-fifteen, the sun already showing every promise of a fine spring day.

The only details she remembered from Sheila Whiteacre's directions were that she was seeking a farm on the left-hand side of the road which ran westwards out of the village towards Woodmancote. There was a cattle grid across the entrance, but somehow the farm's name had not been mentioned.

It turned out to be perfectly easy because Rags knew the way, and left no room for doubt when her home gateway came into view. They rumbled over the grid and proceeded down the straight approach to a medium-sized stone farmhouse as lovely as any that Thea had ever seen. A stone barn beside it, a cobbled yard and well-kept dovecote all added to the picture-postcard impression. Woodwork was freshly painted, and the ground completely free of muck and mud. The house was shielded by mature trees and a garden to one side was thickly planted with budding daffodils. Long morning shadows lay across the yard and a field beyond.

Rags yapped and leapt from window to window on the back seat. Hepzie began to voice her displeasure at this and Thea hurriedly drew to a halt. She reached back and opened the car door to release the dog, who, after jumping out, stood perfectly still listening for something.

Tempted as she was to simply pull the door shut and drive away, Thea debated with herself for a moment. What if the house were empty, and liable to remain so for days? Did the farm have livestock that had to be tended? It was the lambing season, and it seemed very unlikely that there were no sheep on the property.

The dilemma was resolved by the front door of the house opening and a woman appearing. 'Hello?' she called.

Rags manifested extreme relief and affection, bounding up to the woman and sitting down at her feet, tail wagging. Unlike Hepzie, Thea noted. Her dog would have leapt and bounced, leaving muddy marks on the woman's clothes. There was a lot to be said for a collie, who did as it was trained to do, however extreme its emotions might be.

She pushed open her door and got out of the car. 'I hope you weren't worried about her,' she said. 'The police knew I had her.'

'I'm afraid I never gave her a thought.'

Thea gave the woman a careful scrutiny. Middle height, wide hips, grey hair. Aged around seventy, wearing old clothes and wellington boots. A pleasant open face, with signs of strain and exhaustion. 'How is he?' Thea asked softly.

'No change. They made me come home at eleven last night. I've only been up a little while. I have to do the hens. I didn't hear you arrive.' Belatedly, she reached down and stroked the collie's head. 'Poor Rags. You must have had quite an adventure.'

'I'm Thea Osborne.' She paused, as if waiting for a gesture of recognition. When none came, she added, 'I met Mr Handy on Saturday. And again yesterday, actually. Just after he was attacked.'

'I'm Sandra. Sandy. I don't know you, do I?'

Thea was mentally reciting *Sandy Handy* to herself, wondering if that really was the woman's name. Jack's stepmother, which was how Sheila Whiteacre had described her, would be the wife of Jack's father, and therefore surely Mrs Handy. She attended to the question distractedly. 'No, no. I'm just here for a couple of weeks. I'm house-sitting in Daglingworth. It was just a fluke that I was driving past where it happened, and—'

'Sorry. I really must do the hens. Come with me if you like.'

She led the way around the house to a very large low building. As they drew near, a warm sound could be heard,

189

flowing like a rich liquid, rising and falling, throaty and calming. 'I'm late,' said Sandy. 'They're getting restless.'

She pulled open a metal door and revealed a scene like nothing Thea had ever witnessed. An ocean of brown and white birds covered every inch of the floor. They simply stood there, moving only slightly, crooning musically. 'Golly!' said Thea. 'How many are there?'

'Two thousand or so. Stay there if you'd rather. It's a bit unnerving walking through them.' She opened a tall metal canister at the top and scooped a bucketful of feed from it. Then another. 'This takes a while. Do you mind? I would like to talk to you.'

'I'll help,' Thea offered. 'What do we have to do?'

The routine was readily explained, with several feeders pointed out, in locations across the vast living floor. 'They're free range, are they?' Thea asked.

'Technically it's called the barn system. They almost never go outside, even though in theory they can. They lay in those boxes.' She pointed out a triple row of nesting boxes all along one wall. 'It's all very low-tech, compared to most. Labour-intensive, I think you'd call it.'

'I can see,' agreed Thea. 'These feeders must take a lot of cleaning, for a start.' The circular contraptions were covered with muck, some of which had fallen into the sections intended for drinking water.

'I do them a few at a time. The ones at the far end are the cleanest at the moment.'

The smell was strong but not unpleasant. The softness of the feathery creatures against her ankles was perfectly tolerable. The building was warm and alive and contentment altogether evident. The birds did not rush for food, but seemed to form orderly queues for a share. Thea had to remind herself that this was far more intensive than anything the hens might experience in nature. They could not scratch about for their own food, nor raise their own chicks. As she looked more closely, she saw how scruffy most of them were, with bald patches and missing tail feathers. She imagined their lives were short, boring and restricted.

'I'll give you some eggs,' said Sandy. 'As a reward for bringing Rags home.'

Thea laughed. 'Just a couple would be nice, thanks.'

They went back to the house together, passing Thea's car. 'Is that your dog?' asked Sandy.

'It is. She's called Hepzibah. She and Rags got along fairly well together, but I doubt they'll miss each other.'

'Is she all right there? I don't allow dogs in the house.'

'She'll be fine, if I'm not too long.' Rags had disappeared, presumably settling down in whichever barn or shed she called home. 'You probably want to get back to Oxford, anyway.'

'Not for a while. If Jack's still in a coma, I'm not sure it makes a lot of sense, anyway. I wasn't designed for hours of sitting by a bedside. It's desperately dull.'

'Apparently they can often hear you if you talk to them.'

'I dare say, but after five minutes I run out of conversation. What am I meant to talk about?'

Thea gave a sympathetic grunt and left it at that. She was trying to work out how distressed this woman was, and therefore how close she was to her stepson. So far, the primary emotion appeared to be exasperation.

'We can sit in here.' Mrs Handy led her visitor into a very large kitchen, boasting a huge pine table and a wall full of shelves stretching to the high ceiling, painted in a duck-egg blue that Thea suspected had been out of fashion for fifteen years or so. Everything was polished and dusted and neatly aligned. Expensive copper pans gleamed from a shelf above a row of Poole pottery. She wondered whether *Cotswold Life* had got around to featuring this room as a classic farmhouse kitchen, and if not, why not.

'What a lovely kitchen!' she gasped.

'Most of it's due to my predecessor, quite honestly. She bought that table, and all those copper things.'

'Jack's mother?' Thea enquired tentatively. 'Is that right?'

Sandy blinked at her. 'You *have* done your homework, haven't you!' There was no hint of annoyance. Rather she seemed mildly flattered. 'Yes, I am the second Mrs Handy. I was married to Jack's father, Roland, for three years before he died. He was twenty years older than me, but I still felt very cheated. Jack's mother had only been dead a year when he married me. Jack himself was married at the time, but his wife moved out not long afterwards. I like to think it wasn't my fault, but there were certainly some tensions. Now he and I are here together, causing all sorts of scandal, I shouldn't wonder.'

Thea almost drooled at these freely given revelations. It was meat and drink to her, as well as implying that she had been deemed a safe and trustworthy confidante by this woman. 'What a story!' she murmured. 'Do you manage the whole farm between you?'

'There's a girl who comes in every couple of days to help

with the house and the food. She's due tomorrow. And a rather decrepit farm worker called Dennis who manages a bit of ditching and tractor work when it's busy. I'm going to have to call him today and see if he can lend a hand.' She wiped a hand across her brow as if to remove sweat.

Thea diagnosed a headache. 'Look – I should go. I'm really sorry this happened. There are obviously some very unpleasant people out there. I liked your stepson when I met him. I hope he gets better quickly.'

'I doubt whether that's going to happen, but thanks for the kind thought. You're right about the people. Those protesters have been gunning for us ever since we put that land on the market.'

'They told me they didn't actually object to it very strongly. Jack wasn't one of their main targets, apparently. But they think it was him who . . .' She bit back the words, unable to voice an accusation of murder, even indirectly. 'I expect you knew about that?' she finished weakly.

'They're so stupid, it makes me want to kill one of them myself,' spat Sandy viciously. 'They can't see anything except for their own dogmatic opinions – which are mostly based on completely false information. Like those idiots who killed the paediatrician by mistake, years ago now. I've never been able to stop thinking about that. It shows how helpless we all are in the face of a mindless mob. No single person takes responsibility, that's the real problem. They think they can get away with anything because there's safety in numbers.'

'Did you know Danny Compton? The one that was killed at the weekend?'

193

Sandy shook her head. 'They were all the same to me – just a crowd of thugs.'

Thea hesitated, with a frown. 'They're actually quite ordinary and respectable, individually,' she argued. 'I don't think they meant to hurt Jack badly.'

'Are you defending them? Because if you are, you're a lot more stupid than you look.'

'Not at all,' she said wretchedly. 'I didn't mean that. I know they were totally wrong to do what they did. It's just that, well . . . Tiffany Whiteacre, for one. I think she's basically okay. She's very young.'

'You've said enough. Thank you for taking the dog. That was a nice thing to do. Here are the eggs. I need to make some phone calls.'

The eggs were in a section of cardboard, like the bottom half of the usual box they came in. It had ragged edges, as if torn from a bigger tray. There were four.

'Thanks,' said Thea. 'I am sorry, honestly. How will you manage – if he's away for a long time?'

'I told you – Dennis can come and help.'

'No other members of the family?' Thea was slowly moving towards the front door, knowing there was much more she'd like to ask. 'There was a chap called Steve who called him Uncle Jack.'

'That's stretching it a bit. Steve Hobbes, he is. His mother's a cousin of some sort. We never see anything of them. But Jack has got two sons, who both live abroad. They're in their thirties. They have no interest in farming – only the money that's tied up in the land. It was their idea to sell the corner field, and see where that's landed us.'

This time Thea swallowed down the reply she would have liked to make. It was one thing for a step-grandmother to criticise, and another for a stranger to agree. As Sandy herself had pointed out, Thea Osborne had already said enough.

'Just one thing,' she remembered, as she crossed the threshold. 'Don't the protesters object to your intensive chicken farming? I mean – it's a long way from free range, isn't it?' The image of the packed floor and docile birds had stayed with her. 'I would think they'd find it unacceptable.'

'Not your problem,' said Sandy Handy, and closed the door between them.

Chapter Sixteen

It was almost eleven on a sunny spring morning, and Thea had no obligations for a while, apart from lonely old Gwennie asleep in her kitchen. Elderly dogs, however, liked to sleep a lot. They liked a quiet life in a warm place with very little excitement. Staying away for much of the day was probably the best thing Thea and her spaniel could do. If the afternoon continued warm and sunny, she would move the tortoise outside and see if it woke up. Meanwhile, there was a lot of exploring she could cheerfully do. She would forget all about the belligerent Sophie and Nella and Ricky, and let them stew in whatever perverse ways they might choose. As they had quite rightly told her, it was none of her business.

There was nothing more she could do for Jack Handy or his stepmother, having returned the dog. The only person she could be remotely useful to was Drew, who was very slowly inching towards a decision about his property in Broad Campden and might be helped along the way by somebody on the ground.

The house was of substantial value and had been left to Drew a year before. There were, however, conditions. His benefactor had added a proviso that he open a natural burial ground on land she had regarded as hers, before taking full possession of the house. In compliance with this, he had obtained outline consent for just such a burial ground, and then simply stalled. The house stood empty and the consent was time-limited. Whilst potentially crucial to his long-term finances, in the short term it would require investment that he did not possess. Various strategies had been discussed, all of them featuring Maggs as a prominent participant. Now, if Maggs was to be interrupted by a baby, she could not be guaranteed as an active partner for a significant period of time. Her husband was already stating flatly that he was against any removal to the Cotswolds.

'At least I can go and make sure the house is all right,' said Thea to her dog. 'And I promise we won't go to that pub that refuses to let you in.'

Broad Campden was at the diagonally opposite extremity of the Cotswolds to Daglingworth, requiring a drive of several miles along the A429 through Bourton and Stow. It was a road she did not often use, despite a familiarity with some of the villages and towns bordering it. In recent months, she had barely strayed from the 436 and the smaller roads running northwards from it. But the 429 was the old Fosse Way, with its glimpses of Roman presence still discernible in the straightness of the road and something ancient about the bordering walls and hilltops. The road had been built in a startlingly straight line from Exeter to Lincoln, something even modern highway builders might well find challenging. The place names often reinforced the fact of the road, from Fossebridge to Stretton-on-Fosse up beyond Moreton-in-Marsh.

She hummed as she drove, muttering sometimes to Hepzie when a thought occurred to her. Life always felt less complicated when she was out on the open road. Her phone was turned off for the duration of the journey, nobody knew where she was and the possibilities were almost infinite. A car was a marvellous source of freedom, just as a fast horse must have been in bygone times.

At Stow she forked left and followed the A424 towards Broadway. Here was very familiar territory. Blockley, Snowshill and Stanton were all within a very few miles, and all contained properties that Thea had presided over during the past three years. Broad Campden comprised a fourth in the same area, and Temple Guiting was only a short distance further off. Memories flooded in as she passed signs to the various villages, with Stanton the most recent and Snowshill perhaps the most agonising.

She kept seeing signs to Oxford, which reminded her of poor Jack Handy lying unconscious in the hospital there. The way was not direct, but she knew that it was a short hop from Stow to the A34, and from there a scant fifteen minutes into the city itself. Of course, even if she were to be crazy enough to make the detour, she would not be allowed to approach the bedside. And if she managed that, then what? Why in the world did she even feel tempted to try? Unwillingly she allowed herself to delve into the thought processes and motivations that had given rise to such an idea in the first place.

It was something to do with the way she and Jessica had found him, she concluded; his helplessness against a gang of attackers, and his futile anger. Nobody should lose dignity like that, unless as a fully deserved punishment for a proven crime. It was a premature revenge, by any reckoning. She would have liked to be certain precisely which of the campaign group had been there, adding their pushes and punches to the blows that had most probably been dealt by Ricky Whiteacre. The conversation that Jessica had overheard certainly made that a very reasonable assumption – but as many people had told her in recent times, hearsay evidence was not enough to convict a person of a crime.

Besides, they had already told the police about it. The warning given by Sophie and her henchwomen had come too late, and only served to render Thea more determined to follow her own promptings when it came to making moral choices.

But she turned away from any idea of going to Oxford and followed instead the little road into Broad Campden. Past the topiary hedge and the upmarket holiday accommodation and down the cul-de-sac to the left, memories of her first meeting with Drew came with every yard of the way. They had walked through the village deep in conversation, horrified by a violent death nearby, sharing the anxiety that came with it. Ever since that time, she had harboured a secret unacknowledged hope that she and he might one day find themselves permanently together in this very place.

The house looked chilly and forlorn. By local standards

it was nothing special, standing four-square to the road, with a modest garden at the front. A garden that was now full of straggling weeds and a layer of blackened leaves that had been left where they'd lain for the whole of the winter. 'Good news for the worms,' Thea muttered. In a region obsessed with tidiness, there was seldom a dead leaf to be found in any garden. No doubt the lawn here would benefit in the long run. Looking closer, she found many of the usual spring flowers flourishing beneath the debris, and fat buds on all the shrubs. In essence, it was a good garden that would quickly forgive a year of neglect.

She did not have a key, and knew there was no longer one hidden under the obvious flowerpot by the back door. All she could do was walk around and make a cursory inspection of drainpipes, roof tiles and pointing. And when it came to pointing, she couldn't guarantee to identify a genuine problem. The back garden had been mainly devoted to fruit trees, a patio and a pond. Between the trees, long grass was mushy underfoot and the patio was slippery with moss. Gazing up at the house, she could not see any sign of structural problems. Inside, when she peered through the streaky windows, the original furniture still stood, with curtains, carpets and fittings all as they were left when the owner died. There would be dust and cobwebs and dripping taps. She moved to the kitchen window. She could see a table and chairs, clear surfaces and closed doors. 'Like the *Marie Celeste*,' she murmured.

It was dreadful of Drew to just leave it like this. He had visited perhaps four or five times through the past year, tidying everything into cupboards and helping himself to a few items such as a lamp and a good saucepan. Thea understood that he was having difficulty in accepting that it really did all belong to him, legally and beyond challenge. He had not been related to the woman who left it to him, and those relatives she did possess had not been happy. They had made threats about challenging the will, but eventually they found themselves in no position to argue. In an effort to avoid outright hostility, Drew had offered them anything they wanted from inside the house, but they had rejected the gesture. 'Who would want any of that old stuff?' said the nephew disdainfully.

Perhaps because of the unpleasant events of the past few days, Thea found herself feeling nervous. The house seemed impossibly vulnerable to her after the fire at the Fosters'. Anybody could burn it down, any time they liked. Neighbours had complained about the garden, she remembered. Where, she wondered, was the giant hogweed they'd found so objectionable? Either chopped down or destroyed by winter weather, she supposed, finding no sign of it as she scanned the garden.

But of course nobody who lived close by would risk setting fire to it. There was a lot of thatch in Broad Campden, and a single stray spark could bring devastation. Besides, these were law-abiding God-fearing people, who might write letters to the council, but certainly wouldn't take anything like direct action. It was silly to imagine rural warriors and activists in every little Cotswold village. Daglingworth and Bagendon were different, lying so close to Cirencester. There, the clash of town and country became much more of an issue, the depredations on the land and its wildlife much more apparent. The contrast with sleepy northern Gloucestershire, where Chipping Campden and Blockley drifted dreamily and complacently through the days, was unmistakable.

And yet, she mused, nobody would have claimed that Cirencester was exactly an urban jungle. It only went to show what darkness could lurk just below the surface. She closed the front gate securely behind her and went back to the car, thinking it must be time for lunch. Never too happy to eat alone in public, she wondered what to do about it. There had been a nice little eatery in Blockley, but the last time she'd been there, it had disappeared. Perhaps, she thought, something new had sprung up in its place, making it worth a small detour to go for a look.

The lane was narrow but fairly straight, enabling a degree of speed that was probably unwise. On the outskirts of the village she saw a sign, in large black lettering on a white background: HEDGEHOGS USE THIS ROAD. Then, fifty yards further on, another, reading PLEASE DO NOT KILL THEM. Finally, a third, to complete the request. we REGARD THEM AS OUR FRIENDS. How sweet, thought Thea. But was it effective, she wondered? At night a lorry driver was unlikely to notice a small scuttling creature under his wheels. But a car might slow down, she supposed. The plight of hedgehogs was just one of many facts of British life that saddened her. She had heard that their numbers were steadily falling, thanks partly to traffic. Why the wretched things couldn't learn to keep off roads was a futile question. Like frogs, they found the smooth surface convenient for travelling, and persisted in using it. Coming out of hibernation, they would be intent on finding food, with grass verges a rich source, she supposed.

The signs worked on her, anyway. Even though hedgehogs were nocturnal, and she had never once seen one out in the middle of the day, she slowed down. Her thoughts turned to the tortoise in the Fosters' garage. The emergence from hibernation was a little miracle, like a rebirth, which ought to be supervised carefully. According to the notes she'd been left, it could be a hazardous business. Perhaps, after all, she was in dereliction of duty by wandering around the countryside miles from Daglingworth. She had no obligation to stay indoors the entire time, but equally she should remain close by. The rules might not be carved in stone, but they were easy enough to understand. She ought to go back and make herself a sandwich. Then she should take Gwennie for a gentle stroll around by the church, where she could sniff familiar scents and reassure herself that all was well. Blockley could wait.

She left the car outside, thinking it would be easier to examine the tortoise with the extra space. It was not a large building, with shelving all down one side and tools hanging on the wall facing the entrance. Rags had been given a cramped corner, which was now just a tangle of bedding that she must have struggled to make comfortable. It was to be hoped that she was a lot happier back in her own familiar barn. It had not occurred to Thea until that moment that there could have been trouble for the tortoise if the collie had jumped around too much. The glass tank was on a shelf about four feet from the ground, at the back of the garage, where the warmth of a car engine ought not to make a significant impression.

The tank was two-thirds full of soil, with a tiny area of shell just visible. The animal had buried itself almost completely, which increased Thea's sense of a rebirth – even a resurrection. Hibernation was as close to being dead as she could imagine, especially submerged in cold dark earth like this. She did hope it would emerge while she was there, so she could greet it with food and sunshine and welcoming words. It might compensate in some small foolish way for the death of Danny Compton. He would surely have appreciated the notion, even if ambivalent about the keeping of a non-indigenous reptile as a pet in the first place.

While she was there, she supposed she could tidy away the temporary dog bed. Picking up the muddy blankets and shaking them out, she noticed a small object fall out and roll away. Going after it, she slowly identified it as a slimy scrap of material, barely two inches square. There was something on it that looked like blood, as well as mucus, and her first thought was that Rags had been injured and bleeding, without anyone noticing. Then she thought of how the dog had been coughing, and wondered if this had been an obstruction in its throat. The stuff appeared to be denim, with three ragged edges and a hem. She frowned, trying to account for it to herself. Had Rags torn it from the leg of Jack's attacker's jeans and then kept it in her mouth all the way to Daglingworth?

She remembered Jack's criticism of the dog and her own defence of it. She had, he said, caught his attacker by the ankle, at one point. Was it possible that Rags would now provide a slender piece of evidence against one of the protesters, where none existed before? Carefully, she carried the scrap to the house and slipped it into a plastic bag. It could easily turn out to be nothing, a bit of rubbish already in the garage, but she thought not.

In the kitchen, stroking Gwennie's head and promising a change of scene in a little while, she wondered what she should do about her discovery. She could either phone or go in person to the Cirencester police station. Higgins would probably be preoccupied, not wanting to speak to her. He was the detective inspector on the local team. His superior was Detective Superintendent Sonia Gladwin, who was almost certain to be the senior investigating officer on the case of the murder of Danny Compton. And yet nobody had mentioned her, and she had failed to make an informal visit, as she sometimes did when Thea found herself drawn into a criminal investigation. The two had become friends in Hampnett, a bond that had survived through events in Snowshill and Winchcombe. She could call Gladwin and tell her about the discovery, making it only semi-official. But as she rehearsed what she might say, it began to seem foolish. Any meaningful evidence must surely have been lost amidst dog spit and garage dust. Any torn jeans would have been destroyed already. Besides, the identities of Jack's attackers were pretty obvious. Without Tiffany Whiteacre or Sophie or Nella – assuming their denials were truthful – there surely could not be so very many remaining candidates? It was possible that Tiffany could be readily persuaded to reveal their names, under a degree of police and parental pressure, even if – or maybe *especially* if – her own brother had been the prime aggressor. The girl would want to make a mitigating plea, explaining how Ricky was really a sweet chap, with no intention of causing real harm.

'You're getting carried away,' she told herself sternly. It happened a lot, when she was alone in a strange house. Imagination ran riot. The trouble was, it often turned out to be alarmingly accurate. All the same, she was reluctant to bother the police with her small discovery, for a number of reasons ranging from fear of looking silly to an inability to forget the warnings of the previous evening. She had refused to be cowed by the three young women while they were in the house, but the abiding memory of Sophie's words and expression was certainly intimidating.

She left it a while, lunching on a cheese sandwich and a mug of coffee. Outside it was clouding over and the temperature had dropped. Disappointing news tortoise-wise, she realised.

Then she compromised by sending a cowardly text to Gladwin, using the mobile number she already had in her phone.

ME AGAIN. HAVE A POSSIBLE LITTLE CLUE TO THE ATTACK ON HANDY. HOPE YOU'RE OK? THEA.

Within three minutes an answering text came back:

SORRY I CAN'T HELP. I'M ON HOLIDAY. ALL MESSAGES WILL BE FORWARDED TO A COLLEAGUE. THIS IS AN AUTOMATED REPLY.

The idea of Gladwin on holiday in term time did not ring true. She had two school-age boys, so it was hardly a family excursion. Was she perhaps ill? Or seconded to a different police force for some reason? Or had she simply awarded herself a week or two on a sunny Greek island, without husband or sons? The word 'holiday' was more exact than 'leave' would have been. It conjured Gladwin's informal style, her distaste for jargon and obfuscation. *You better believe it*, Thea could hear her saying. *I'm away from the lot of you, enjoying myself.*

Which left Thea's feeble message floating around the Gloucestershire Constabulary, very likely to end up on the desk or screen of DI Higgins. Or even, possibly, another detective superintendent unknown to Thea.

Persuading herself that her conscience was now perfectly clear, she contemplated the rest of the day. There were two urges making themselves felt. One was to phone Drew and simply talk to him about all and anything, for the pleasure of hearing his voice. The other was closer at hand – the Whiteacre family was very much calling to her. Not just Tiffany, who was rapidly becoming a sort of protégée in Thea's mind, a young girl to be saved from bad company and destructive mistakes. As well as her, there was Sheila, Ricky and the bearded husband, whose name she had forgotten already. The whole family had got beneath her skin more than anybody else she had met since Saturday. Sheila had been gracious and civilised. The *house* was gracious and civilised – all the more so for its lived-in atmosphere. It was very difficult to believe that anything criminal or antisocial could emanate from such a home. Somehow, somewhere, things had gone wrong. And the son, barely glimpsed so far, was most likely at the heart of it.

But she did not dare just go to Baunton and knock on their door. Such a level of intrusion was plainly out of the question. No viable pretext came to mind for doing such a thing.

'Right!' she announced. 'We're going for a walk.'

The word that every dog in the English-speaking world understood had a galvanising effect, even on Gwennie. She wagged her tiny stump of a tail and did a little dance. Thea fetched the leads and attached them firmly before opening the front door. Down the drive, into the small road, and then on to the path that led around to the church. It was short, undemanding and unexpectedly interesting, despite the growing familiarity with it. A few houses were scattered along the way, their backs to the footpath. The ground rose gently to the minor elevation that the Saxons had selected for their place of worship. Everything was quiet and still, apart from a few hyperactive birds in the throes of the breeding season. Dawdling at Gwennie's pace, there was ample time to peer into the gardens and windows of the houses they passed. Everything was orderly, as was usual in the Cotswolds. Thea sometimes suspected there was a local law that decreed that gardens should be tidy and buildings kept in perfect repair. Nature was kept firmly at bay. The transgression exemplified by the giant hogweed in Broad Campden must be considerable. Nettles or brambles would be even worse.

Someone was walking down the path between the graves towards the church. Thea paused to watch, thinking the figure was familiar. Bony shoulders, expensive boots, above average height. Without even thinking, she steered the dogs through the gate and followed. Here was a providential opportunity to have a quiet talk with one of the more intriguing locals, offering a listening ear, or even a comforting hug, if it came to that.

She pushed in through the door, less than a minute after the person ahead of her, having hung back deliberately. The dogs went with her, regardless of any edict that might prevent them.

Chapter Seventeen

Nella was sitting in a pew at the front, just below the altar. Her head was bowed and her hands clasped. *Fenella*, Thea remembered – a name that made much more sense in every way than the one everybody used. She let the door close gently, hoping there would be no sound. Already she was reproaching herself for being so crass as to pursue a bereaved young woman, with two dogs at her side. It was an awful thing to do. But too late now. There was no going back. Nella had heard her and was looking round.

'What the hell do *you* want? And how dare you bring dogs in here?'

'Sorry. I wanted to see the church. I didn't know you were here. The dogs won't do any harm. I daren't let Gwennie out of my sight. Sorry.' She was babbling.

'Go away.'

'Listen – I know how you must be feeling . . .' She felt the usual flicker of complacency as she said this. It really was the case that she understood the shock, rage, despair and sickness that came from a sudden death. 'My husband was killed four years ago, without warning. I know how mad it can make you.'

'Mad?' Nella looked at her across the rows of pews in the small ancient church. 'As in angry, or insane?'

'Both. And a lot more.' She tasted again the acid that had remained at the back of her mouth for weeks after Carl died. The gall of helplessness and misery. The inability to construct a coherent thought. 'You wonder how you can possibly set one foot in front of the other.'

But as she spoke, she was aware that Nella Davidson showed every sign of functioning a great deal better than Thea herself had done. She had, after all, joined with Sophie and Tiffany in making direct threats against her, Thea. She might not have said a great deal, but several times she had formed sentences and appeared perfectly focused. Had that been a sort of autopilot, that was now being overtaken by real emotion? Was the truth finally sinking in? And how unusual, these days, for a person in such a state to seek solace in a church!

'Leave me alone,' the girl said quietly. 'I mean it. You can't say anything that would help.'

'That's probably true. But don't be alone too much, okay? You've got friends. What about family?'

Nella turned away without answering. Thea hovered another minute, holding the subdued dogs close. They both seemed to find the church atmosphere oppressive, their heads and tail drooping. 'Come on, then,' she said to them. 'We'll go home, shall we?'

Just before closing the door, she took another look at Nella. The angular figure was bent forward, head in hands, rocking slightly. Thea's heart gave a heavy thump of helpless sympathy. She hoped that something she'd managed to say would bring at least a crumb of comfort.

Completing the circular walk by going down to the small crossroads at the centre of Daglingworth and turning right to get back to Galanthus, Thea gradually realised that she now had a credible reason to visit the Whiteacres. She could express concern about Nella, ask whether there was any family available to support her, and offer any help she could for the short time she expected to be in the area. She could be open and innocent and direct, staying well away from dangerous topics and completely overlooking the unpleasantness of the previous evening. It all looked entirely feasible, as she examined the plan.

But it was a weekday. People would be at work, school or college. It was just past three o'clock and Thea fancied a cup of tea. The day had been far less eventful than the previous one, but all the same it had yielded enough food for thought to keep her mind occupied for a while. A moment of honest self-awareness suggested that she really could do no good at all by calling in on the Whiteacres or anybody else. Her role was as nothing more than silent bystander, with moments of engagement that led nowhere. Would she never learn to stay clear? Following Nella just now had been a stupid intrusion, unkind and unnecessary.

Indecision and self-doubt filled the next ten minutes, to be interrupted and dispelled by DI Higgins himself coming to the door.

'"Possible little clue" I think you said,' he began,

standing as before just inside the threshold, one foot on the blackened patch of carpet.

'What? Oh – the text. Yes. Look, come into the kitchen and I'll make some tea. I didn't expect you to turn up in person.'

'We learn from experience, I hope, Mrs Osborne. And experience suggests that such a message from you is best not ignored.' He followed her into the kitchen, and sat down heavily on one of the chairs.

She filled the kettle and switched it on. 'I'm not sure how to take that,' she said frostily. It was back to the same old accusations, she thought, with a sinking stomach. Gladwin would have made a joke of it, but Higgins was too direct, and in too much of a hurry, for that.

'Sorry. I didn't mean anything. So . . .' He waited.

'Oh. It's probably nothing. But you know I brought Mr Handy's dog back here last night? Well, today I found this—' She proffered the plastic bag that had been left lying on a worktop. 'In the dog's bed in the garage. I wondered if she'd torn it off the jeans of the man who hit her master. She was coughing in the car, and I think it might have been stuck in her throat. She must have expelled it during the night, poor thing. Something like that, anyway. It is a bit disgusting.' Leaving it in his hand, she moved away to make the tea. Two tea bags in two mugs, milk and a spoon was the unceremonious method she used. 'Do you want sugar?' she asked.

Higgins tentatively fingered the shred of material through the plastic, and then gave her a look. 'No sugar, thanks. This could be anything,' he said. 'How do you expect us to make use of it?'

'I don't know. It might match something, somehow.'
The vagueness was a deliberate attempt at self-protection.
'And I didn't like the way Mr Handy was so scornful of his
dog,' she added crossly. 'When she might have been doing
her best to protect him.'

Higgins held her gaze. 'Explain,' he invited.

'Before he blacked out, he said something about her
being useless. Said she just ran round in circles – although
he added that she grabbed one of the men by the hem of his
trousers, as well as a chunk of ankle. I defended her. She's a
sheepdog, for heaven's sake. Bred not to bite man or beast.
If she *did* bite someone, the marks on his leg will help make
a case against him, won't it? She sounds quite brave to me.'

'You won't have heard the latest news, then,' Higgins
observed.

'No. What?'

'He came round – Jack Handy, that is. We don't need
any special forensics to identify the people who attacked
him. We've already got quite a few names and addresses. He
poured it all out this morning. Couldn't be more helpful.'

'Oh.' She frowned, and drank half the tea. 'So why did
you come here, then?'

He sighed. 'I came here because there is still a murder
investigation ongoing. Or had you forgotten that?'

'It had rather faded in significance,' she said carefully.
'How's it going?'

'Well, he definitely was Daniel Compton. We were
starting to have a few doubts, the way he covered his tracks
so well. The parents have confirmed it's him.'

'Did they come back from Dubai?'

Higgins shook his head. 'We did it electronically. Wonders of modern science. They're in the middle of some highly important survey of migrating birds, apparently, and insist their son would wish them to carry on with it, instead of dropping everything to come and cry over his dead body.'

'Sounds as if there's a family commitment to ecology.' She thought she quite approved of such dedication, on the whole. 'Besides, he's got his fiancée here to do all that, hasn't he? I saw her today,' she added. 'She's absolutely grief-stricken. I hadn't thought so until now.'

The detective cocked his head in a familiar gesture that said *Here we go again – you obviously know things that we don't.*

'Oh?' he said.

'She was in the church, *clenched* with misery. She told me to go away. Not for the first time, actually.'

'Explain.'

'Well, she was here last night, with her two friends. They weren't very nice, to be honest. Told me I was interfering, and to stay away from them.'

'They threatened you?'

'Sort of,' she admitted. 'But I don't think they meant anything too awful. Tiffany for one, is really quite sweet. I mean – her heart's definitely in the right place.'

'They're vigilantes,' he snapped. 'Something the police force regards in a very bad light.'

'Why buy a dog and bark yourself?' said Thea fatuously.

'Something like that. But more along the lines of ordinary citizens jumping to conclusions and doing a great deal of needless harm.'

'They said none of them was there yesterday, where Handy was attacked. Did he name any of them?'

'Can't tell you that. Best for you if I don't.'

'Are they wrong, then, to think Jack Handy killed Danny?'

'Too soon to say. He fits in a lot of ways, but there's no evidence worth mentioning. And his manner . . . it's not professional, I know, but he doesn't strike me as a killer. He's too . . . outraged. Looks you in the eye. The fact is, the protest group make enemies everywhere they go. They're an irritation and an embarrassment right across the whole region. And they were getting a lot worse. Harassment on a major scale, disruption verging on terrorism at times. The badger thing really escalated their methods to whole new levels. That gives us a wide selection of suspects for the killer of one of them.'

'Handy's got two thousand hens packed together in a barn. I saw them this morning. When I asked his stepmother what the protesters thought of that, she wouldn't say.'

The head cocked again. 'Mrs Handy? You've met her?'

'I had to take the dog back, remember? She showed me around and gave me some eggs. But she didn't like me very much,' she ended regretfully.

'What did you say to her?'

'Nothing. Honestly – nothing you could possibly object to. I *had* to go, didn't I?' The defensiveness was automatic, born of a growing sense that she was seen as trouble by almost everybody. She gave herself a determined shake. 'Do you know she's called Sandy Handy? I've been wanting to say that out loud all day.' She giggled. 'People do have daft names, don't they? But she must have really loved the old man to saddle herself with that. Or she could have kept her original name.'

Higgins smiled tightly and drained his mug. 'I must go,' he said. 'It's been nice to chat.'

'But you don't rate my little clue very highly, do you? Will you take it with you?'

'Oh yes. You never know. It just seems a bit unlikely the dog would have carried it all the way here? You think she was choking on it, do you?'

'I told you – she was coughing. I don't know any more than that, but I can't see the Fosters having such a thing in the garage. They're not obsessively tidy, but it was fairly neat and brushed.'

He shrugged. 'Anything useful that might have been on it will have been sucked off, then.'

'Yes,' she agreed patiently. 'But the material itself – you could tell where it was torn from, if you had the jeans or whatever. It would put their owner at the scene.'

They were on the doorstep, and he had turned to go back to his car. Then he hesitated, and rubbed a finger across one eyebrow as if chasing a thought. 'Okay,' he muttered. 'Right. Thanks.'

'Bye, then,' she chirped at him in her brightest voice. 'Thanks for coming.'

He flipped a valedictory hand and got into his car.

She closed the door, feeling genuinely pleased by his visit. He had passed some time, bringing her nightly call to Drew that bit closer. Soon she could feed the dogs, take them into the garden, close the curtains and find herself something to eat. All that would take them to nearly six, if she did it slowly and cleaned the kitchen up thoroughly after herself. She also had quite a lot to think about. The pleasant task of ordering her account of the day for Drew's benefit gave a little spring to her step and found her humming softly now and then.

The fact that Jack Handy had regained consciousness brought mixed implications. He presumably wasn't going to die, which meant nobody would be prosecuted for his murder. But despite Higgins's gut reaction, Handy was highly likely to find himself under suspicion once again for the killing of Danny Compton. It was a strange balancing act, and she wondered what the local people made of it. What degree of popularity did the Handys enjoy in the area? Did everyone go to the farm for their eggs? Were there sheep on the land, as well? The presence of a collie suggested so. In which case, who was overseeing the lambing? Her thoughts drifted sideways into a slew of questions to which she had no answers. She remembered Higgins's reproach that the first and unambiguous murder had slipped out of sight with the attack on Handy.

And – a new thought zinged somewhere in the middle of her head – what if Handy himself had been meant as a diversion, a new victim in the form of a callous red herring designed to dilute the quality of attention the police devoted to Danny's death? She had no idea where the idea had come from. It made no sense, given what everyone already believed. If not Handy, then some other outraged Cotswold resident – most likely a farmer – had taken his chance to slaughter one of the most prominent and annoying of the protesters, by breaking his head and then throwing him into the quarry. His friends had drawn their own conclusion as to who had done it, and taken their revenge, worried that there would be insufficient evidence for a prosecution. The notion that this might be a deliberate smokescreen was ridiculous. She couldn't think what could possibly have sown the seed of any alternative explanation in her mind.

Chapter Eighteen

The phone call that evening to Drew completely ruined her mood. 'Sorry, love,' he panted. 'I can't talk now. It's utter chaos here this evening. Timmy had an accident at school, and spent all afternoon in A&E. I had a funeral, so Maggs went to sit with him. I had to call on an extra mourner to carry, which didn't go down very well. Stephanie got sent off to a little friend's house, and that went down even less well. You get the idea.'

'Is Timmy okay now?'

'Cracked his elbow. Hurts like hell, poor little chap. Not a lot to be done, other than leave it to mend. He's got a sling, but can't wear it in bed. Says he can't find a way to lie that doesn't hurt. There – hear that?' A distant wail came down the line.

'Just about. You must go, then. Give him some kisses from me.'

'You're all right, aren't you?'

She could hear his need for an affirmative reply. 'I'm absolutely fine. Nothing to worry about at all. Good luck with everything. I'll call again tomorrow.'

He groaned. 'I don't promise it'll be any better. If Maggs doesn't get over being sick all the time, she's not going to be much use at funerals.'

I need to be there, Thea wanted to say. But too much stood in the way. Not least her obligations to Mr and Mrs Foster.

'She'll soon be over that,' she said confidently. 'Any time now.'

'Let's hope so,' he said gloomily.

Poor Timmy, Thea repeated to herself throughout the evening, crushing down the threads of resentment at the wretched child and his carelessness. She had an awful feeling that there had been a similar hint in Drew's voice, too. Timmy should be seen as an innocent victim of circumstance, not a cause for irritation. From what she had gathered, his conception and birth had been unplanned and not particularly convenient. His mother's injury, followed by a prolonged malaise and eventual death, had blighted his early years. A vulnerable male child, perpetually compared to his infinitely more robust sister, never getting his needs met, was unlikely to grow up confident and secure. He would be a withdrawn, antisocial adolescent. He would perplex his teachers and disappoint his family. A dropout, addicted to the comfort and predictability of computer games, he would become fat and unfit and sociopathic. There were plenty of examples of just such a scenario amongst people Thea knew. The raising of boys was a far more complicated and demanding task than that of girls, she was convinced. Girls recovered. They went out and met people. They found the whole business of education much easier and more congenial than boys did.

'Poor Timmy,' she sighed aloud. She had no relish for the prospect of becoming a substitute parent to him in his most difficult years. But love Drew, love his kids, she admitted to herself. Only the saddest of people reached the age of forty with no baggage, after all.

Meanwhile, there was Gwennie and the tortoise. It occurred to her that the creature should have a name, but it had not been disclosed to her. If it woke up and showed some character, she would have to call it 'Torty' or something equally unimaginative. Idly, she turned on the television in the hope of hearing a weather forecast. Watching TV news had become a slightly nerve-wracking exercise during some of her house-sits. Local events could sometimes find their way into national headlines, and although it was desirable to keep abreast of developments, there was something awful about seeing your own temporary home village on camera. It never looked right, and the people looked fatter and more tanned than they were in reality.

On this midweek evening, however, there was not a word about any crimes committed in the West Midlands. There was, however, something every bit as alarming.

'A large police operation in Manchester got off to a bad start when a young police constable was injured early this morning during a raid on a house in Bowden. Her arm was broken, but no further information is yet available.' Footage was shown of a generic breaking-down-the-door in a typical street, which added nothing to the story.

It wasn't Jessica – of course it wasn't. Somebody would have phoned to tell her. She'd checked the phone for messages and found nothing. But even so, the police activity was almost certainly connected to the operation her daughter had told her about the previous day. It had been scheduled to start early that morning, and Jess was to be part of it.

She grabbed the phone out of her bag and checked again for a text or voicemail. With nothing to see or hear, she keyed her daughter's number.

There was no reply, and she was directed to voicemail. 'Hey, Jess – I just saw your operation on the news. At least I assume it's the same thing. Do you know the girl who was hurt? Can you call me sometime and let me know everything's okay?'

It was all she could do, she told herself. There was no possible justification for calling the very senior police officer who happened to be her brother-in-law, and who also happened to be part of the same force as Jessica, thanks to a recent transfer that he insisted had not been due to Jessica at all. The fact that she had the same surname had worried them both at first, but it seemed there had been no cause for concern. After all, many families had a strong tradition for police work, with uncles and brothers, fathers and cousins popping up on all sides. James had been both sensible and conscientious, keeping an eye on his niece without ever causing her embarrassment.

And yet she very much wanted to know where her daughter was and whether she was all right. It was a little after nine o'clock, much too soon to go to bed, however early the morning start might have been. So why didn't Jess answer her phone? Plenty of rational explanations came to mind. The operation, whatever it was, might require long hours of complete focus, with personal phones kept off for whole days at a time. There would be briefings, reports, *de*briefings and actual work out there in the real world. Thea could not properly imagine any of it, but she knew enough to understand there was no place for reassuring conversations with one's mother.

The world so quickly turned hostile and dangerous. She was aware of an association between her vulnerable daughter and Drew's injured Timmy; an association which expanded outwards to the unborn offspring of Damien and Maggs. Everybody became a hostage to every kind of disaster, once they had children.

But it wasn't so simple, of course. Danny Compton had parents who sounded as if concern for his death was secondary to their passion for birdwatching. Jack Handy had sons who had failed to rush to his bedside. Not everybody accepted the full burden of the parent/child relationship. Even Thea herself had been less than perfectly attentive at times.

She was saved from further gloomy thoughts by her phone ringing.

'Mum? Just got your voicemail. You've got it all wrong.' Jessica sounded irritated, if not downright annoyed.

'Have I?'

'Yes. That thing on the news had nothing whatever to do with what I'm working on. You ought to know better.' Her voice lowered to a hiss. 'I should never have said anything about it. It's *covert*. Do you know what that means?'

'More or less. So – what was I meant to think?'

'Don't think *anything*. Just forget I ever said what I did. It's going to be hard enough as it is, without you . . .' She tailed off, apparently speechless with frustration.

'Okay, okay. I get it. You're right – I was panicking for no reason. Not like me, you have to admit.'

'Right. Which is why I'm calling. Don't do it again. I might have to use this phone – oh, I can't go into all that. But just for a bit, please forget all about me. You'd soon hear if there was anything to worry about. No news is good news, remember. Now I need to get to bed. Have you got it, Mum? Don't call me. Don't email, either. I'm disappearing for a little while.'

Thea kept a firm grip. 'Sounds terribly exciting,' she said.

'Now you just sound like Granny. Oh – what happened to that man, by the way?'

'He came out of the coma, so he can tell the police the whole thing for himself. I met his stepmother. Everything's still very up in the air.'

'Well, you stay out of it. Just . . . you know. Walk the dogs or something.'

'I'll try.'

'Must go now. Bye, Mum. I'll let you know when things are normal again.'

'Bye, sweetheart.'

All the legions of devoted mothers through the centuries crowded in on her. Mothers of serving soldiers; mothers of unhappy sons and daughters – wringing their hands and gaining approval from society by so doing. She did not want to be like that. Worry was not a virtue; it was a waste of time and energy. The object of the worry was burdened by it, rather than supported and reassured. She felt fierce and defiant and very slightly in the wrong, for reacting in such a way. Jessica was an adult, and had made the position very clear. This was not some back-to-front game where what was said meant the opposite. Until further notice, Thea was to remain quiet and unworried.

Okay, she promised herself. She could do that. Except she still felt concerned about little Timmy Slocombe.

And she was still eager to know who had killed Danny Compton, too. She found herself very much not wanting it to have been Jack Handy, for reasons she could not pin down. She had not especially liked his stepmother, whose story of how she came to the farm, and who else might lay claim to it in the future was not entirely trustworthy. She had married a man who had been nearly twenty years her senior and effectively ejected the woman who had been mistress of the house until then. Her account of events had been dispassionate with a small hint of complacency. She showed scant signs of distress at her stepson's injury at the hands of local people. Rightly or wrongly, Thea had mentally fitted the woman into a pattern she was constructing to explain the people and events of Daglingworth and Bagendon and adjacent settlements. She could draw it, if requested: Danny at the centre, with Sophie, Nella and Tiffany ranged above him; Ricky and Steve joined them on one side and Jack Handy on the other. At a remove were Sheila Whiteacre and her husband. A satellite cluster comprised the Fosters and the Tanners, with the arson attack linking them. Nothing joined the two crimes, as far as she could see. The police had shown no sign of thinking there might be a connection. Even Thea herself could hardly qualify for that role, she silently insisted.

After all that thinking and patterning, the Whiteacre family persistently remained at the forefront. The house itself had appealed to her so strongly that she hated to think she might never see it again. Perhaps she would brave it the next morning, clinging to the flimsy pretext of checking that they were aware of how unhappy Nella was. Perhaps by then she would have found something persuasive to say that would allow her over the threshold, despite the repeated warnings to do no such thing.

All was well with the dogs, at least. The weather forecast predicted a mild day to come, which was encouraging news for the tortoise. There were elaborate instructions for transferring him into the much larger living space that Mr Foster had called a 'vivarium'. It had temperature control, which was designed to avoid any confusion brought about by fickle English weather. 'After all, it can snow in April,' Mr Foster had said. 'And once he's woken up, he won't go back into hibernation, whatever happens.'

Thea had been distracted by the notion of snow in April, at the time, and given less attention to the tortoise than she ought. The main point she registered was that Mrs Foster called the creature 'she' and her husband referred to it as a male. Now Thea resolved to make up for her defective attention by ensuring the transition from death-like sleep to revival and animation would go smoothly.

She went to bed early, reviewing the day with some relief. She might well decide to stay close to Daglingworth the whole of the next day, simply pottering around the lanes, or enjoying spring sunshine in the garden. Everybody from Jessica to Higgins, via Sophie and her associates, had told her to stay clear of whatever crimes and misdemeanours might be taking place. Obviously she should quell her own instinctive nosiness and do as they advised. And equally obviously, she wasn't going to.

Her final thoughts, as usual, were of Drew. Drew was the exception. He would understand how difficult it was to just remain quietly unobtrusive in a stranger's house. He himself was driven to question and probe into matters that were not directly his concern. He liked to set things straight and restore order, just as Thea did. It was this shared urge that had first forged the bond between them.

Drew was never going to tell her to keep away and avert her gaze when something terrible was going on.

Chapter Nineteen

Thursday exceeded even the optimistic predictions of the weatherman. Sunlight streamed through the open curtains onto Thea's bed. The room was on a corner of the house, with windows in two walls. One faced north and the other east. Between them, they gave her a good view of much of Daglingworth, despite the presence of a lot of trees. She could see the church, and a handsome barn conversion, as well as the little road into the heart of the village, with its raised walkway for pedestrians. The buds on the bushes and trees all seemed to have grown fatter and greener overnight.

Throwing on some clothes, she skipped downstairs to awaken Gwennie and take her outside. Her spirits were suddenly much higher than they had been for weeks. The sight of the burnt patch in the hall did nothing to lower them, nor did the events of the past few days.

The corgi seemed glad to participate in whatever rite of spring her temporary mistress had in mind. She snatched her breakfast biscuit and raised her pointed snout in a plea for more. 'You are a pretty dog,' Thea told her. 'Such a lovely coat.'

Hepzibah wagged competitively, and pushed past the older dog to be first into the garden at the back of the house. It was a routine Thea had performed several times in numerous house-sits, and she watched the animals with half an eye as she debated what to have for breakfast.

She should, she knew, keep a closer watch on her own dog, who had something of a record for volatile behaviour in recent times. Sudden excitement could spark a moment of madness that had at least once led to expensive and embarrassing damage to another animal. But calmly mooching about under old apple trees was unlikely to set her off. The two dogs were ignoring each other, anyway, sniffing around in different parts of the garden.

It would be pleasant to walk once more down the pathways and over the fields to the house in Bagendon, for a final visit. The people were due back late the next day, which would mark the halfway point in Thea's occupation of Galanthus House. She thought of the Fosters in Australia, surrounded by relatives and enjoying the exotic wildlife and vegetation. She never did hear exactly how they responded to being told by the police that their house had been fire-bombed – but assumed they were suitably mollified by assurances that no real harm had been done.

It was a shame that Gwennie couldn't manage such a long walk. She was obviously happy to be out in the sunshine, and had doubtless benefited from the gentle circular stroll around Daglingworth the day before. It was plainly Thea's duty to take her for a similar outing again today.

A slice of toast and a mug of coffee were quickly consumed, and then she clapped her hands decisively. 'Okay – a short walk to start with, then Gwennie comes home and we go off for the rest of the morning.' She addressed her spaniel. 'And this time, we won't accept any lifts back. It's not far – we can easily do both ways.'

For a change she kept along the road leading to a different church, standing beside the junction with the road through Stratton – the place where she and Jessica had missed the turning, thanks to the drama of Jack Handy's troubles. It was probably a mile each way, if she went the whole length, which was far too much for the elderly corgi. 'We'll turn back in ten minutes,' Thea promised.

The road was quiet, but there was no proper pavement and when cars did pass by, they moved quickly. The dogs had to be kept close on their leads, which Hepzie found thoroughly frustrating. 'I should have left you behind and just taken Gwennie,' Thea muttered crossly.

The next car to appear was coming towards them. The driver ducked his head to get a better view of Thea's face, and she met his eyes. It was the same bearded young man, and the same car, that she and Jessica had met two days before, in the gateway to a field where a man lay bleeding. Without thinking, she flapped a hand at him, but he was already pulling to a stop.

Twisting to get a view from the rear window, he reversed the ten yards or so to where she stood. One of his big ears was visible, and Thea wondered foolishly why he kept his hair so short. It only emphasised the less-than-attractive feature.

'Steve,' she said, through the open passenger window. 'We meet again.'

'Yeah. I knew you were staying along here somewhere.'

'Were you looking for me?'

'No way! Why'd I want to do that?'

Good question, she thought. 'So . . . ?' she invited.

'Just wondered how you were doing. And that girl – your daughter, was she? Must have been a bit of a shock for her.'

Thea put her head through the window and gave him a straight look. 'You drove off without waiting for the ambulance. The man's your *uncle*, or so you said. You didn't know if he'd live or die, and you just drove off. What was that all about?'

He returned the look, completely unabashed. 'I got a phone call. So I had to go. I knew he'd be okay. I saw the ambulance on its way. I called in later and gave them my name and address and all that.'

'Who called you?'

His face darkened. 'None of your business. Anyway, he's getting better now. Panic over.'

'You could have taken the dog. I had to keep it all night, and then find out where she lived and take her back the next day. Why should *I* get all that hassle?'

He left a beat before replying, his eyes on hers. She could read his thoughts as clearly as if he'd shouted them. Hadn't she asked for it, pushing in where she wasn't wanted, concerning herself in other people's business? Any hassle she got landed with was entirely of her own making. 'Looked to me as if you fancied a bit of hassle,' he said. 'Must be boring, watching out for someone's house day after day. Nothing like a bit of violence to brighten the day – ain't that right?' He laughed nastily. 'You think you know such a lot about us, after five minutes, don't you? And you haven't a bloody clue, really.'

If it had not been such a lovely day, she might have responded in kind. As it was, she found it almost easy to deflect the abuse. 'You're probably right. So why did you stop to talk to me?'

He laughed again, with more genuine amusement than before. 'Good question. They told me you were different. I can see what they meant now.'

'Who's "they"?'

'The girls,' he said vaguely. 'Listen, if you're not doing anything, we could go and have a bit of a chat. Set you straight.'

It dawned on Thea that he had heard a report of the visitation on Tuesday evening, with accompanying doubts as to how effective the warning to stay clear had been. Perhaps this Steve was trying again, along a new tack. 'Okay,' she said. 'Where do you want to go?'

'Back to yours? It's closest.'

'It's not *mine*,' she corrected. 'And I thought you said you didn't know which house it was, anyway.'

'I don't. But it's along here somewhere. You can't have walked far with that dog. Looks as if it'd drop dead if you made it go more than a quarter of a mile.'

He couldn't see Gwennie, where she was sitting patiently almost under his car. Hepzie was more restless, even jumping up at the window to get a glimpse of the man

233

inside. Thea supposed that Steve had got a good look at both dogs as he drove towards them.

'That's true,' she agreed, maintaining an affable manner despite small flickers of anxiety somewhere inside her. Would it be utter madness to let him into the house, when there had been so much unexplained violence going on?

'So?'

'Can we have a lift? Or do you want to crawl along behind us?' There had been no passing traffic at all during their conversation, but now a fair-sized lorry came up behind Steve's car and hooted. 'You'll have to move.'

'Jump in, then. Put the dogs in the back.'

The lorry waited with poor grace while she bundled Gwennie onto the seat and suffered Hepzie to sit on her lap, contrary to Steve's instructions. 'She won't stay in the back,' she said, knowing that this was a lie. She felt faintly protected by the spaniel, which was ludicrous. Hepzie had no concept of protection. She was soft and brainless and not entirely predictable.

It took less than two minutes to reach Galanthus House. Steve left the car at the bottom of the drive, effectively preventing any other vehicle coming in or going out. 'Nice day,' he said fatuously, as they walked up to the door. 'We could sit out here if you'd rather.'

It was a tempting idea. 'I suppose that would be nice,' she said. 'The dogs can come in and out as they like.' She assumed that Gwennie knew better than to escape into the road. There was no gate across the entrance, which for the first time struck Thea as unusual. Most Cotswolds properties made it very clear where their boundaries lay, and just how they regarded potential intruders. The openness of the Fosters' house was an appealing detail, and another way in which it was very different from the one in Bagendon.

'I can't stay long,' said Steve. 'As you're probably pleased to hear.' He plonked himself down on a wrought-iron seat positioned to one side of the small lawn. Thea saw no alternative but to sit beside him, but she hesitated.

'Shall I get some coffee?' she asked him.

'Don't bother. I've just had some. Let's get on with it.'

'You're going to set me straight,' she nodded.

'Sit down and listen, then.' He waited a moment while she obeyed. 'Okay – for a start, let me tell you about our group. All you've got so far is what Sophie's said, by all accounts. And Sophie's the extreme one. You can't take her as typical.'

'That's a relief.'

'We're a big collection of like-minded people, mostly young, but not entirely. We've *activists*. That's the word we use. We use direct action where everything else has failed. But we're mostly trying to change minds with reason. Most of the time we're blogging and tweeting and putting the case for better environmental awareness. We don't hurt people.'

'Jack Handy was hurt,' she objected.

He paused and closed his eyes. 'You think that was us?'

'He *told* us it was. We're fairly sure it was Ricky Whiteacre who hit him.'

'Uncle Jack doesn't know who's who. He's never bothered to learn anyone's name or ask them what they want. He's always been on the defensive, ever since his dad died. He thinks everyone's talking about him and out to get

235

him. Those hens of his – he knows it's wrong. And selling that field was deliberate provocation. The whole village was against him doing it. But those aren't things we get concerned about.'

'He knows you, though.'

Steve nodded. 'Only because I was at school with his boys and spent half my time on his farm. That was when he was milking. Ages ago now.'

'So what are you saying? You think it wasn't Ricky?'

'Ricky Whiteacre is a law unto himself. He's not properly with us, never comes to the meetings.'

'His father knows it was him. We heard them talking. You're just trying to keep me from knowing the truth. Well, it's too late now, isn't it? Jack's going to tell the police it was Ricky. Even if he doesn't know names, he can describe them. He said there was a gang of girls pushing and punching him.'

'All I know is it wasn't Tiffany or Nella or Sophie.'

'So they tell me.'

'It's true. Nella and Sophie can both prove they were nowhere near that field. So can Tiffany, come to that. She was at home. If you must know, that was the phone call I got. Sophie was calling to ask if I was coming or not. I was late, see.'

She nodded slowly. 'But you'd already stopped by that gateway. You'd seen Jack and were horrified. That's why I stopped – the look on your face.'

'Right. What's wrong with that?'

'Nothing, I suppose. Except – why were you there, at that very spot, and just the right moment? And then it still strikes me as very odd the way you disappeared – as if you didn't want to get involved with the police.'

'Right,' he repeated. 'What's surprising about that? We're not on good terms with the cops. And, as I told you already, I didn't see there was anything I could do. There were two of you, and that girl seemed pretty capable.'

'My daughter. She's a police officer.'

'Yes, you said at the time. So why would you need me?'

'Didn't you *care* about him? He's a relative, isn't he?'

'Distant cousin. What can I say? I didn't think he was badly hurt.'

'I'm still confused. Who *were* those people, then? Why would they attack him like that?'

'As you just said, he can tell us himself, now he's woken up. Someone's going to get a knock on their door – if they haven't already.'

'The assumption is it's most likely to be revenge for the death of Danny Compton,' she said. 'Everyone seems to think Jack Handy killed him.'

Steve said nothing for a minute, simply staring thoughtfully at the road beyond his car. Then he forced an artificial cough, as if the silence had to be filled somehow. 'Everyone liked Danny,' he said after another minute. 'He was everyone's friend. Willing, cheerful, capable. All the girls fell for him.'

'And he chose Nella,' Thea nodded, thinking the bony, sharp-spoken young woman was an unlikely selection.

'He did. They were mad about each other. They were getting married.'

'I don't suppose I've seen her at her best.' Then she

237

remembered that when she first saw Nella and the others on Saturday, nobody knew Danny was dead. She tried in vain to recall her first impression of the dead man's fiancée. 'I heard Tiffany saying that Danny was dragging his heels about a date for the wedding and Nella was cross about it.'

'What man doesn't drag his feet in that situation?' Steve laughed. 'He was just being sensible. They didn't have anywhere to live, for a start. And there was something weird about his parents. He left home very young and hardly ever saw them – something like that.'

'Must have had some money, though – with that nice car.'

'Yeah. We did wonder about that. He said he got it at a massive discount somewhere. Never did hear the full story. We used it for off-road operations. S'pose there'll be no more of that now. Unless Nella gets to inherit it.'

'So you believe your distant cousin Jack bashed him on the head and tipped him into the quarry, then?' she persisted.

He shook his head heavily. 'I don't know,' he said. 'Better people than me say he did, so they're probably right. After all, it wouldn't have taken much to provoke him.'

'Wouldn't Danny have resisted, fought back, left scratches or bruises?'

'Who says he didn't? What do you know of the details?'

She smiled ruefully. 'Not much. They know for sure it wasn't an accident. I think Higgins said he was bashed on the head before being thrown into the quarry.'

He gave her a startled stare. 'That wasn't it,' he said. 'I thought it was common knowledge.'

'What?'

'He was stabbed.'

'No! Who told you that?' She was furious at her own ignorance, at Higgins having wilfully withheld the fact, even suggesting something quite different, whilst apparently telling all sorts of other people the real truth of the matter. 'And don't tell me your brother works at the local mortuary.'

He laughed. 'Not quite. It was the chap who found the body on Sunday. He tweeted about it, damn fool. There was a lot of blood. Somebody in the group retweeted it, Sophie saw it and told some of us.'

'Did she tell Nella?'

'I doubt it, but she might have done. I'm trying to tell you – I'm not part of the inner circle. None of them's my best mate.'

She frowned at him. 'And yet you were right there, in Bagendon, monitoring the police radio, on Sunday. I saw you myself.'

'And I saw you,' he said loudly. 'I thought at the time you were trouble, and I turned out to be right, didn't I?'

'How am I trouble?' she asked, in all innocence. 'Did I disrupt some horrible plan?'

'Don't be stupid.' He heaved a profound sigh. 'Sorry. But just by *being* here, you're causing trouble. Nobody knows where you'll pop up next, or which of your copper friends you'll have trailing after you. Even your bloody *daughter* is one of them.'

'She is. Not that I ever encouraged her. It gets worse – my brother-in-law's a detective superintendent. And I'm quite matey with another of them, in this region. Luckily for you, she's on holiday.' She gave a wry laugh. 'I'm sort of on your side, you know. I mean, I agree with a lot of your aims.'

'Big deal,' he grumbled, which increased her sneaking liking for him. A solid young man, with large hands and hair the colour of oak furniture, he had a wit and integrity that had taken a while to recognise.

Again he gazed off down the drive, seeming to conjure a slow-moving, silver-coloured car approaching from the west. The driver was shamelessly peering up at the house, in an attitude that Thea was beginning to find annoying. The twisted neck and hunched shoulders that were necessary to see through the passenger window exemplified an excessive level of intrusion. Even Thea at her most nosy had never done it.

'It's Sheila Whiteacre,' she noted. 'Again. Hasn't she got better things to do than keep snooping up here? She did it on Monday, as well.'

'Sheila's all right,' he said softly. 'So long as she's on the same side. She's got a lot of influence.'

'Oh, damn it.' The woman had pulled her car awkwardly behind Steve's and was getting out. She waved cheerfully, which reminded Thea that their last encounter had led to a very uncomfortable piece of knowledge about her son. The two waited on their seat for the newcomer to come closer.

'Just thought I'd ask how you got on with that dog,' Sheila chirped, when she was a few yards away. 'Did you find the farm all right?'

'No problem. Mrs Handy showed me round.' There were undercurrents in operation that could take them into all kinds of deep water. Tiffany's hostility; Ricky's misdeeds; Sheila's own uninvited appearance – they were all potential areas of conflict.

'Oh good. Hi, Steve,' she greeted him fondly. 'Fancy meeting you here.'

Another possible minefield opened up – had Sheila stopped because she'd spotted Steve, and wanted to check up on what was being said? Something guarded in his eyes suggested this might be the case. 'Hi,' he said.

'Look – I have to go over to Bagendon,' Thea said firmly. 'I'm not being paid to sit about and chat like this.'

They both looked at her in astonishment. 'Aren't you?' said Sheila. 'I'd have thought this is *exactly* what they want from you. Better than getting yourself embroiled in local trouble that you understand nothing about.'

Here we go, thought Thea. 'You mean, I should shut myself away in here and ignore everything going on outside?' Anger was slowly building somewhere in her chest. 'All I did was go for a walk on Saturday, you know. Tiffany and Sophie were in the little wood, and it seemed entirely natural to have a little chat with them.'

Sheila let her shoulders drop in an attitude of exasperation. She breathed out slowly. 'And then you cadged a lift off Jack Handy. After that, you went back again and pushed into a group of people you didn't know. You just keep turning up, time after time, don't you? You're like a witch. Or a bad fairy.'

'A jinx,' muttered Steve.

'Or a spy,' Sheila finished. 'Deliberately informing the police about everything you hear us say.'

'Oh, for heaven's sake,' Thea shouted. 'That's all absolute nonsense. I had no idea your protest group even existed until I came here. Sophie told me a whole lot about it, five minutes after I first met her. If you're worried about spies, maybe you should tell her to keep her mouth shut.'

'She thought you might make a likely recruit,' Steve explained. 'She's always on the lookout for new people.'

Thea got up. 'Well, tell her she's useless as a recruiting officer. She comes across as borderline insane. Now, I do have to get on. The morning's half gone already.' Part of her regretted the curtailment of the conversation, but a larger part was eager to be done with it. 'Thanks for putting me straight, Steve,' she added with some irony. It would take a good deal of hard thinking before she could truthfully say she was any closer to understanding what had been going on.

'He put you straight, did he?' Sheila said sharply. 'How, exactly?'

'Never mind,' said Steve. 'If you move your car, I can go. We can't stay if she doesn't want us here.' Again, Thea pegged him as essentially decent, although evidently not entirely law-abiding, given his eavesdropping on police radio exchanges. She would have liked longer to try to assess his character and motives. A murder had been committed, after all – and anybody with a strong arm and sufficient reason might have done it.

242

Chapter Twenty

The two cars manoeuvred away and Thea was left feeling overwrought and slightly foolish. She wasn't actually in any rush to get to Bagendon. It was perfectly pleasant here at Galanthus House in the spring sunshine, the dogs pottering idly back and forth, birds singing on all sides. Instead of setting off across the countryside, she could bring the tortoise out into the warmth and hope he stirred from his slumbers. She was more and more eager to meet him . . . her . . . whatever it was. She had never been on close acquaintance with a tortoise before.

Acting on the idea, she carefully carried the tank from the back of the garage. It was much heavier than she'd expected, and she had not planned in advance where to put it, so she simply plonked it down on the ground just outside the garage door. It contained almost a foot of dense soil, which obviously weighed quite a lot, she realised belatedly. She didn't think she would be able to lift it back onto its original shelf, which was rather a worry. No way could it stay outside all night, getting cold and vulnerable to passing predators. Did foxes eat tortoises, she wondered? A badger might well have a try, if it detected something alive inside the tank. More than that, she would have to be careful not to drive into it when she got the car out. 'What an idiot,' she muttered. She would have to find somebody to help her put it back, before the end of the day. From recent experience, she had good reason to hope a likely assistant would turn up before very long.

Meanwhile it was definitely time for more coffee. It would help her to think, which felt like a fairly urgent priority. Impressions, hunches, suspicions were all snaking around inside her head, thanks to Steve and his 'setting her straight'. Nothing was remotely straight any more – even the few facts she had believed to be fully established now felt rocky and fragile. Somewhere deep inside all the talk was a core detail or connection that might explain the whole business.

Her phone had to trill for several seconds before she grasped the import of the sound. She had left it in the kitchen, next to the sink, and was a million miles from expecting a call. *Jessica*, she thought with a stab of anxiety.

But it wasn't Jessica. 'Hello? It's me,' said a welcome voice. 'Sorry about last night. I've got a quiet half hour, with any luck. How about you?'

'All the time in the world,' she said, with a sensation of sinking into a deep feather bed, far away from the world and its worries.

He told her about his stressful evening, dealing with a damaged child. 'He's asleep now. They said he should take the rest of the week off school.'

'But how will you manage? Can you still do funerals?'

'Just about. There's one later today, and another tomorrow. Timmy can stay indoors while I do them. He'll be able to see me from the window. I'll rig up a signal system, so he can let me know if anything happens.'

'Sounds like fun,' she said doubtfully. What if the child fell, or blacked out? He wouldn't manage to send a signal then.

'He'll be okay. It's only for half an hour or so, each time. Tell me what you've been doing.'

'I didn't get a chance to tell you I went to see your house.' She'd almost forgotten about Broad Campden. 'It's looking a bit sad.'

'But it still has a roof?'

'Oh, yes. But it seems such a terrible *waste*, Drew. It's worth a small fortune, and you know you could do with the money.'

'I can't just *sell* it.' He sounded horrified. 'What would happen to the field, if I did that?'

'I have no idea, but you ought to find out what the precise legal position is. As far as I can see, you've satisfied the original condition, and it's up to you what you do with it now.'

'It's not that simple. I just need to . . . get myself a bit straighter. Now there's this uncertainty about Maggs as well, I have to wait and see how that goes. She can't make any firm commitments for a year or more, the way things are.'

'That's a long time.'

'I know. Change the subject. How's the murder going?'

She gave him a disjointed summary of events since they last spoke, adding points out of sequence, as she remembered them. It took almost five minutes.

'I can't throw much light on any of that,' he said. 'Most of it seems obvious, on the face of it. Local residents fed up with the activists, to the point where one of them stabbed a leading member and threw him into a quarry. Possibly on the spur of the moment. Maybe just came across him by chance and took the opportunity.'

'Not many people carry a knife big enough to kill someone with.'

'Farmers do. They're always having to cut baler twine or brambles or something.'

'I'm cross that Higgins never said anything about there being a knife. I'm sure he told me it was a bash on the head. A knife seems much nastier somehow.'

'They are. Did I tell you about the time when I—'

'You did. I know how you feel about knives. Anyway, the good news is that Jack Handy can speak for himself, so they'll know by now who it was who attacked him.'

'It still feels like a case of revenge,' he said thoughtfully. 'Maggs said something, years ago, that I've never forgotten. It keeps coming back to me.'

'What?'

'"We fear those we hurt". It's obvious when you think about it, but I don't think people take it into account enough. Like me, with that nursing home. I'm scared stiff they'll find a way to get back at me. It's the reason why revenge is such a powerful thing – it has a sort of inevitability to it, even for the victim. Because the victim was the perpetrator as well. It's symmetrical. Balanced. Half expected. You need to find out what that Danny did to somebody in particular. It feels more personal to me than what you've been saying.'

'We know he annoyed any number of locals. Probably threatened their livelihoods in some cases. Isn't that enough?'

'It might be, yes. But there must be a reason why it was him and not one of the others. And maybe the quarry is significant in some way. Quite often the place is important, as well as the means of doing the killing.'

'I expect the protest group regards the quarry as some kind of desecration of the countryside. It is, after all, even though it's been there for decades, at least. There are quarries all over the place, going back to the Middle Ages. How else could they build all these lovely houses?'

'It's just a thought,' he said mildly.

'Sorry. Was I shouting?'

'A bit.'

She laughed. 'It's a bad sign when I do that. Shows I've got myself emotionally involved – again. Every time, I resolve to just stay quietly in the background, ignoring all the goings-on around me. But it never works.'

'Of course it doesn't. How boring would that be?'

'Right. You know – the Steve person who was here just now – he seemed to understand. I rather liked him. He said everybody liked Danny, as well.'

Drew let that lie, and followed another thought. 'When's

the funeral? Danny's, I mean. They should be releasing the body about now.'

'No idea. His parents can't be bothered to come, apparently, so it's all down to Nella. Does a fiancée count as kin?'

'Not really. She wouldn't be able to sign cremation papers, strictly speaking. Where are the parents?'

'Dubai, watching bird migrations.'

'There'll be a way around it, then. And maybe it'll be a burial,' he added hopefully. 'The paperwork's much easier if that's the case.'

'Do you want me to put in a word for a green burial?' She was half joking, but it wouldn't be the first time the idea had arisen.

'No, no. There's no way at all I could undertake that.' He chuckled. 'Pun.'

She was too engaged in thoughts of etymology to laugh back. 'Aren't words amazing?' she said instead. 'The way they can carry such layers of meaning.'

'Don't start,' he said, still giggling. 'I must go. Somebody might be trying to get through. Thanks, Thea. You've cheered me up enormously.'

'All part of the service,' she said lightly. 'When will I see you, I wonder?' There had been a number of occasions where he had brought his children for a visit to the Cotswolds during one of her house-sitting jobs. Wistfully, she realised that there was scant chance of that happening this time.

'When you've finished there, I guess. Is there anything else in the pipeline?'

'I had an email from a man in Farmington, a few weeks ago, but he hasn't come back to me. It's nice there.' She thought of her wintry stay in Hampnett, a year before, and the handsome little town of Northleach. They were close to Farmington. 'I don't know a single thing about it,' she said blithely. 'There'd be plenty of scope for learning new things.'

'Sounds good. When would that be?'

'July, I think. But he might have changed his mind.'

There was a small silence, before Drew said, 'Well . . .'

'Yes, you must go. Me too. I should pay one last visit to the Bagendon house, before the people come back tomorrow.'

'You work too hard,' he said with outrageous irony.

'Go away. I'll speak to you soon.'

'Bye, my love,' he murmured, leaving her warm and frustrated and reassured.

She'd go in the car, at two o'clock, she decided. Walking there and back was too much, after all. Passing the quarry on foot felt risky, for some reason she wasn't able to pin down. Nobody was likely to hang around hoping for a second victim to kill. It was the last place anyone would select in which to act suspiciously. Except, didn't they say that murderers always revisited the scene of the crime? Knowing her luck, she was highly likely to coincide with a surreptitious return of the killer and get herself chucked into the quarry, along with her dog.

She was also reluctant to cross the fields and traverse the little woodland just south of the village. It was too redolent of Sophie and Tiffany and the overheard remarks which had begun the whole sorry involvement with them and their group. There were factors she still didn't understand – badger setts and ancient sheepfolds, which meant more to local people than she could ever properly grasp. In spite of all her defiance, she fully intended to drive directly to the Bagendon house, water its plants and drive straight back again. She would not speak to a single person, nor stop for any reason at all.

Before that, there was lunch. Giving it the label of an actual meal made her feel she was adhering to a proper routine, like a civilised person. In reality, she simply carved a slice of cheese from a block she'd brought with her, added slices of somewhat elderly and utterly tasteless tomato, and wrapped it all in two slices of brown bread. She didn't bother to sit down to eat it. Afterwards she ate an apple that had come from the other side of the world, and which hardly tasted of anything, either. Food, she reflected, had become even less interesting to her than it had been for much of her life. Being small and not especially active meant she could survive on a very low intake. It saved money, anyway.

She knew people who ate as a way of filling the time – something she could well understand. It would be easy to devote hours every day to planning and preparing meals which would be consumed in solitude. Pointless, unhealthy and sad, perhaps, but all too temptingly easy. No way was she going to fall into that trap.

Such thoughts, if she wasn't careful, could lead swiftly to self-pity, which could be difficult to shake off. Before that could happen she forced herself to think about house-sitting, money and the coming summer. But then she slipped into images of the Bagendon house, so well secured and yet so vulnerable. As before, she visualised it burnt to the ground by the same arsonist who tried to burn Galanthus House. No house was truly invulnerable. They had windows which could be broken, doors that could be smashed or penetrated via the letter box or cat flap. If sufficient malevolence existed, anything was possible.

Switching to another track, she found herself thirsting for the latest news about Jack Handy's progress, as well as confirmation that it was the renegade Tanner family that really had set light to the Fosters' house. She also wondered about Danny Compton's parents and Nella Davidson's state of mind. And quite a lot of other things, once she got started.

When the phone vibrated on the kitchen worktop, her mind zipped through the half-dozen or so possible callers before she picked it up.

It was a text from Damien – something she had never expected to receive. She hadn't thought her brother capable of such a thing. It said:

SCAN THIS MORNING. BABY GIRL. ALL WELL.

At least it's not twins, thought Thea, with far less enthusiasm than custom demanded. She quickly replied,

CONGRATULATIONS. ALL VERY EXCITING. KEEP ME POSTED.

Texts were the new telegrams, she reflected. Just as emails were the new letters. Length and content were very similar, as any visit to a Victorian archive would reveal. In the 1890s, business people despatched short notes on a single sheet of paper, often no more than two sentences. They arrived the same day in London and other cities. Communications were admittedly much more all-pervading now, but not a great deal faster, for all the technology available. And who was going to go to the bother of keeping and storing all those emails for posterity? If Damien had sent a telegram, she might have retained it as a piece of family history. As it was, the text would evaporate as if it had never been. It seemed rather a shame.

It was also a disappointment that the message had not been from Drew, Jessica, Higgins or the Fosters. In that order, she had hoped for some words from those people before needing anything from Damien. But a new niece was important. Nieces were special. This one was likely to need all the auntly input she could get.

Gwennie was more than happy to remain curled up in her basket while Thea and Hepzie went off for a drive. She didn't even open an eye as they left. Mindful of the tortoise tank beside the garage door, Thea reversed the car with extreme care, turning in the wide area in front of the house. She really would have to attend to the hibernating pet as soon as she got back – if it escaped the predations of fox or badger, there might be a risk that it would wake up and disappear if she didn't do something about it. There was no lid on the tank, but she hoped four inches of slippery glass between the soil and the top would deter it from climbing out. It had been folly, really, to move it at all.

Back across the main road by means of the convoluted roundabouts and tunnels, it seemed almost as slow and varied a route as it would have been on foot. After three left turns, she drew up at the house, thinking how different it was to arrive somewhere by car rather than as a pedestrian. Now she was a more significant person, in possession of a car, in no way suspicious. In the light of recent events, she supposed there would be a strong police presence, watching out for unusual movements – in particular anybody walking over the fields with no immediately obvious purpose.

The house was fine. Silent, clean, empty, it waited contentedly for its people. Thea ran a perfunctory duster over a few surfaces, doing her best to quell complex emotions of disapproval, envy and relief. She found a notepad in the hall, and wrote a brief message. *Welcome home. All seems to be in order. Thank you for the commission – I gather Mrs Foster will be paying me? Best wishes Thea Osborne.* And she added her mobile number for good measure. Another emotion pushed through: a hint of guilt at taking a hundred pounds for so little work.

But it would surely be worth it for the relief the owners would feel when they got back and found everything in such perfect order. That was worth any amount of money, especially with crime raging through the village and no prosecutions yet made. Complacency crept into the mix, as she gave the place a final review, before locking the door.

* * *

It was half past two on a Thursday afternoon and the sun still shone invitingly. The Cotswolds were gorgeous in all seasons, but spring came close to the top for perfection. All dead leaves had long been eradicated from gardens – except for Drew's property in Broad Campden. Everything was pruned and staked and mulched, ready for the coming months of colour and texture, carefully designed. She had occasionally thought of spending a day with a camera, capturing the stone and the landscape and the gardens, but it had never really happened. The few pictures she'd taken were never as she'd hoped. Shadows fell in the wrong place, or vital details got chopped in half. Photography really wasn't one of her strong points, she had long ago concluded. So instead, she used her eyes, pausing for long looks at a view or an ancient wall. She still remembered them, at least as well as if she'd taken a picture with a camera. Standing on Cleeve Hill overlooking Winchcombe, or examining Painswick from a distant elevation, and deciding the church was ill-fitting – she could still recall almost every detail.

So far on this job, she had found the big houses of Stratton and Caunton the most appealing; perhaps all the more so because it was hardly a settlement in its own right, dismissed as an offshoot of Cirencester and given short shrift. In fact, she had a feeling the houses could tell some gripping tales of former times, with the traffic along the Gloucester Road to and from the ancient city close by. The Whiteacres' home was a prime example, with which she had quite fallen in love at first sight.

The Whiteacre family felt very central to the business of the murder, as well as the attack on Farmer Handy, on the basis of very little hard evidence. Sheila showed up at crucial moments, and Tiffany was closely involved with all the people concerned. Then Jessica had heard Ricky virtually confessing to having committed grievous bodily harm. But Thea herself was cast out to the borders of ignorance, with no news updates and no real insights into what had happened or why.

Yet again there were no people to be seen; no feeling that work was going on in the fields, or even in the silent houses. Bedrooms might be converted into studies, with computers and scanners and high-speed connections, but she saw very little evidence of their being much used. These villages were increasingly treated as weekend hideaways, rather than permanent homes for ordinary families. Affluent, retired people bought lovely stone houses and then spent much of their time on cruises or visiting relatives in Australia, as Thea knew from her own experience.

All this, she supposed, was included in the range of things that Sophie and her group found so outrageous. Second homes, pretentious gardens using peat from irreplaceable bogs, enormous greedy vehicles, inessential travel – everything these rich Cotswolds dwellers did must surely fuel the fury of an eco-activist. Thea felt she had glimpsed the makings of something not far from warfare in the glittering eyes of the fanatical Sophie and her sidekick Nella. After all, it did happen. Generations of antagonism could simmer invisibly until something occurred to spark a wholesale conflagration. The police took campaign groups seriously, after all. And now there had been a murder, tensions were quite possibly at breaking point. Hence the attack on Jack Handy. Chances were, then, that it was not going to stop there.

But Drew had not seen it in the same way. He said it was personal. He said people fear those they hurt and there was something inevitable about revenge. But Higgins had implied that investigations into who Danny Compton might have feared were minimal, if they existed at all. Or had he? She tried to recall everything the detective inspector had told her, and came up with only the scrappiest of facts. A new idea floated up – that the murder was not demanding an especially intense degree of focus. Granted there were additional officers drafted in to help prosecute the usual enquiries, there was still nothing of the horror or fervour she had seen on previous occasions. The absence of the victim's parents made a difference, too. Just a traumatised fiancée, who was apparently being duly helpful with the enquiries. At heart, the police were not going to care too desperately that a semi-criminal protester had died at the hands of a local landowner after unbearable provocation. The landowner quite possibly belonged to the same clubs as the chief of police, anyway. Without the slightest suggestion of corruption, human nature was likely to decree that no special effort need be made this time.

This line of thinking almost persuaded Thea herself that she could simply leave it, as most people said she should. But then her phone rang, just as she was getting back into the car, and everything was sent in quite another direction.

'Mrs Osborne? This is WPC Gordon. We met the other day? DI Higgins asked me to call, to tell you that Ricky

Whiteacre has been arrested. He thought we owed it to you to keep you informed.'

'Oh! That's a surprise. How thoughtful. But it *isn't* a surprise, really, is it? We knew he was the one who hit Mr Handy.'

'No, you don't understand. He's been arrested for murder.'

Chapter Twenty-One

'What?' She struggled to grasp all the implications. 'You think he killed Danny? But why?'

'Sorry – I can't tell you any more. But the DI thought you should know. He says you can just sit back and enjoy the sunshine now.'

'Oh, did he? Well, thanks for calling. I don't suppose I'll see you again.'

She hadn't much liked the Gordon girl anyway, she remembered. Now she discerned a definite hint of smugness in the voice. It made her miss Gladwin with a sudden passion.

Everything swirled around her head, with nothing approaching a logical pattern. Ricky Whiteacre, the brother of young Tiffany, son of such nice parents, a murderer? So he had bashed Jack Handy because . . . Handy had seen him kill Danny? Or somehow knew the truth, even if not from directly witnessing it? Or because he was on a list of people Ricky wanted dead? Had there been a struggle between the two men for the role of leader in the group? Or what?

She couldn't possibly follow Higgins's advice and return to Daglingworth for a quiet week sitting in the sunshine. How little he knew her if he thought there was any chance of that. She had to know *why*. She had to discover how Nella had reacted to the news. And poor Tiffany!

What about Steve? He hadn't shown much liking for Ricky – or his mother, come to that. She had interrupted them, when Steve might have gone on to reveal more about the people involved in what had happened. Had she done that deliberately? Anything now seemed possible. There could be conspiracies on every side. Steve knew about the knife that killed Danny, saying it had been broadcast on Twitter. Was that the evidence that incriminated Ricky, then? And who was the nameless man who had first found Danny's body?

She made no attempt to start the engine, simply sitting in the driver's seat, with Hepzie slumped half on her lap as questions flooded through her mind. The big change in her thinking dawned slowly. None of the explanations she could think of involved any sort of revenge. At what point had it seemed clear that this was in fact the motive, anyway? Had it been Drew's idea? Instead, it was something about the internal politics of the protest group, and therefore of no real cause for concern. There would be quiet chuckles from locals at this evidence that there was trouble in the ranks and every prospect of less harassment and campaigning as a result. Perhaps the whole edifice would collapse. The shelf life of such groups was never very long anyway, as far as she was aware. The sheer level of intensity ensured they would soon burn out, in most cases. People grew up and lost heart, too.

Young recruits like Tiffany would recognise the brainwashing they were subjected to, and make a bid for freedom.

All of which only further piqued her curiosity. What was Sophie saying now? It was impossible to refrain from such questions, and even more impossible to resist the compulsion to go and find out.

But go where? She definitely would not be welcome at the Whiteacres' home, and had no idea where Nella, Sophie or Steve lived. That left the Handys' farm, and she could see no point in going there. Jack was still in hospital and Sandra wouldn't welcome a visit. Nor was she likely to know anything.

She drove around the loop of Upper End, down past the church and back through the lanes to the big roundabout. Arriving in the middle of Daglingworth, she felt mildly disappointed not to have met anyone interesting, nor witnessed any further violence.

But she didn't remain disappointed for long. Outside the open entrance to Galanthus House was a man. He was dark-haired, in his forties and appeared to be waiting for something. He simply stood passively, not looking at anything in particular, until he heard her car slowing down and indicating right. Then he transformed into a caricature of alertness, head up, mouth smiling, hand raised. He trotted across to her side of the car, plainly eager to speak to her. She wound down the window.

'Are you Mrs Osborne? The house-sitter?'

'That's right.'

'I was just about to give up. I need to speak to you, you see. Would that be all right?'

'I don't see why not. Who are you?'

'Jim Tanner. I live in Stratton. Only a mile away. They might have told you about me.'

'Tanner! The—' She could hardly say *the benefits cheat* and even less *the arsonist*. 'Um, yes. I think I know who you are. Why do you want to see me?'

'It wasn't me, you see. Nor any of my family or friends. It had nothing to do with us. I need you to know that.'

'Okay. Wait a sec.' She drove hurriedly up to the garage, intending to put the car inside it. Then she thought perhaps it would be more sensible to leave it out, where she might get at it quickly if necessary. Such caution was unnatural to her, and she knew a small pang of regret at its onset.

'Careful!' came a shout, a millisecond before she hit the glass tank containing the tortoise. It made a telltale sound, a sound that universally signalled calamity. Broken glass meant wastage at the very least, and a terrorist bomb at worst. In this case it spelt bad news for a sleeping tortoise.

She let the car run back a yard or so, and then got out. 'Stay here,' she told the spaniel. 'You might cut your feet.'

The man was already squatting down to inspect the damage. 'Is this a tortoise?' he asked.

'Yes. Have I killed it?'

'Don't panic. You didn't hit it hard. It's buried in all this dirt – was it like that before?'

'Yes. It's hibernating. Due to wake up any day now.'

He scooped away some soil, and delicately extracted shards of glass from one side of the reptile. 'Look at that!' he said, with wonder distinct in his voice.

A narrow stripy head raised miraculously out of the

earthy bed and very slowly turned from side to side. The man worked his hands down either side, and gently lifted the whole creature aloft. 'He's awake,' he said. The shell was domed, four stumpy legs sticking out and the head raised. It blinked and opened its mouth, in a perfect imitation of a long yawn.

'So he is. I guess even hibernation can't withstand being hit by a car.'

'What happens now?'

'Um . . . warm bath and relocation to a nice big thing called a vivarium. Are you sure he's not hurt?'

'Probably takes quite a lot to damage that shell. A warm bath, eh? Then a nice big meal, I expect. Maybe he'd like a little walk, just to stretch his legs.' He bent down to set the tortoise on the ground, only to emit a shrill cry of pain.

'What?' Thea could see no cause for concern. 'What's the matter?'

'My back. Oh Christ – it's gone into spasm. Wait a minute. Oh!' He staggered to the car and leant over it, gasping. Thea remained where she was, her mind blank.

'Sorry,' panted Jim Tanner. 'It does this. Never any warning. I won't be able to walk until it eases off. Sorry,' he repeated.

'Can you sit?'

'Where?'

'Over there.' She pointed out the wrought iron seat that she and Steve had used that morning.

'If you help me.'

Unselfconsciously she supported him the few yards to the seat, and lowered him slowly into it. Then she collected the tortoise and her dog. Inside the house, Gwennie was yapping.

'Thanks,' he said, and then gave a muted howl. 'Oh, God. It always does it at the wrong moment. You wouldn't believe the pain.' There was sweat on his brow and he held himself tight from neck to knee.

'Have you got pills or anything?'

'Not with me. They're not very good, anyway. Just take the edge off it.'

The whole episode was reminding Thea powerfully of an earlier instance where a man with a bad back had looked to her for sympathy and support. She had failed him in a big way. Now she had a second chance to get it right. 'You poor thing,' she murmured. 'Is there anyone I can phone?'

'Give it a few minutes, okay? Just let me sit.'

'A drink?'

'No thanks. Go and do what you need to with the tortoise or the dog. I'm all right.'

'I'll be ten minutes. Shout if you want me.'

She left him sitting in full view of the road, his whole body rigid with pain. Anyone passing would see a puzzling figure, but she doubted whether they'd stop to learn more. Tucking the tortoise under one arm, she unlocked the front door and let Gwennie out. She made directly for Jim Tanner, but didn't touch him. Instead she stood two feet away and gave him a thorough inspection. 'She can't see very well,' Thea called. 'But she's quite friendly.'

She went into the kitchen, with her spaniel at her heels, and gave some thought to the task of bathing a sleepy tortoise. Mr Foster's instructions were invaluable. *Use the big red bowl from under the sink. Water should be comfortably warm. No soap. Just fill it to within a couple of inches and slowly immerse him. Leave him for five minutes maximum and then remove him onto a towel and pat him dry. Quickly take him to the vivarium, which should be set at 65 degrees F, and offer fruit, salad – whatever you can find. Apple is good.*

All of which was easily accomplished. But first she ran upstairs to plug in the vivarium, hoping it would warm up soon enough to keep the animal at the desired temperature. Outside, the afternoon was waning and with the disappearing sun the air was cooling quite noticeably. Poor Jim Tanner would get chilly too, at this rate.

'I've done it,' she reported, finally going back outside. 'One revived tortoise, munching on a slice of apple. It does seem a bit like a miracle. How are you feeling now?'

'Not quite so bad, thanks. I'm sorry to cause such a nuisance.'

'No problem. Do you want to try and come into the house? You'll get cold out here.'

'All right, then,' he said with apprehension clear on his face. 'If I stay here I'll only seize up, anyway.'

She took him past the scorched carpet in the hall – where he stopped for a long thoughtful look – and into the kitchen and made tea, despite his protests. 'It looks to me as if you really do deserve the disability benefit,' she said, without preamble. 'Which isn't what I heard. In fact I was told you'd spent time in prison for fraud.'

'Thirty days,' he nodded ruefully. 'Nobody believes me, because it comes and goes, see.' He smiled sadly. 'I can't really blame them.'

'But surely you can? That was an awful thing Mrs Foster did to you. People took her side. You must have been completely ostracised.'

'I've been okay for a while now. I even started to think she was right. They tested me, and I could do almost all of it – all the things they throw at you. So I lost the case and did the time. I only got out a couple of weeks ago. They sent me to the Job Centre. I've got a job, trying to sell ice cream.'

'What – in a van? Driving round to housing estates and schools?'

'No, no. There's a big place that makes it out towards Cricklade. They wanted someone to get new business for them. I quite enjoy it, to be honest.' He moaned. 'The back's been playing up for years, you know. I did something to it, ages ago. If it gets bad again now, and I have to pack in the job, I'll never persuade them to put me back on benefits.'

'But Mrs Foster,' Thea prompted, trying not to get drawn into the complexity of the benefit system and its apparent injustices. 'Is it right that she reported you to the welfare payment people, whatever they're called?'

'Seems so. She told enough of her friends about it that word got back to me. Didn't take the cops long to conclude it was me tried to burn this house down. Lucky I could prove I was miles away at the time. Likewise both my boys. Not that any of us would have much idea how to make a firebomb anyway. If that's what it was.'

'I could have died,' she said softly. 'It was a terrible thing to do.'

He looked at her, moving his neck carefully. 'Not the only terrible thing, then.'

'You mean the murder? Or the assault on Jack Handy? Or both?'

'There's a lot going on. And you seem to know all about it. How's that, then?'

She flushed. 'Purely by accident, I met some of the people involved. And now they've made an arrest. It'll be on tonight's local news, I suppose.'

He jerked forward and then stopped with a noisy intake of breath. 'Aarghh,' he groaned. 'There it goes again.' He exhaled slowly, and took two more shallow breaths. 'I can hardly breathe when it's like this.'

'There must be something they can do for you. You can't carry on like this.'

'They've tried a couple of things, but backs are tricky and nothing comes near it. It'll be a wheelchair before long, at this rate. Did you say someone's been arrested? Who?'

She debated briefly with herself, and saw no reason to withhold what she knew. 'Ricky Whiteacre. Do you know him?'

'Everybody knows the Whiteacres. The young one's been in trouble once or twice. Got herself in the paper.' He frowned and blew out his cheeks. 'They'll be wrong, though. It wouldn't have been him that they want.'

'Pardon?'

'Murder.' He said the word thoughtfully, the frown deepening. 'Stabbing, I heard. Very nasty.'

'Indeed. Even nastier than cracking a man's skull with his own walking stick. Ricky did that – apparently. It's not so different, really. He must be a violent character.' She realised she had not properly considered the implications of Ricky's arrest for his family. Being accused of murder was about as bad as it got. How would they ever recover?

'I don't know. All I wanted . . . well, I said it already.'

'Yes. So, who *did* start the fire? Have you any idea?'

'Mrs Foster was a social worker. Everybody hates social workers. There was a forced adoption just before she retired. The baby was taken away at birth, because they said it was likely to be harmed by the mother. A lot of fuss was kicked up. She was wrong.' He looked up again. 'She's a stupid woman. I won't say more than that. But if I were a copper, I'd have a look at where those people were when the fire was set.'

Thea was wide-eyed at this imputation, not so much on the victimised parents, but the woman she had met and liked. 'She seemed all right to me.'

'She had too much power. That's the truth of it. A stupid powerful woman can cause a lot of harm.'

'You think it was this mother – the one whose baby was taken away? Did you tell the police?'

'No need. They'll work it out for themselves eventually. It took them until today to confirm my story. It's not their top priority just now.'

'And you thought they'd have left me thinking it was you?'

'Everyone's talking about you. I guessed you'd have heard my name from someone by this time. And I was right, wasn't I?'

She nodded. 'Seems we're both rather famous, for different reasons.'

'Those girls,' he suddenly snarled. 'Like witches, they are, poking their noses into other people's lives. Shouting their rubbish about badgers and the rest of it. Always some new thing to make trouble over. Nobody's safe from them. Poor old Jack Handy – just trying to make a living as best he can. If anybody's going to commit a murder, I'd stake money on it being one of them.'

'You mean Sophie . . . what's her surname? Wells! She does seem very fanatical.'

'I don't know one from another. Except the little Whiteacre lass. She's going to regret getting entangled with them, silly kid. My Graham took a fancy to her when they were in the sixth form together. He still carries a candle for her, tries to talk sense into her. I tell him, it's a lost cause.'

'She might need his friendship, then, when all this is finally sorted out. I mean – her brother! It's going to be dreadful for them, isn't it.' Her thoughts remained centred on the Whiteacre family and its sudden tragedy. 'They seemed so . . . *carefree* . . . only a day or two ago.'

'Nice people,' he nodded. 'No side to them. They might have that dirty great house, but they never flaunt it. Look at us, living in a poky little terrace – they've never made us feel beneath them at all.'

'I liked them,' she agreed.

'I should go,' he said suddenly. 'They'll be wondering where I am.'

'Why aren't you selling ice cream today?' she wondered.

'It's only part-time. I thought I said. Not exactly a brilliant career move. They just needed to prove a point, basically. Now that's buggered, as well.' He put a hand to his lower back, pressing himself hard, then slapping the place angrily. 'No way can I go back like this. How would I even get there?'

'How will you get *home*? I'll drive you if you can get in and out of the car.'

'I can't. Call my wife. She knows what to do. We've got an adapted vehicle, so I can swing in and out.'

'And with all that, you still got accused of fraud? That's appalling.'

'It's the times we live in,' he said, fatalistically. 'And plenty of people do swing the lead, after all. Can't expect the system to know which is which – it's too big and too rule-bound. They don't see the real person – just tick a lot of boxes.'

It was certainly enlightening, Thea thought. She had known, in theory, that her experience seldom brought her close to deprivation; life on welfare payouts, even living in a poky terrace house was strange to her. Jim Tanner was making her feel ashamed of herself and everybody like her.

'I'll call her, then. What's the number?'

Chapter Twenty-Two

It was five o'clock before Mrs Tanner drove away with her groaning husband. She had been upset, and frosty with Thea, who readily understood what a blow his relapse must be to her. The brief encounter with her made Thea feel even more ashamed of the unkindness that prevailed throughout the country. A callous attitude towards the less fortunate had blossomed in recent times, allied to a complacency among those who did have their health and a job and a decent house.

Far better for Sophie and her comrades to fight against such inequity and ill usage, thought Thea, uncertainly. She had to concede that it would also be less glamorous and far less exciting. The task of improving the lot of the poor and disadvantaged demanded political engagement, persistent dogged work on points of law and hard cases. There was little or no scope for direct action when it came to ensuring decent provision of social security. Saving badgers was a lot more straightforward, and infinitely more romantic.

And now they'd arrested Ricky. They would not have

done that without compelling evidence against him. On the other hand, there was a big difference between 'arrest' and 'charge'. People were often arrested and then released again *without* charge. It could yet turn out to be a mistake, despite Higgins's message implying that the whole thing was over and Thea could safely settle down and forget all about it. He just wanted her out of his way, she suspected, and who could blame him? He was going to have his hands full with Sheila Whiteacre, who was highly likely to turn into a ferociously protective mother, employing skilled lawyers and ensuring there was no undue pressure or excessive questioning of her beloved son.

She was strongly tempted to defy Higgins and barge in somewhere asking questions of her own. But where? Even Thea Osborne had more sense than to try to speak to anybody in the Whiteacre family. Nor did there seem to be much chance of finding Nella or Sophie or Steve, since she had no idea of where they lived.

The only person left, it seemed, was Sandy Handy – and what could Thea possibly have to say to her? She gave it some thought, and came up with nothing other than a pleasing diversion into other possible names the woman could have been landed with. Candy, Mandy – even Pandy. Wendy would have been almost as bad.

It all required an extended meditation, possibly with notes. She needed to go back over the week and try to figure out what truths, if any, could be established. If Ricky was the murderer, did that explain the reason for the visitation on Tuesday evening from his sister and her friends? Did they all know it was him, and were closing ranks? Where were the clues that she had missed? Was she being childish and naïve to think there was anything of the sort? Wasn't plodding police procedure far more likely to arrive at the facts of the case?

She tried a succession of character analyses, starting with Sophie Wells, who was relatively easy to label as well intentioned but uncontrolled. Influential over others, but also often embarrassing. Impatient, intelligent and probably indulged as a child. Nella Davidson was less easy. Likely to be rich and at least as spoilt as Sophie, she must possess lovable qualities, since Danny had chosen her as his lifetime partner. Thea had seen small indications of passion – all her emotions had been exaggerated, from grief to impatience and anger. And yet somewhere there was an anomaly that Thea could not quite identify. Nella had said almost nothing about the environment or the reasons for being an activist in the first place. She had been detached when Thea first saw her, leaning carelessly against her fiancé's – or officially her, as Higgins had disclosed – big car. Again, the next day, she had shrugged off the drama at the quarry as nothing important. Nella, then, went her own way and was wary of following the crowd. Perhaps that had been her attraction for Danny.

Tiffany was another spoilt daughter. Her mother had ineffectually reproached her for being with the group on Sunday morning, but had all too easily abandoned her complaints and let the girl do as she pleased. There had been a suggestion of mutual trust, and an overall relaxation of rules, despite Jim Tanner's disclosure that Tiffany had been in trouble not so long ago. Tiffany was, after all, the youngest of five. The worries and problems of raising children would all have been worked through already by the time it came to her. Mr and Mrs Whiteacre were probably just keen to focus on being grandparents, cruising towards retirement with a sense of a job well done.

Steve, with the big ears and the straggly beard, had endeared himself to her with his straight talking. He seemed to be a well-balanced young man, comfortable with his place in the world, while still immersing himself in the grey areas of activism. He conveyed a sense of invulnerability, impervious to the usual laws of society, with his eavesdropping app. Steve, she supposed, could all too easily fit the profile of a deliberate killer. Clever, amoral, and pleased with himself. Physically unappealing, he had developed a disarming manner to compensate. Steve knew everybody – probably including the Tanner family.

Jack Handy, of course, might yet turn out to have murdered Danny. He remained the most convincing suspect in some ways, despite Thea's liking for him. It would not be the first time she'd liked a killer, although she had yet to reach a position whereby the very fact of liking them became an indication of guilt. Laughing silently to herself, she gave up the whole task as a bad job. It was impossible without talking it through with someone else, someone who would point out any lack of logic or remind her of comments or incidents that might change her whole approach.

She had fed the dogs and visited the tortoise. Outside it was almost dark. Very little traffic passed the gate, even at the time of day generally regarded as busy. Anybody coming home from work in Gloucester or Oxford or Stratford would use the main road and come off at the roundabout. Only those from the Cirencester direction might choose the smaller road via Stratton. Presumably there were barely a handful of commuters living in Daglingworth anyway – nowhere near enough to constitute a rush hour. She had seen nothing of the people living either side of Galanthus House, their properties strung out sufficiently for there to be no unavoidable contact. *I'm in limbo*, she thought, with a wave of self-pity. Nobody was going to come and cheer her up. She'd be lucky to get five minutes' chat with Drew, with all the other calls on his time. Jessica had told her to keep away, and Gladwin was on holiday.

So she did what she hoped would earn her some sort of cosmic brownie point and called her mother.

It was a year and a half since her father had died, and all the old balances and alliances in the family had shifted as a result. Maureen Johnstone had spent very little time in lonely grieving and even less waiting for attention from her children. She had picked herself up, made new friends, reminded herself of her former interests and abilities and given everybody a series of surprises. But she continued to live alone and to make it clear that she expected to be kept closely apprised of all family news. She was aware of Thea's attachment to Drew Slocombe, but had not yet met him. Damien was the most dutiful, and Thea probably the least when it came to sustaining good-quality contact.

'Maureen Johnstone,' came the familiar voice, businesslike and very slightly suspicious.

'It's me.'

'Thea? Or Jocelyn?'

It was always irritating to be confused with her younger sister, and always her own fault for not announcing her name. 'Thea,' she said.

'You've heard from Damien? Talk about a surprise. I'd completely given up on them. Of course, it could still go wrong. She *is* terribly old for a first one.'

'He sounds pretty confident. You're well, then, are you?'

'Same as usual. Where are you? Not at home, I'll be bound.'

'It's a very small village called Daglingworth.'

'Anywhere near Winchcombe?'

'Not really.' Her mother had joined her at a house-sit in Winchcombe the year before, having originally introduced her to the homeowner. She had shown little interest in subsequent commissions and even less approval. Somewhere under the surface there was always a flicker of disdain at the whole business.

'I hope there hasn't been any trouble?'

'Well . . .' Already she was asking herself why in the world she had made this call. What had she been thinking?

'Thea! What is it this time?'

'Nothing to worry about. It's all sorted out now, anyway. Jessica came to see me on Tuesday. We had a nice pub lunch.'

'How is she? I haven't heard anything from her for a long time.'

Thea swallowed down an urge to defend her daughter. How she related to her grandmother was her own business, and *a long time* might easily be a mere two or three weeks. 'She's fine,' she said, crossing her fingers. Until that

275

moment, she hadn't grasped quite how unfine Jessica might be. The girl had been anxious, uncomfortable, trying to say something that never quite emerged as a lucid account.

'Good. There was a thing in Manchester, wasn't there? A young policewoman got hurt. I saw it on the news.'

'So did I. Nothing to do with Jess. I called her to check.'

'You know something?' Maureen burst out. 'I don't like the police. I don't trust them. They tell awful lies when it suits them. They think the end justifies the means. Nasty people. She shouldn't ever have joined them.'

'Blimey, Mum! Where did that come from? You of all people.'

'My friend Annie – you remember her? She's got a grandson with long hair and tattoos. He was stopped and searched, for no reason at all. When he complained, they just made up a story that was *totally* untrue. What sort of a society is it, where that can happen?'

'I know,' Thea agreed vaguely. She *did* know, on some level. But it wasn't anything she could hope to tackle. Like most people, she more or less believed that justice would prevail in the long run. 'Although there are some very decent police officers. I know a few, after all. In fact,' she went on, 'I don't know a single bad one. Some are rather thick, but that's a different thing.'

'Too thick to know how to behave with integrity,' said Maureen sourly.

'Anyway – it's exciting about Damien's baby.' She changed the subject determinedly. 'Something to look forward to. Especially a girl. A girl's going to cope much better than a boy would.'

Her mother laughed. 'I agree with you there,' she said. 'We'll all have to make sure she's not too brainwashed.'

'Right.'

They parted with promises to meet up soon and Thea felt the glow of having done a good thing. There were times when she and her mother argued, where the essence of their relationship slipped back into criticism and self-defence, uncomfortable truths and a bitter feeling of falling short. But that seemed to have faded away almost completely now. It gave her hope that from that point on, she and her mother would become closer, more affectionate and of much more mutual support.

But there had been elements of the conversation that niggled, too. There was a sense that she had been lazy and evasive in her consideration of the place of the police in society, given that she often had dealings with enforcers of the law. It had been a shock to hear her mother state so flatly that she did not trust them, because Thea herself had never reached such a point of cynicism. Thinking of Phil Hollis, Jeremy Higgins, Sonia Gladwin, and her own brother-in-law, James Osborne, she knew she would trust any one of them with her life. Literally. The police in general might be defective, but the individuals of her acquaintance were remarkably decent.

She filed the whole matter away, to be given further attention. It did matter, she was sure. It connected with everything that had been happening in the past few days, but not in any way that she could properly distinguish. She would think about it when she went to bed, when she felt warm and safe and relaxed.

Meanwhile, she dithered about phoning Drew. An ill-timed call could cause stress and irritation, and if the children were still awake and wanting him, it would put her in the role of importunate girlfriend, wanting attention that rightfully belonged to Timmy and Stephanie. It would pull him in two directions, which could in no way be a positive thing. She could text him instead, but she wasn't sure he would see it. He had never fully acquired the mobile phone habit, apart from keeping a dedicated number for the funeral work and never straying out of earshot of it ringing. Thea was not privy to that number.

Then Gwennie yapped, and the doorbell rang, and the clock in the living room struck seven.

Chapter Twenty-Three

It was Tiffany Whiteacre, looking smaller and paler than Thea remembered. 'Can I come in?' she said. 'It's raining.'

'Is it?' Thea peered out in surprise. 'After such a lovely day?'

'Drizzle, anyway. I didn't bring a coat.'

Thea threw the door wider and ushered the girl inside. 'Have you walked, then?'

'I rushed out. I've never done that before. I thought it was only people in books. But I couldn't help it. It was like being blown by a fierce wind. I had to get away. I just ran.' She was almost crying, her voice broken and breathless. 'I didn't bring a phone or anything.' She seemed amazed at herself, reporting her actions with an air of wonderment.

'What happened?'

'They arrested Ricky. They say he killed Danny. My mother's gone berserk. She's trying to phone the MP. She kept shouting at me, asking about a thousand questions. My head was exploding with it.'

'Why come here, though?'

'I didn't mean to. I just walked this way. I did think of hiding in the church for a bit – the one on the corner. But it was cold and dark and horrible, so I changed my mind. Then I couldn't go home, so I kept on walking. When I saw the name Galanthus I remembered this is where you are, so I just thought . . .' She trailed off miserably. 'Sorry.'

'You must have friends around here, who'd be more help to you.'

'Not really. You know more about it all than anyone else.'

'How can you say that? That's ridiculous.' The anger took Thea herself by surprise.

'I mean, apart from Sophie and Nella and another girl called Polly. She's away, travelling.' She sniffed and looked around the room for somewhere to sit. Thea had led her into the living room without thinking and now waved towards the sofa where she sank down like a collapsed puppet.

'Your parents will be panicking about you. Wasn't it terribly thoughtless to add to their worries, when everything's in such chaos about Ricky?'

'Nobody understands,' Tiffany burst out. 'Except I think *you* might. Ricky didn't kill Danny. Why would he? They *liked* each other. Danny was trying to get the group to accept Ricky as a full member, even though they weren't sure.'

'For a start, I don't understand that at all. Is Ricky in the group or isn't he?' She remembered something Steve had said on the subject. 'And how come he nearly killed Jack Handy?'

'He didn't mean to hit him hard.'

'So perhaps he didn't *mean* to stab Danny to death, either? Maybe he doesn't know his own strength.'

'Stop it. Let me try to explain.'

'Go on then.'

'Well – Ricky and Nella were . . . together for years before Danny turned up.' She held up a hand to stop Thea's automatic response. 'Yes, I know that sounds as if there'd be reason for Ricky to hate Danny, but it wasn't like that at all. They'd already split up and Ricky had a new girlfriend. He was *glad* when Nella got somebody else as well. She's terribly *intense*, as you might have noticed. But very sweet and clever and everything, as well. It was magic the way she and Danny just clicked from the start. I don't think he ever meant it to happen. He kept his distance for weeks before it all got too strong for him. And then it was all-consuming and he proposed and it was really lovely.'

'Okay. Got that. So – Ricky,' Thea prompted.

'Ricky's got a job with the canal people. CRT, they're called. They do rivers as well and they've got a project connected to the Churn. You know it?'

'Not really.'

'Doesn't matter. But there's a tributary that joins it not far from Bagendon, and *that* runs through Mr Handy's land. He's been polluting it with his chicken shit and causing all sorts of trouble. They've got to take him to court over it, but he's making everything as difficult as he can, and Ricky's the main person dealing with him. He went for him on Tuesday. They didn't want me to know about it, but I found out anyway.'

'Why can't he just tell all this to the police?'

'I suppose he will, but they're still going to think he killed Danny. It suits them, doesn't it? Gets everything nicely sewn up. That's what my mum says.'

'And mine,' said Thea ruefully. 'It's not my experience.'

'Steve says your daughter's a cop. You're biased.'

'I don't think so.' But she wasn't able to inject complete conviction into her words. Jessica herself had hinted that the truth might be otherwise at times. 'Anyway – what do you want me to do? I can drive you home, I suppose.'

'Drive me to Sophie's,' Tiffany said impulsively. 'She might not have heard about Ricky yet.'

'Unlikely. It was hours ago now. Why haven't you told her already?'

Tiffany blinked. 'How do *you* know when it was?' She pressed herself back into the cushions. 'You've been spying on us for the police, haven't you? Sophie said you had. Right from that first time we saw you in the woods. Said you were following us and listening in to what we were saying.'

'If you believe that, wasn't it rather stupid to come here now?'

'I didn't believe her. She gets a bit paranoid at times. There've been a few incidents when the police already knew what we were planning and where we were going. Nella and Danny said it was just coincidence, and most of our targets were obvious all along.'

'And you probably put everything on Facebook anyway.'

'No, we don't. And we don't send emails or texts, either. Not when it's something important. I mean – those men culling the badgers aren't funny. They've got guns. We had to

282

be cleverer than them, if we had any hope of disrupting them.'

'And did you? Disrupt them, I mean?'

'Sometimes. Not enough.'

Thea sighed. She did not want to take the girl to her friends, even though she was undeniably hooked by everything Tiffany had to say. On the face of it, there did seem to be good reason for arresting Ricky – and how reliable would a sister's protests be, anyway? Of course she would insist on his innocence. She thought of another topic she wanted to discuss. 'You know you said Jim Tanner was the one who set fire to this house,' she began.

Tiffany nodded slightly, with a befuddled look.

'Well, he didn't. He came here to tell me. Mrs Foster was quite wrong in reporting him to the benefits people. His back is incurably diseased. He was in agony when he was here.'

'So?'

'So you get things wrong. *People* get things wrong. You might well be wrong about Jack Handy, Ricky, Danny – the whole lot of them.'

'How could anybody be wrong about *Danny*? He was an active and committed member of our group. He worked with us for a year. We all knew him and liked him.'

'Like a brother,' Thea murmured.

'What?'

'I thought you were going to say you knew and loved him like a brother.'

'Well – yes, we did.'

'And see what brothers can do.'

Tiffany scowled. 'Except he didn't. There's no way Ricky

283

could stab somebody. Especially not somebody he liked.'

'Okay.' They were going round in circles, Tiffany's mind in a single track like a toy train. 'So what now?'

'I told you – I want to go and see Sophie. She'll know what to do. She's got a friend who's a solicitor.'

'I expect your parents are better placed to see to that side of things. Where does Sophie live, anyway?'

'Cirencester. The south side. Well, it's Siddington, actually.'

'Where there's another stretch of abandoned canal? I've heard of it, but never been.'

Tiffany waved this away as altogether irrelevant. 'Will you take me?'

It was time to be decisive. 'No. Sorry. I'll take you home, but nowhere else. You're too young to get any further involved than you are already. I wouldn't trust Sophie to keep you safe.'

'That's stupid.'

'Very likely. But I'm not risking it. You should call your parents right away and tell them you're okay. It's mean of you to cause them any further worry, on top of the business with Ricky. I should have made you do it the moment you got here,' she realised. 'Or done it for you. They'd have come and collected you.'

'I'm not *twelve*. I can go where I like.'

'You sound twelve when you talk like that.'

'Okay, then. Give me a phone and I'll do it.'

Thea produced her own mobile and handed it over. The girl keyed in a number and waited. 'Hey, Mum – it's me,' she said eventually. 'Yes, I'm with the house-sitting lady in

Daglingworth. Can you come and get me, do you think? She said she'd drive me if necessary, but I don't think she really wants to . . . yes, that's right . . . I know . . . good . . . fine. It's fine . . . see you in a bit, then. Bye.'

'She'll come?' asked Thea.

'Ten minutes or so.'

'They must be furious with you.'

'Not really. Can I use the loo, do you think?'

The original cupboard under the stairs had been converted to a tiny downstairs toilet, which Thea carelessly indicated. She was feeling flat and superfluous, unsettled by the sudden arrival of the girl and her own failure to behave as a fully responsible adult. As always, her primary motive had been to glean information, fitting more pieces into the puzzle and jumping to some imprecise but persistent conclusions.

Back in the living room, with both dogs reacting to the minutes of waiting as if they were centrally concerned, Tiffany perched on the edge of the chair closest to the window. When a car horn softly hooted, she leapt up and headed for the front door.

'Thanks!' she called, and pulled it open.

'Mind the dogs!' Thea called after her.

Hepzibah always regarded an open door as an invitation. This one was no different, especially as it had been a pretty lazy day as far as she was concerned. Far too much sitting around for her liking. She ran between Tiffany's legs and shot down the driveway.

Thea grabbed Gwennie before she could follow, and bundled her into the kitchen. 'Sorry, old girl,' she panted.

'But I need to keep you safe, okay?' Then she shouted after her own disobedient animal, which had vanished from sight. 'Catch her, will you?' she yelled at Tiffany.

But Tiffany had already reached the car, and was opening its back door. Thea could see three heads inside it. *Three?* Even two would be a surprise. She dashed down to it, getting there just as Tiffany was pulling the door shut again. 'Hey! Wait a minute!' Thea yelled. She wrenched the door wide and peered into the car.

The driver was Sophie Wells. Next to her was a woman Thea had never seen before, and on the back seat was Steve of the big ears.

'Hey!' said Thea again. 'What's going on? We were expecting Sheila. Tiffany phoned her mother, not you.'

'No, she didn't,' said Sophie calmly. 'She called me, and here I am. It's not a problem. Mind your own business, will you?'

Thea had had enough. 'Stop saying that,' she grated furiously. 'How can I mind my own business when a girl arrives on the doorstep without a coat and tells me a whole lot of terrible things?'

'What terrible things?' Tiffany blinked at her. 'I never said anything like that.'

'Never mind. I've got to get my dog. But I can't just let you—'

'You can't very well stop us, can you? There's four of us and one of you. We've got something very important to do. You'd approve, actually, if you knew what it was.'

'What is it, Soph?' asked Tiffany, transparently bewildered. 'And who is this?' She indicated the woman in the front passenger seat.

286

'We'll explain on the way. You just caught us, when you phoned. It'll be good to have you with us. Given what's happened to Ricky, it'll be an excellent bonus. Now shut that door and let's get going.'

There ensued a tug of war with the door, which was easily won by the passengers once Steve leant across and added his weight. Thea let go when the car began to move, simultaneously furious and afraid for her dog, which could well be under the wheels.

But she wasn't. She emerged from somewhere in the shadows and jumped up at Thea's legs. 'Bloody dog!' she said. 'Get in the house, will you.'

She watched the car intently as it disappeared towards the centre of the village, memorising its number plate and model. A black Volvo estate, the number starting with CN12, she would recognise it again. For a few seconds she considered giving chase in her own car, but it would take too long to find the keys, lock the dogs in, and reverse out into the road. They'd be miles away by then.

But she kept thinking it might be possible. The chances were that they were going back towards Cirencester, along the main road. If Thea dashed down to the Stratton road and turned left, she'd get on to the straight stretch to the big roundabout in a minute or two – possibly soon enough to coincide with them. 'Get in the house,' she ordered her dog again, and flew to find her keys. Coat pocket. Good. No need to lock the house up – just flick the Yale and slam it shut. The car was still outside, because she'd forgotten to come out again and put it away properly. It was definitely worth a try.

Everything seemed to move hopelessly slowly, and when she finally got to the junction beside the Stratton church, she calculated that it was actually hopeless. Sophie would have long since passed the point where she could hope to intercept her. But then a miracle happened. A black Volvo came towards her from the left, heading towards Stratton. Frustratingly hazy about the precise geography, Thea concluded that as a local resident, Sophie would choose the smaller roads, on a more direct route through Cirencester. At this time of day, it would be quiet and clear.

'Thank you, God,' breathed Thea, and pulled out behind the oblivious black car.

Chapter Twenty-Four

There was so little traffic that Thea expected her presence to be immediately detected by the car she was following. But there was no discernible reaction – no sudden deviations down a side road or increase in speed. Instead they proceeded at a normal pace down into Cirencester via the road that must once have been the main highway. Traffic lights and roundabouts were successfully navigated without any other vehicles interposing themselves and Thea found herself with time to think. What was she planning to do? What were the most likely scenarios, once the Volvo reached its destination? How was she going to explain herself – or even *defend* herself, if things got nasty?

Because something nasty was definitely possible.

She had come without her phone. It was still at Galanthus House, on the little table in the living room. If she'd had it with her, she might have called Higgins. Perhaps not quite yet, because nothing so far had actually happened. But it would have been nice to think she had that option to fall back on. Even if she got hold of another phone, she didn't know his number in her head. Calling 999 would have to be the last resort, then.

Nobody would be looking for her. It wasn't even certain that anyone was looking for Tiffany. The whole story about rushing out of the house could have been an invention. If she was sneaky enough to pretend to call her mother, anything was possible.

Then they were suddenly there. The Volvo stopped outside a modest house in a row of similar properties, somewhere in the backstreets of Cirencester. She hadn't noticed any street names, the whole place feeling like a jumbled warren of houses dating back nearly a hundred years. She drove on to the next junction, noting a sign announcing Lewis Lane, and parked in the first gap she could find. Then she walked cautiously back the way she'd come, staying on the opposite side of the street from the Volvo, hoping nobody would notice her.

It seemed that there was already some trouble. Tiffany was speaking loudly, and Steve was holding her arm. 'I won't believe you!' she said, as if not for the first time. 'It's impossible.'

'Just come with us, and listen,' ordered the man. 'We know how you feel. We were the same, a few hours ago. It's awful, Tiff. But it looks as if it must be true, just the same. And stop making a noise, will you? You'll make it all a whole lot worse if you keep on like this.'

Thea had no need to worry about being spotted. The four people were much too intent on their own business to worry about passers-by in the street. They were all facing the house, and starting to move towards the front door.

'She might not be in,' said Sophie. Steve muttered a reply that Thea couldn't hear.

They stood in a huddle on the doorstep, and a light went on in what must have been a hallway. Then the door opened and they all trooped in. It looked to Thea as if the person inside had been rather roughly pushed out of their way. The unknown woman went last, and Thea heard Nella's voice on a high note, saying, 'Who's this?' No answer was audible.

The door closed, and Thea was left safe but frustrated. It was not an unfamiliar situation, she slowly admitted to herself. She had developed a habit of confronting people, once she had developed a theory as to who was guilty of what. But rarely had she done it on her own. And rarely had one of her theories felt so unstable. One of the people inside that house was a killer – of that she was reasonably sure. Sophie was the one she distrusted most strongly, but Steve had behaved in ways anyone would find suspicious. Nella and Tiffany had both presented starkly straightforward emotions that Thea had believed herself to be fully aware of and in sympathy with. As for the unknown woman, anything was possible.

There really wasn't any choice. She needed to know what was happening with a visceral urgency that would be impossible to explain. She was the only witness available to what could quite possibly lead to another murder, or at best some sort of violence. She ought, of course, to summon the police – and she would, if necessary. Somehow. In the olden days she might have found a public phone box on the street corner. Now she would have to accost a total stranger and demand to use their mobile in order to summon help. That ought not to be unduly difficult, on reflection. But first she needed to know whether help was in fact required. Perhaps there was a perfectly amicable and civilised conversation going on inside the house. There certainly weren't any crashes or screams or gunshots emanating from it.

It was a semi-detached property, with an alleyway leading around to the back, on the left-hand side. But a solid wooden door barred the way at the further end, so any thoughts of creeping in through the kitchen or utility room had to be abandoned. Nor was there any possibility of lingering under a front-room window, hoping to catch what was being said inside. The street was quiet, but not entirely deserted. A responsible citizen was bound to see her and enquire as to her intentions.

In deep frustration, she walked slowly back to her car, trying to think of a course of action. Coming towards her was a muddy Land Rover, looking out of place in the spruce little town. As it passed her, she was standing beneath a street lamp and the driver saw her face clearly lit.

The vehicle stopped and the driver called something from inside it. No electric windows, Thea noted. And too far to lean over and wind the one on the passenger side down. She couldn't hear what was being said, but she understood that this was Sandra Handy, who had also grasped who she was. Thea grabbed the door and yanked it open.

'Hello,' she said. 'Fancy meeting you here.'

Mrs Handy was in no mood for pleasantries. 'Bloody hell – it's true what they say about you, isn't it?'

For once, Thea could not deny it. 'I suppose it must be,'

she agreed. 'And I guess you know who this house belongs to and who's in there as we speak.'

'Steve called me. They're having a sort of meeting. He thought I should hear what they say. I'm late. I really hate driving at night. I can't see well enough to do it safely.'

'They've only been there for ten minutes at most. I followed them,' Thea explained without shame. 'But now I can't get in.'

'Did you try the doorbell?'

'They wouldn't want me. Believe me, I'm quite sure on that point, at least.'

'That's probably true. Best go away, then.'

'Tiffany came to me this evening, in a state. And that's not the only time I've been dragged into whatever's going on. I think I've earned a right to an explanation. They might accept me if I'm with you.'

'I doubt it.'

'Do *you* know who killed Danny?'

'Steve said they'd arrested Ricky Whiteacre. I never did like him, self-righteous little sod. Now he's raising Cain over the so-called river pollution, as if we didn't have enough trouble. He's underhand, too. If there was some third columnist in the protest group, I shouldn't be a bit surprised if it was him.'

Could a person be self-righteous *and* underhand, Thea wondered, as she processed this little speech. Presumably so. But another element stood out as more significant. 'Third columnist?' she repeated.

'Never mind now. Come on. Nothing ventured. United front, or something.' Sandy marched up to the front door and pressed a button that set a bell loudly jangling inside.

Thea did not feel united to Sandra Handy. She was of another generation, not just to the young protesters, but to Thea herself. She said things like *raising Cain*, which surely dropped out of the language decades ago. There was every sign that she could be a very disruptive influence, all by herself.

Steve opened the door, which Thea supposed was a blessing. Of all the members of the group, he was the only one who hadn't shown overt hostility towards her at any stage. But it looked as if that was about to change. He stared at her for a few seconds and then scowled. 'What the hell are *you* doing here?' He looked to Sandy for an explanation.

'I found her outside. She followed you. She wants to know who killed Danny. Can't imagine what it's got to do with her, but there it is.'

The scowl did not relax. 'We all want to know *that*,' he said. 'That's why we're here.'

'Who, exactly?' asked Sandy.

'Tiff and Sophie. Nella's upstairs. Says she's got a migraine.'

'And the other woman,' Thea reminded him. 'There was another woman in the car.'

'Ah, yes.' He pulled an odd face that came close to an expression of fear. 'She's called Carol.'

'Who *is* she?'

'We were just getting to that when you rang the doorbell. Better come in, then. Safety in numbers, or something.'

He *was* scared! A lone man amongst a houseful of women – perhaps that was all it was. Unnerved by uncontrolled emotions or appeals for support. Thea felt rather sorry for him, remembering that she had liked him earlier in the day.

Three women were seated around a small room that looked more like a study or office than a lounge. The chairs were small and utilitarian. A large table took up a quarter of the floor space, piled high with papers, leaflets, posters and a computer. There was also a printer on its own little table. Shelves of books and magazines filled a shallow alcove. There was no television.

'What the hell is *she* doing here?' snarled Sophie. So predictable, thought Thea with a quiet sigh. Sophie no longer worried her, because she was almost completely occupied with an examination of the woman called Carol, who was sitting restlessly on a hard little chair beside the fireplace. She was very obviously pregnant.

'Never mind,' said Steve tiredly. 'She's here now, and she's not going to do any harm, is she?'

'Of course she is,' Sophie shouted. 'She's a *witness*. She'll go straight to the cops with everything she hears us say. What's the matter with you, Steve? Don't you get it yet?'

Tiffany, from another hard chair pulled up to the laden table, swallowed with a visible effort, and tried to assert herself. 'Sophie,' she said. 'Don't get started. Go and fetch Nella – she really should be here. Why isn't she? She was well enough to let us in. What's going on with her?'

Sandra laughed, much too loudly, and said with gross irony, 'Hello, Mrs Handy, welcome to our abode. Pleased you could come. Would you like a cup of coffee? Or something stronger? Did none of you bloody kids ever learn any manners?'

Steve cleared his throat. 'Listen – this can't be allowed to turn nasty. Let's take it one step at a time. Sophie, I really think you need to calm down and mind what you say. And before we go any further, you have to explain where Carol fits in. Why bring a total stranger along to something like this? She doesn't know any of us, does she? What's she here for?'

'Looks as if it's an open meeting,' quipped Thea, trying to catch Carol's eye. The woman was big and fair and oddly lethargic, despite the restless wriggling on the chair. Her shoulders and head drooped, and her legs stuck out in front of her, showing swollen ankles. 'Except there aren't enough chairs.' Sandra Handy had taken the last one, leaving Thea to stand awkwardly by the door. 'Where's Nella going to sit?'

Sophie got up. 'I think Nella knows who Carol is. If she doesn't now, she'll soon work it out.'

A ripple went round the room. The atmosphere was increasingly strained, with an acute sense of waiting for something to happen. Thea felt the start of a headache, which she fancied might be shared by most if not all the others.

'I'd have thought it was obvious,' said Sandra. 'So it wasn't Ricky, after all. Jack got that wrong, didn't he?'

'What?' said Tiffany.

'Don't you people read the papers? Have you no idea what the police are capable of? Or is it that you never understood how much of a threat you've been to a lot of highly respectable local businesses? It was obvious that you had to be stopped. And how do you suppose that was going to be best achieved?'

Everyone stared at her, including Carol. 'How did you find them, then?' Sandy asked Carol. 'I don't imagine you were told what he was up to, were you? But he's been missing for nearly a week – no nightly phone calls or whatever it was. I bet you haven't seen much of him these past months, either. And you won't live within a hundred miles of here.' She gave a slow look around at each face in turn. 'God, you're thick,' she told them.

To Thea's surprise, Tiffany was the first to explode. 'We are *not* thick,' she protested. 'We knew somebody was leaking our plans. And yes, most of the group thought it was Ricky, which is why he was excluded from the last few operations. So – what are you saying? Surely not that the informant was *Danny*?' She shouted his name, following it with a wild laugh. 'That would be insane.'

'True, though,' said Carol in a whisper. 'He was a police detective sergeant with the Kent Constabulary. There's a system where they second people to other areas, to reduce the chances of them being recognised. I *did* know about it,' she flashed at Sandra. 'Why wouldn't I? At least – I worked it out after the first couple of jobs. I knew he was up here – so I came to look for him.'

'And found me,' said Sophie. 'Called me on my mobile this morning.'

Thea's mind was flitting from one awful idea to another. The word *operation*, uttered by Tiffany, had sparked a realisation that had nothing to do with the people in the room. Her thoughts were all on Jessica, who was working undercover. She was being asked to spy or sneak, to pretend to be someone she wasn't, and entrap some unwary criminal into betraying himself. And spies ran terrible risks. Just see what had happened to Danny Compton.

Steve stood up slowly and approached Sophie, who was frozen in position between Tiffany and Sandra. 'Did *you* kill him, then?' he asked her. 'You figured it out and killed him.'

'Of course she didn't,' said Tiffany. 'Don't you understand? Go and fetch her, Soph. She has to come down and face us.'

'She won't come.'

Alarm simultaneously filled Steve and Sandra's faces, and Thea thought her own might not be dissimilar. 'She's not . . . She wouldn't . . . ?' Steve spluttered.

'What do you think? You know what she's like.' Sophie spoke coldly, lacking all emotion. 'She asked me to make sure she had enough time.'

'Call an ambulance,' Thea ordered Sandra. 'Come on, Steve – we've got to stop her.'

'It's okay – I didn't have the nerve when it came to it.' A voice spoke from just beyond the door, which opened before she'd finished speaking. 'And why should I let the bastard wreck my entire life, anyway? He's done enough damage as it is.'

Nella entered the room with her head held high. Dark shades ringed her eyes, and grooves joined the corners of her mouth to her nose. 'You must be his wife,' she greeted Carol. 'I thought that was going to be me, you see.'

'Hell hath no fury like a woman scorned,' said Sandra, much too brightly. 'I guess I don't have to call an ambulance after all. Should I make it the police instead?'

Nobody answered for a long moment. Then Tiffany broke into loud sobs and threw herself at her friend. 'Oh, Nella! You poor, poor thing! How did you discover what he was doing? I'd have stabbed him myself if I'd known. Oh, Nell . . .'

'I saw his texts to his wife,' Nella said hollowly. 'He kept a special phone just for her, but he forgot to hide it one night. Just one little mistake. It wasn't even as if I didn't trust him. I just automatically picked it up, and was going to use it, and there were all his messages to and from his *wife*. He never even had the sense to delete them.'

Again a silence, before Steve said, 'I find that rather hard to believe, actually. It would be an instinctive thing, covering his tracks.'

'You're right,' said Carol. 'He never kept any messages.'

'More likely, you googled him, found his picture somewhere,' Steve went on.

'Shut up. I *did* see texts. Why should I lie about it?' Nella's jaw clenched tightly. 'I'm not going to tell any more lies. There's no point now.'

Thea was still trying to grapple with the details of how the whole business worked. 'Was he using a different name?' she asked Carol.

'His name was Daniel Compton,' Carol confirmed. 'As far as I know, that's the only name he ever used. It gets too complicated to change it, I suppose. Car registration, bills . . .' She shook her head miserably. 'I don't really know the reasoning behind it. Someone's bound to explain it to me before long.' She rallied and looked from face to face. 'It was a dirty business. Isn't that enough for you?'

Thea was still breathless with anxiety for her daughter. 'Sorry,' she said, 'but no, it isn't quite enough. For a start, did the Gloucester police know who he was? Did he report to them?'

'I'm not sure, but I wouldn't think so. It would be too likely to get out, if they gossiped to wives or girlfriends. I didn't dare approach them to ask about him, in case he was all right, and just needing to stay quiet for some reason. I had no idea until last night that he was *dead*.'

'Wasn't his name on the news?' Thea wondered.

Everyone shook their heads at that. 'It was kept pretty low-key,' said Sophie. 'Never made the national headlines at all.'

'So how did you find out?' Thea asked Carol, thinking the woman was manifesting a surprisingly low level of shock.

'I googled him and got the online version of the local paper here.' She grimaced. 'After going into meltdown, not knowing who I could talk to, all I could think of doing was to come up here and see for myself and the first thing I found was one of your leaflets' – she looked at Sophie – 'with your mobile number on it. Those leaflets are everywhere,' she added. 'And there was a poster in the library.'

'Makes you wonder why anyone thought there was a need for undercover work, then,' said Sandra dourly. 'Now – do you want me to call anybody?' She held up her mobile questioningly.

'I'll go and hand myself in,' said Nella. 'Get it over and done with.'

'Somebody ought to go with you,' said Steve, suddenly gallant. He was almost as pale and drawn as Nella herself.

'I'll go,' said Thea, decisively. 'I have things I want to ask the detective inspector. And I know the way to the police station. We can probably walk it from here.'

'It's about two minutes away,' said Nella with a grim smile.

'But they close at five,' said Sandra. 'I have reason to know that for a fact.'

'So they do.' Thea smacked herself lightly on the head. 'So what happens now? If I had my phone I could call Higgins. I've got his direct number. But I can't remember it.'

A sudden howl filled the room, freezing everyone in place. To Thea it felt as if everyone then became crowded together, bonded by a sort of cosmic magnet connecting them all into one amorphous body. An arm brandishing a poker flew out and impacted on Nella's head. 'You bitch!' screamed a voice. 'You *killed* him, and now you're *smiling* about it.' The poker struck again, and blood began to pour down Nella's face.

'Stop it!' Another raised female voice rang out, full of authority. The poker was wrenched away, and Carol bundled across the room by Sophie and Steve. Tiffany and Thea found themselves cravenly clinging together, pressed against the table.

'*Now* shall I call an ambulance?' said Sandy Handy.

Chapter Twenty-Five

It was midnight when she got back to Galanthus – much too late to speak to either Jessica or Drew. She had no great wish to do any further talking, anyway. There had been hours of explaining and questioning, going round and around in maddening circles. Nella's head had consumed all official attentions for far too long, given that it was not very badly hurt. There was blood, admittedly, and the paramedics were very much insistent on taking things one at a time. The policemen who turned up were equally slow to allow any other subject past their ears. Only when DI Higgins was finally summoned, ages later, did sense slowly start to filter in.

Then there was a search of Nella's house; concerted efforts to ensure that Carol was safe and not liable to go into premature labour; tight-lipped blushes at repeated questions concerning undercover police work – and a whole lot more. It was all utterly exhausting.

Both dogs had peed on the kitchen floor, and regarded her with full-on reproach when she finally returned to them. 'Sorry, girls,' she sighed. 'Not your fault.'

Weighing her down like a stone in her chest was anxiety over Jessica. It was irrational and inconsistent, but knowing that didn't shift it. The fact that a police officer working undercover had been killed in the Cotswolds inevitably suggested that the same thing could happen to Jess. This simple idea screamed and shouted at her unbearably – all the more so because she could do nothing about it. Even if she could reach the girl and speak to her, that wouldn't help. Her operation, whatever it was, would probably last for weeks, with no guarantees of safety or a good outcome in all that time.

'Serves me right,' she muttered. What were those daft ideas of a few days ago about the uselessness of worry? Fate had taken its revenge on her for such hubris. Worry was like being trapped in a treadmill, with no way out. Jessica's career choices were beyond her control. All she could do was wait and watch and hope.

She crawled into bed, convinced that she wouldn't be able to sleep, after all the dramatic events of the evening. There were still a lot of unanswered questions, too. And she planned to rehearse an account of the whole business for Drew, next day.

Instead she fell into a deep oblivion fifteen seconds after switching off the light and closing her eyes.

When she woke up, it was half past seven and sunny. She rolled out of bed with a sense of extreme urgency that lacked all shape or plan. Her phone! She needed to find her phone, for a start. She needed to feel connected and involved. To be kept in ignorance felt like the worst possible position to be in – which was another irrational development, she realised. And anyway, who was going to contact her? Who among all those people cared tuppence whether the house-sitter knew what was going on? She ought not to have been included in the first place. None of it was remotely her business.

Gwennie brought her down to earth by whining and scratching at the back door. When Thea let her out, she began to run as fast as her little legs would permit towards a corner of the garden. Hepzie followed for a half-hearted few yards, before losing interest. A big ginger cat jumped onto the fence, leaving the corgi bouncing and yapping five feet below. 'Stop it, Gwennie!' Thea pleaded. 'You'll give yourself a heart attack.' The dog ignored her, much as the cat was ignoring the dog.

It was all reassuringly normal. Whatever might have been going on a few miles away, with a tangle of betrayal and vengeance and ultimate violence, all was simple and predictable here at Galanthus House. It was a view she did not often entertain: that her house-sits might be seen as a series of sanctuaries, somewhere to draw breath and catch up with books and films and plans for the future. Instead, she often found them boring and repetitive. That way lay her downfall, as she had gradually become aware. 'We can't go on like this,' she muttered to her spaniel.

A yap from Gwennie alerted her to a muted clatter at the front door. When she went to look, a letter was lying under the flap, face down. When she picked it up, she saw it had no stamp, and simply said 'Thea' on the front.

Dear Thea Osborne,

I don't expect you want to speak to me again, at least for a while, so I simply wanted to say how much I admire you. I believe in speaking as I find, and this definitely needs to be said. You are the least foolish person I've met in a long time.

For the record, Jack is making a magnificent recovery now, and is likely to come home on Monday. I telephoned him this morning and gave him a summary of last night's events. He says he will not press charges against Ricky Whiteacre, but I suspect that could yet change. He has to decide whether or not to regard himself as an innocent victim. I've never been too sure that such people even exist, but they tell me I'm wrong.

I am now wondering what the activists will do with themselves. The police have behaved abominably, of course. What's new? Although it did seem last night that the local lot were kept in the dark and never had much of a hope of working out just what happened and why. I felt rather sorry for them, to be honest.

Well, I won't go on. Do feel free to phone me if you want to chat. I think you and I could be friends.

All best

Sandra Handy

Thea wasn't sure what to make of this. She almost termed it a *billet doux* to herself, given the opening lines. Sandra's phone number was at the top of the note, suggesting she really would appreciate a call.

It was at least contact from a friendly local, which was liable to have some value over the coming week. It was proving difficult to adapt to the abrupt cessation of drama, and the inescapable isolation of the coming day.

But some of this self-pity evaporated when she found her phone. It offered her two messages. One of them was from the man in Farmington who had enquired about house-sitting. He suggested three weeks in July, caring for five Siamese cats. A well-behaved dog might just be acceptable as companion to the house-sitter. Thea suspected he had tried to find somebody else, minus dog, and failed. Thea had the advantage of not belonging to an agency, and therefore making lower charges. She smiled ruefully. Three summer weeks in yet another contender for Most Lovely Village in the Cotswolds was hard to refuse. And perhaps Drew could join her with the children, if it ran into the start of the school holidays.

The other message was from Jessica.

NO NEED TO WORRY. I'M OFF THE JOB.

She sat down on the sofa with a thump. Did Jess mean she'd been suspended? Or the job was prematurely aborted? Or what? Slowly she recognised the way her feelings were mutating from worry to curiosity. That was better! Curiosity was, after all, her default emotion. Curiosity was warm and alive and buoyant and, above all, under her own control – at least partially. She did not even try to resist the compulsion to phone for further information.

Jessica sounded sleepy, but comparatively cheerful. 'Mum? Did you get the text?'

'Yes. What happened?'

'It's a long story, but basically Uncle James had to rescue me. I was in over my head. I make a rubbish spy.'

'They wanted you to spy for them?'

'Not really. I had to tell a lot of lies and try to win the trust of some bad people. I knew I'd be useless and I was.'

'You don't sound too sorry about it.'

'Well – Uncle James pointed out that being a good liar wasn't exactly something to be proud of.'

'He's right. But are you in trouble? What happens now?'

'Too soon to say. It's still ongoing. What about you? How's the murder going?'

'All sorted. I think.'

'Thank goodness. And what about the firebomb?'

'Gosh, I'd forgotten about that. Apparently it was some people whose child was removed by Mrs Foster being unduly officious. That's what the original suspect told me. Mrs Foster has just retired as a social worker, and she's made a lot of enemies, or so I gathered.'

'Pretty extreme revenge, though – burning her house down.'

'True,' said Thea, thinking of all the ways a person could be violently killed, and how dangerous life could feel at times. Then she shook herself. 'Anyway, everything's okay now. I'll ring you again in a day or two, when we can have a nice long chat. I can't say too much for now.'

'Okay, Mum. Bye, then.'

Which left the unanswered questions concerning Nella and the Handys and the wretched Carol Compton. The way she had risen up like an avenging angel made a lingering image that Thea guessed would stay with her for a very

307

long time. She had seemed so together, explaining what she knew and how she'd traced Sophie, until some small thing suddenly triggered the attack on Nella. Nobody could blame her, of course. And nobody did.

But nobody quite blamed Nella, either. After the protracted explanations and statements at the specially opened police station, Thea and Steve and Tiffany had gone to a pub, where they sat until nearly midnight, debriefing each other and obsessing about the whole story. Sophie went miserably home to Siddington and Sandy drove off with yet another quip. 'What a weird woman!' Thea had burst out, the moment she'd gone. 'Doesn't she take anything seriously?'

Neither of the others replied.

'You ought to get home,' Thea told Tiffany. 'They'll be missing you.'

'Past my bedtime?' challenged the girl.

'No, no . . .'

'They'll be much too taken up with Ricky to bother about me. I've told them where I am. You can take me home when we finish here.'

They talked mainly about Nella, with Tiffany shedding tears and Steve sighing a lot. 'She really did love him,' Tiffany insisted. 'Imagine how she must have felt when she discovered what he was doing. I mean – that's betrayal on so many levels. Not just her, but the whole group.'

'Sandy was right,' said Steve. 'We should have clocked him ourselves. It's almost a cliché, isn't it? Undercover bloke gets it together with one of the girls in the group under surveillance, to give himself even better cover. Happens all the time.'

'But *Danny*,' Tiffany wailed. 'He was such a lovely man. Always cheerful and helpful and ready for anything. Nobody's ever going to convince me he didn't care about the badgers. Out there in the rain, night after night, checking on them. How could any of us ever have guessed? And he *proposed* to Nella. He didn't need to do that, did he? Surely he must have loved her a bit? How could anybody *pretend* like that?'

Steve fidgeted. 'You mean sex, I suppose. It's not so difficult, actually. And Nella's attractive.'

'Is she?' said Thea. 'I'm not sure I can see it.'

'You didn't see her as she really is.'

'I saw her at about three o'clock on Saturday. Had she killed him by then, I wonder? Was she putting on an act, leaning against that great big car, as if nothing was worrying her?'

'I've been thinking about that too,' said Tiffany. 'I think she must just have come from doing it. There were probably bloodstained clothes in the car boot. If you stab someone, there's lots of blood, right?' She shuddered. 'And what we all thought was grief was really *guilt* at what she'd done. I still can't believe it.'

'I think she must have gone and done it after you were together at the church,' said Thea. 'When did you leave her?'

'Five minutes later. She said she'd have to go and find Danny, because she was sick of waiting. Maybe that's more likely. I hope it is,' she finished. 'That sounds silly, I know.'

'I know what you mean,' said Thea. 'And you're right about the blood. She'd have had to go somewhere for a wash, and I can't see she would have had enough time. And if it had already happened, I might have seen something. I was walking down that road, just before I caught up with you and Sophie in the woods.'

'But how *cold*. And calculating. She'd have to wait until she was sure nobody was around – no traffic coming. Then just stab him and push him into the quarry.'

Steve coughed. 'Get him into a clinch, do the business, and heave him backwards. Even if someone saw them, they wouldn't understand what was happening.'

'They'd remember afterwards, though. When they heard he was dead,' said Thea.

'What you said about grief and guilt,' Steve said to Tiffany. 'Don't you think it could have been both together? Each making the other worse.'

Thea thought about the scene in the church, with Nella so clenched and inward-looking. 'I think you've got that exactly right,' she told Steve.

Much more along similar lines was voiced, the lines becoming circles and spirals of speculation and gradual acceptance.

'But what about the people in Dubai?' Thea asked at one point. 'They can't really have been his parents, can they? Or they'd have told Nella about Carol.'

'It wouldn't matter, though, would it, once he was dead?'

This called for some serious thinking. 'But they'd never talk to Nella about the funeral and everything, would they? They'd want to know why it wasn't Carol. And then they'd call Carol, right away, and she'd have known he was dead days earlier than she did.'

'Right,' nodded Tiffany and Steve slowly. 'You're right.' Thea could tell that Steve especially was finding it an uphill struggle to follow all the implications of the story. For him, the mere fact of Danny's betrayal was a giant boulder in the way of any further understanding.

'Might they have been planted somehow, by the police, then? The Kent police, that is. Just voices on the end of a line, acting a part? That would be easy to arrange. If Nella asked, Danny could just let her think they really were two middle-aged people on a birdwatching project. And another thing – the Kent police must have provided him with that locksmith's van, full of equipment, to give him a credible source of income. They really thought of everything, so that Nella had no reason to doubt him.'

'She *did* doubt him, though,' Steve insisted. 'As I said at the house – she must have been checking up on him. That stuff about finding texts on his phone can't be true.'

'Doesn't really matter, does it?' said Tiffany. Of the three, she was drinking the most. Her third large white wine was disappearing fast.

'Why did Ricky hit Jack, then?' Thea asked. 'Tell me that.'

'Jack provoked him. No big mystery. Ricky's furious about the muck in the river, and Jack just played with him, getting away with it.'

'So who were the girls with him? Not you or Sophie?'

'We *told* you. I expect they were Sally and Emma and Leanne. Everybody was *sure* he'd killed Danny. It's as simple as that.'

'They'll be more careful in future, then,' said Thea irritably.

'It all pointed to Jack Handy,' Tiffany persisted.

'You know,' said Thea haltingly, 'the police haven't been very diligent in their investigations, as far as I can see. They just let you all believe it was Jack, without saying anything. Admittedly, I have missed a lot of it, but even so. If they'd done the full panoply of forensic analysis, wouldn't they have caught on right away that it was Nella who killed Danny? I doubt if they even took that big car in for a proper look. It would have had Danny's blood in it, I imagine.'

'They probably thought they could sew the whole thing up quickly, because Handy was clearly the killer,' said Steve bitterly. 'If he'd died in hospital, that would have made it all very convenient.'

'Handy,' murmured Thea, hoping to raise a smile.

All she got was a groan. 'Don't you start,' Steve begged.

'Sorry.'

They had stumbled wearily away, Steve and Thea both hoping their beers wouldn't render them illegal to drive. They'd had a pint and a half each. Tiffany almost had to be carried to Thea's car, and bundled out at the Baunton house with very little ceremony. 'I'm not going to speak to your parents,' Thea announced. 'I'm far too tired for that.'

And now it was Friday and Jessica no longer a cause of such painful anxiety. Drew had left no message or text, which was disappointing. Also, when she let it sink in, another reason to worry. There were too many things that could go wrong in his life.

But then, at ten-thirty, he phoned. 'Where were you?' he started without preliminaries. 'I called four times last night.'

'You never left a message.'

'No.'

'I was having an adventure,' she said and took a deep breath.

Five minutes later, the whole story had been told. Drew asked a few questions and made a few interested noises, and waited for her to finish. 'Revenge,' he said then. 'What a complicated emotion it is.'

'Is it?'

'Don't you think? You sound as if Danny had it coming, for what he did. And look at the consequences for the police! What's the trial going to look like, if she pleads not guilty? The media will absolutely love it. The nation will back Nella, with petitions for clemency, the whole works.'

'I suppose so.'

'But if *Handy* had killed him because he was having such hassle with the protesting activities, how would that have looked? Which side would people be on, then?'

'I don't know.' Drew's habit of seeking for the philosophical meanings behind crimes such as this could be rather demanding.

'They'd have stuck up for Danny. Dead just for defending animal rights, or highlighting pollution. The farmer would be vilified. Do you see?'

'Yes, Drew, I see. So what?'

'So morality's a troublesome thing. Who was right and who was wrong here?'

'Danny was wrong. He told lies and deceived Nella in particular. But she was wrong to kill him. And *she* must have told nearly as many lies afterwards, trying to get away with it. It's all perfectly obvious, Drew. I don't think we need get too analytical about it.'

'The victim now is Carol, though. She didn't do anything wrong at all. She sounds quite brave and sensible to me. And what about that poor baby, never knowing its father?'

'He should have thought of that.'

'They were probably paying him a huge bonus, danger money or something. He'd have used it to give his child a good start in life.'

The third pregnancy, Thea suddenly realised. So it was true that these things always went in threes. 'How's Maggs?' she asked.

'Maggs is in hospital with a threatened miscarriage. Den's distraught.'

'Oh, God! There really isn't any justice, is there?'

'We keep looking for it, though, don't we. We can't face the implications of a random universe, even if that's the basic truth of it all.'

'Give her my love. Tell her about what's happened here – she'll appreciate the distraction, if they're making her lie still for weeks on end.'

'It won't be weeks. They think if she's still intact by this evening, it'll all be okay. It happened to Karen with Timmy, and she carried on perfectly easily, once the panic died down.'

'Hard on you, then.'

'Mmm.'

Life in general was hard on Drew, she thought with a pang. Her role was to make it better, as much as she could.

'Listen,' she said. 'You're going to have a holiday. My Farmington job is on, after all. Three weeks in July with cats. You and the kids absolutely must come and join me for at least one week of it. That's an order.'

'Actually,' he said slowly, 'I've been having a proper think about the Broad Campden house. Whatever happens with Maggs, I've got to come to a decision. In fact, I think I already have.'

'Oh?' Thea noticed her hand had started to sweat onto her phone. Whatever Drew was about to say suddenly mattered enormously.

'I think I'm going to move us all there. Me and the kids. I might sell this place as a going concern, and make a fresh start. I think it's what we all need.'

'Oh,' said Thea weakly. 'Gosh.'

He laughed. 'Don't panic. We can talk about it when I see you.'

'Okay,' she said and rang off. Her mood was euphoric. Already she was mentally putting her own little house on the market, and throwing in her lot with the Slocombes in Broad Campden. She could see the whole idyllic picture quite clearly. In a flash, all money worries would disappear, along with other difficulties. Then she caught up with herself, and forced her thoughts on to matters immediately in hand. There was the tortoise, for a start, needing lots of food to build

315

up its strength after long months of starvation. There would be suggestions in the notes left by the Fosters, so she went to find them.

The list included items the animal was *not* to be given, such as cabbage. But dandelions and clover were okay. And, to her relief, there turned out to be a bag of special tortoise food in a small cupboard beneath the vivarium. She took considerable satisfaction from the enthusiastic reception of a small handful of this stuff.

Then she read the notes again, in their entirety, and found a line she had previously missed.

'Feel free to do some needlepoint, if you like that sort of thing. There's a big canvas in the box of craft stuff in the dining room. I'll never finish it. You'd be doing me a favour!'

On investigation, she found the canvas. It was very big, and depicted a highly coloured village street, complete with hay cart, skipping children and animals. About a tenth of it had been done thus far.

'That's me catered for, then,' she muttered, thinking of another week of empty evenings ahead. She looked at Gwennie, who was close to her feet, staring up with trust and affection. 'That's my girl,' said Thea fondly. 'What a nice dog you are.'

Hepzie approached jealously and nudged her hand. 'And you,' Thea assured her. 'You're a nice dog as well.'

She'd be all right for the remainder of her stay, she repeated to herself. She could visit Jim Tanner and see how he was, perhaps even offering some practical help. She could do all the things a normal house-sitter was meant to do. And at the end of the week, she would go and see Drew and they would talk endlessly and deliciously about the future.

She patted the old corgi again and counted herself lucky.

Rebecca Tope is the author of three bestselling crime series, set in the stunning Cotswolds, Lake District and West Country. She lives on a smallholding in rural Herefordshire, where she enjoys the silence and plants a lot of trees, but also manages to travel the world and enjoy civilisation from time to time. Most of her varied experiences and activities find their way into her books, sooner or later.

rebeccatope.com